BLAZING CHRISTMAS

Printed in the United States of America.

FIRST EDITION

Library of Congress Cataloging-in-Publication Data

Risenhoover, C.C.
     Blazing Christmas / C.C. Risenhoover. - 1st ed.

AUTHOR'S NOTE: This is a work of fiction. The individual characters who appear in this book are wholly fictional. Any apparent resemblance of a character to any person alive or dead is purely coincidental. Names of businesses, places, events, locales and incidents are either the products of the author's imagination or are used in a fictitious manner.

BLAZING CHRISTMAS

C.C. Risenhoover

OTHER BOOKS BY C.C. RISENHOOVER

Blood Bath
Child Stalker
Death Angel
Dead Even
Happy Birthday Jesus
Hitler's Children
Hitler's Pigsty
Hitler's Seed
Hoofbeats Across America
Imminent Evil
Larry Hagman
Liar, Lunatic or Lord (Ghosted)
Make Some Noise
Matt McCall: An Introduction
Murder at the Final Four
Murdering America: One White Man at a Time
Once Upon a Texas Train (Ghosted)
Outside the Lines
Proud to be an American
Reluctant Killer
Satan's Mark
Techniques of Great Bass Fishermen
The Beauty Makers
The Suicide Lawyers
Trestles Over Darkness
White Heat
Wine, Murder and Blueberry Sundaes

ONE

There are many drawbacks to being eighty-four years old, not the least of which is that many of the people that I once talked to regularly have left this life. And others have disappeared into the oblivion of what many refer to as assisted living or retirement centers. Not many younger people want to talk to old folks, and I now realize that not many, old or young, even wanted to talk to me when I was younger.

Fortunately, I do have a Golden Retriever named Luke who acts as if he is listening to everything I say, whether he is or not, so I felt it important to take him on one of my recent fishing trips and to tell him about the man who called himself Jesus that I met more than forty years ago.

Now, with Luke being a dog, I do not know that he will ever be able to share the story with anyone other than other dogs, but that is okay.

Being a journalist and investigative reporter for a daily newspaper for all my professional life, this is not my first attempt at sharing this story. I wrote a book about this encounter and submitted it to thirteen different publishers, all of whom sent me rejection letters.

This was hard to take since many people over the years have said that that I am the best writer to ever come out of Baylor University. Granted, most of these people have been confined in mental institutions, but this does not detract from their assessment of my considerable talent, with which I agree.

So, Luke, here we are on a beautiful summer day fishing in one of the best lakes in

Texas, of which they are many. And here is my story:

I met this guy who called himself Jesus twelve days before Christmas, and prior to the Dallas Cowboys playing the Philadelphia Eagles in a critically important game. Obviously, all Cowboys games are critical for people who live in Dallas.

As I recall, it was about nine-thirty in the evening on a Sunday. I was perched on a barstool in one of my favorite eating and drinking establishments adjacent to the LBJ Freeway.

The fact that I was close to the LBJ Freeway is not an endorsement of the former President, but I must admit that I admired a politician who was able to be elected by the votes of more dead than live people.

You might say that I was crying in my beer, but the truth was that I was having margaritas, not beer, along with beef nachos. Most of my friends considered themselves connoisseurs of Mexican beer, but I knew what passed for water in brewing Mexican beer. So, I did not want to chance what might have floated to the top when Mexican beer was being brewed.

Although I have forgotten why I was downing margaritas at what some would consider a rapid clip, it was probably because I had been dumped by some wench whose name I have long since forgotten. That was usually my reason for becoming inebriated.

The bar area was lean of customers, which was not unusual for a Sunday night since most people were resting and readying themselves for Monday morning and the weekly grind of work. Back in the day most people worked. They did not count on welfare checks from the government to cover their lifestyle.

Being a reporter, my job did not require sobriety, so like an old-time American Indian I simply ate when I was hungry and slept when I was sleepy.

Anyway, as previously stated, I was probably lamenting my most recent dumping by someone of the female gender and getting angrier by the minute. Expletives were dancing like sugar plums in my mind, even though to this day I do not know what a sugar plum looks like.

Most people reared in Texas do not know much, if anything, about sugar plums or roasting chestnuts on an open fire, although both sound nice in both poem and song, neither of which are my strong suites.

Spelling is one of my specialties, so I have never been able to accept texting. And back then I was always irritated by MERRY XMAS signs. I always figured that if something was worth writing, it was worth spelling correctly.

The mirror on the wall across from the bar at which I was sitting had a MERRY XMAS sign and a lot of scribbly stuff on it, including Dallas Cowboys and Texas Rangers decals. For some reason there was nothing about Baylor, SMU or TCU, but plenty of decals and paraphernalia about Texas A&M and the University of Texas, the evil empire. There was even Oklahoma University stuff.

Obviously, I was irritated that no Baylor memorabilia was in the establishment but was too overwrought that I had been dumped by old what was her name to raise any objection with the management of the bar. Besides, the bartender was the only one available to protest to, and he looked as if he was having a worse day than me.

Rejection is not easy to take, whether from a woman whose name you do not remember or from a publisher you remember even less. I was not about to shed any tears over my situation, or as some people say, "Get my panties in a wad." I cried, Luke, when Cowboy, your grandad died, but all that being rejected by some airheaded chick did to my psyche was give me an excuse for a few more margaritas.

I do not really like the alcohol in a margarita. I just like the salt on the rim of the glass.

As I recall, the chill of winter had set in that evening when I met the man who called himself Jesus. Of course, Texas weather can be as temperamental as a woman who is surprised to learn that she has exceeded all the limits on her credit cards.

Anyway, the temperature was hovering around thirty degrees and the north wind had pushed the chill factor down around zero. The previous day had been a complete contradiction, with a warm southerly wind blowing up from the Gulf of Mexico and bringing with it all sorts of wonderful pollen for the nostrils of those who attract allergies like molasses attracts flies.

Unfortunately, I am one of those and had only recently spent a fortune on allergy treatments. Otherwise my head might have been hurting worse that it did. As it was, it felt like a basketball must feel when dribbled on concrete.

It is a good thing allergy doctors do not have to guarantee their work. But then, it is a good thing that all of us do not have to guarantee our work.

There was no way I was going to blame my headache on the margarita that was setting in front of me, or on the ones I had already consumed. For me margaritas have always had a healing effect, especially on allergies that cause a stuffy head and runny nose, Take an order of beef nachos covered with jalapeno peppers, wash the nachos down with a margarita, and you have a cure for just about anything that ails you, including a broken heart.

At least that is what I thought at the time.

When the man who called himself, Jesus walked into the place, I was nursing a margarita and contemplating my good looks in the mirror on the wall behind the bar. This was a little difficult because of all the scribbly stuff on the mirror, and all the sports stuff, but it could not hide my handsomeness.

Sure I had, and still have, a crooked nose, the result of a misspent youth proving myself in Golden Gloves competition and football, but that only added to my mystique back in the day, as does my current white hair, lines in my face similar to a roadmap, and bags under my eyes that look as if they need to be checked in when I take a flight.

The man who called himself Jesus walked right up to where I was sitting and asked, "Mind if I take this stool?"

Now the only people in the bar other than me was a couple sitting at a table in the back of the place who should have gotten a room in the motel next to the bar. They were drunk and beyond the mere kissing stage.

So, the man's request was a bit strange and caused me some concern because of the city's homosexual population, but I replied, "Sure, it's a free country."

He must have read my thought because he said, "I'm not gay."

I responded, "I didn't accuse you of being.

"Mentally, you thought I might be," he said.

He was right as rain, but I looked into his eyes and immediately decided that he was straight arrow. His eyes looked honest and true, not shifty and evil like those of a media person. And because of the kindness and softness I saw in his eyes, I knew he could not be a college professor, doctor, lawyer, banker or clergyman.

Because he was dressed in generic attire that looked like it had come off a rack at a Goodwill Store, I figured him for a laborer of some kind, out for a few beers and in hopes of meeting a loose woman. And although there were plenty of them in Dallas, if he hoped to find one in this bar, he was up that well-known creek.

The guy shocked me when he stuck out his paw for a handshake and said, "My name is Jesus."

I shook his extended hand, chuckled and replied a bit nervously, "Of course it is."

"I'm serious," he said.

"And I'm the Apostle Peter," I responded.

"No, you're Mark Luther," he said, smiling.

Obviously suspicious, I asked, "How did you know that?"

He replied, "I know everything about you."

The gears started spinning in my mind, and I glanced furtively about the place, thinking I might see one of my jokester alleged friends. "Alleged" is one of my favorite words, the reason I went into journalism instead of brain surgery.

Back in the day, these "alleged friends" spent considerable time and expense trying to screw up my mind. They were never successful because it was all but impossible to warp something that was already severely bent.

"You don't look Mexican, but that doesn't mean you aren't," I said. "Don't you normally pronounce your name Hay-Seuss?"

"No, I'm not Mexican, and I always pronounce my name Geez-Us.

While I was never into irreverence, I decided to go along with the gag. So, I said, "You mean as in the Son of God?"

"The same," he replied.

"If I were you, pal, I'd be afraid of being hit with a lightning bolt," I said. "Who sent you here? Who was it, Bobby Jack, Joe Don, Billy Bob?"

"None of your friends sent me here," he said.

I asked, "How do you know the guys I just named are my friends?"

He replied, "Like I told you, I know everything about you."

"Okay, tell me something you know that my friends don't know," I said.

"Well, you were a breast-fed baby," he said, "and when your parents decided to wean you, they took you fishing and told you that a hoot owl got your milk."

Although my friends knew I did not like owls, I had never told any of them the reason why.

"What else?" I asked.

"When you were three years old, you were always sneaking off to play with your four-year-old friend Roland," he said. "Your mother once told you that if you sneaked off, you would wet your pants. You tested her, and you wet your pants."

Not wanting to admit to either of these incidents, I changed the subject, laughed and said, "Well, if you're who you say you are, welcome back to earth."

He asked, "What makes you think I just arrived?"

Luke, let me emphasize that there was no arrogance in the man. He was soft-spoken, seemingly self-assured, and his demeanor was beyond calm.

"Sorry," I said, "I just assumed this was your first trip back to earth since you told your disciples goodbye and gave them the Great Commission."

He said, "So, you know about the Great Commission, do you? I'm impressed. You haven't exactly been a pillar of the church for many years."

"I got over Sunday School and Vacation Bible School, along with the cookies and Kool-Aid," I said. "But forgive my manners, would you like a drink?"

"A glass of water will be fine," he replied.

I laughed and said, "That's right, you can turn it into wine, can't you?"

He shrugged, "So, you remember what's recorded in the Bible as the first miracle?"

I signaled the bartender and said "Water" loud enough for him to hear, then replied, "It's hard to forget stories and Scripture that was drilled into you."

"Your paternal grandfather was a wonderful preacher, and both your grandmothers were saintly women," the man said. "They all tried to steer you in the right direction."

"What about my maternal grandfather?" I asked.

"A womanizer from the word go," he replied.

I grinned and responded, "So, I'm more like my maternal grandfather than my paternal grandfather?"

My response did not seem to amuse him. He simply said, "I'm afraid so."

Many alleged "spiritual people" talk about having had some unique religious experience, during which time Jesus came into their heart. Well, I do not recall Jesus coming into my heart, but more than forty years ago he came into one of my favorite bars.

He would later tell me that any bar I happened to be in was my favorite bar.

There had been a time in my childhood when I had supposedly accepted Christ as my personal Savior. My memory of how I felt at that time had long since escaped me by the time I met the man who called himself Jesus. I was able to recall that with cookies and Kool-Aid some well-meaning people had convinced me to say I accepted Jesus, which led to baptism by emersion. This is not an indictment against the people who with cookies and Kool-Aid convinced me to allegedly become a Christian, just a confession that I was easily persuaded.

When the bartender returned with my margarita and his water, I teased the man and questioned, "Why don't you turn that water into wine?"

He smiled and replied, "It would probably be best if I turned your margarita into water."

"That would be a waste," I said. "But fire away. That might convince me that you're who you say you are."

"I don't need to prove anything," he said.

I laughed and sarcastically said, "I figured you would have an answer like that."

I then took a sip of my margarita and did a doubletake because it tasted like water, and good water, too, not like the stuff we usually got from the Trinity River.

But my margarita still looked like a margarita. So, I tasted it again and got the same results.

"Nice trick," I said, "but I didn't fall off a turnip truck. The bartender must be in on the joke, too."

"Maybe thinking your drink tastes like water is just your imagination," the man said. "After all, you're pretty much past just being drunk."

That annoyed me, Luke, because like most drunks, I have never been drunk.

I summoned the bartender and told him my margarita was nothing more than water. He tasted it and said, "It sure tastes like a margarita to me."

So, a bit angrily I said, "I know what a margarita tastes like, and this is nothing but water."

The bartender said, "Don't get your bowels in an uproar, Mark. I'll make you another one."

"Great, and I'm going to watch you make it," I said. "In fact, I'm going to instruct you."

And that is what I did. The result was that the new margarita tasted just like water. I could not even taste the salt on the rim of the glass, even though I could see it.

"I don't know how you did it," I told the man, "but I'll figure it out. Do it again and I might believe you're who you say you are."

"If that's what it takes to get you to believe, you'll just have to remain an unbeliever," he said.

"Don't get bent out of shape," I responded. "If you know all about me, as you claim, you know I'm a cynic and skeptic."

"Yes, and I know you think that makes you a better journalist, but like most journalists you don't know why," the man said.

"Well, it can't hurt," I said.

He laughed and said, "You don't even know that."

"Look, whoever you are," I said, "the joke is over. I'm impressed. Bring in my clown friend who paid you and we can all have a good laugh together."

"There is no clown friend and there is no joke," he said.

I snorted like a bull in a rodeo chute and said, "You're quite a comedian. But I'm going to have the bartender fix me another margarita, and if it doesn't taste like a margarita, I may have to break both your noses."

He laughed and said, "I don't think that would be a good idea because lightning would be a minor worry. Taste the margarita that was like water again."

I did as he asked and it was pure margarita, which caused me to question, "How in the…"

"Don't ask," he said. "In the way you perceive religion, you don't allow for God or Jesus to have a sense of humor, but they do."

"I've never given it much thought," I said, "but I wish you wouldn't come on with that religious act. It does make me a bit nervous."

"My presence usually makes people nervous," he said.

I responded, "I'd say that's a problem you ought to work on."

"I can only be who I am," he said.

"Well, I don't know who you are, pal, but you and whoever of my friends put you up to this tasteless act should be ashamed," I said. "Pretending to be the Son of God, that's about as low as you can get."

He laughed and said, "Since you claim to despise all religion, I don't see why religious claims by anyone should bother you."

The margaritas had made my brain a bit fuzzy, but since I have never been drunk, I was still in complete control of my faculties. My thought processes were not just good, they were, as always, brilliant.

"Just because I'm not a churchgoer doesn't mean I don't believe in God," I contended.

"What does belief in God mean to you?" he asked.

I responded with philosophical logic that took him aback when I said, "Lots of stuff."

It is difficult for anyone to respond to that kind of answer and he was no exception. He said, "When you can honestly answer my question, there might be some hope for you."

I came back with, "What does that mean?"

My question had him on the ropes and reeling, causing him to come up with the weak response, "It means you have to be honest with yourself."

Luke, what I did not understand was my willingness to listen to this fraud who was sitting beside me, but for some reason I was intrigued with his claim that he was the real Jesus. In fact, there was something about him that was so different that it was frightening. It was as if he was able to look right into my soul, whatever a soul is.

"Since you're not going to be truthful with me, and since I've always wanted to question God about a few things, I'm going to go along with who you say you are to make the conversation more interesting," I said.

"Nice of you," he said, smiling. "But if I'm boring you, I can leave."

"No, don't do that," I said. "Would you like another glass of water, or maybe something stronger?"

"I'm fine," he replied.

I ordered another margarita and asked, "Assuming you're the real Jesus, why would you want to visit Dallas, Texas?"

He replied, "It's not a matter of wanting to visit any specific place. Dallas is here, so I'm here."

My response was, "Well, there's not much to do here except to shop and watch the Cowboys. But I guess you know that, being omnipresent an all."

I was getting in the swing of things, so followed up with, "Why did you come see me? Did you think I might get you a little media coverage?"

He laughed and said, "I hardly require media coverage. But if I did, I'm sure all your readers are much more interested in the Cowboys than they would be in me."

"Hey, don't sell me short," I said. "I might even be able to make you seem interesting. A story on you visiting me might even get me a byline in the *National Inquirer*."

He laughed again and joking, I assume, said, "I'm already persona non grata at two other tabloids, *The New York Times* and the *Washington Post*." He then asked, "But what makes you think I'm here just to visit you?"

"Well, I don't think any of my friends would pay you to visit someone else," I replied.

He chuckled and said, "You're a hard case, Mark."

"Damn right," I said. "I might have used a few other expletives, too, Luke, but it was so long ago I've forgotten."

He said, "You are right in thinking that I wanted to make myself known to you. In fact, I want to make myself known to everyone."

I laughed and said, "That's going to require some heavy-duty media coverage. But if you want to get to know me, ask me anything and I'll tell you whatever you want to know."

"I already know everything about you, and have since I created you," he said.

"Wow! You do have some balls," I said. "I wouldn't dare tempt God the way you're doing."

"I know you're afraid of God," he said, "but you need not be."

I responded, "Easy for you to say, but most people are afraid of God."

He said, "God is not cruel, and what most people claim to fear about God is simply man's inhumanity to man."

I laughed and questioned, "What about woman's inhumanity to man?"

"I know you're trying to be funny," he said, "but your problems with women are of your own making."

"And what would those problems be?" I asked.

He answered, "You're an arrogant ass."

Now, Luke, if the man had been the real Jesus, he would not have talked that way, so I challenged him about it. He countered with, "I created asses, and have even rode one on occasion."

He was quicker than a snake ducking a hoe and had an answer for everything. I had to give him credit for that.

So, I grunted and said, "I didn't know I was going to end up debating religion with some clown tonight, but since I am, I think I can give you a run for your money. For example, this inhumanity you speak about, why doesn't God do something about it?"

He responded, "God could have made people like robots, sexless, mindless and nothing more than mechanical devices who would never get hungry, angry or show any type emotion. But He gave people free will, choices, which is one of the most difficult things for people to understand."

I questioned, "So, you're saying that God doesn't have any control over a person's life?"

"In a sense that's true," he replied. "God speaks to people through His Holy Spirit, and He calls them to do certain things, but because each person has free will they do not have to do what He asks."

I argued, "I don't know if that's theologically sound."

He laughed and said, "Man's theology often isn't what's in God's mind. But like most people, Mark, you want to believe that God controls the parts of your life that go wrong so you will have someone to blame. But you're quite willing to believe that you control the parts of your life that go right."

"That's not true," I said.

"And that's a lie," he said.

"You're saying that God doesn't intervene in the affairs of man, which doesn't make sense to me," I said.

"I'm not saying that at all," he said. "God intervenes when you ask or allow him to intervene, but it's your choice. Because of free will, God does not force Himself into your life."

I said, "I don't know if that's theologically sound."

He laughed and said, "Having you lecture me on theology is more than a little humorous."

"I'm glad you think I'm funny, because you sure aren't," I said. "And if what you say is true, what's the point of prayer?"

He laughed again and replied, "Prayer is communion with God, a reassurance of salvation. What is asked for in prayer should be precipitated by a willingness to follow God's directives. In doing that a person's prayers are answered.

"For example, if you pray that hungry children in the world be fed, you can be sure to have that prayer answered by giving your money for that purpose. In other words, God gives you an opportunity to participate in answering your own prayers.

God, through His Holy Spirit, has told you what is important in life, so in prayer you have a chance to talk things over with God and do what's right. Prayer is not just two-way communication between you and God, it's also two-way participation. If you commit to God, He used all your abilities and talents to do His work on earth.

"That's different, of course, than praying for salvation, which is only possible by repenting of your sin and asking God, through me, to forgive your sin."

I argued, "That's not exactly what some churches teach."

He shrugged and said, "True, but it's what I teach."

I cannot tell you why Luke, maybe it was just the way the guy talked or maybe it was the booze, but I was in a dream-like state, remembering everything he said and wanting more.

I questioned, "So, you're saying I shouldn't ask God for a million dollars?"

He shook his head in resignation and said, "If you want to pray for a million dollars, feel free. Your prayer might be answered if you commit your time, energy and ability to achieving that goal. But God doesn't deal in the monetary, He deals in the spiritual."

"So," I asked, "how come every time I go to church the preacher is harping about money?"

"Well, for one thing that isn't true," he said. "You haven't exactly made a nuisance of yourself at church, but when you have gone money hasn't been mentioned a single time. Your mind has tricked you into thinking it has because you don't want to give. And when you've been at church, you did not want to be there, and you're looking for any excuse not to go back."

I argued, "That's not true."

He countered with, "Of course, it is."

"You seem to have a pretty low opinion of me," I said.

"Quite the contrary," he said. "If I were picking apostles again, you would have a shot at being one."

Surprised, I responded with, "You're joking."

He laughed and said, "Of course, I am."

"You're also one crazy dude," I said.

He agreed, saying, "That seems to have been the consensus when I was first sent here, so things haven't changed all that much. And while many have accepted the idea of Christianity, few have ever practiced it."

I said, "I read just the other day that there are almost two billion Christians in the world."

He shrugged and said, "That's nice reading, but how was that count made?"

"What do you mean?" I asked.

"Well, to become a Christian you have to accept and understand that you are a sinner, repent of your sin, and believe in and accept me, Jesus Christ, as your Savior. Tell me, how many babies and children do you think understand that?"

"I have no idea," I said.

"Well," he said, "infants born to Catholic parents are baptized and become Catholics, but they're not Christians. And infants born to Methodist parents are baptized and become Methodists, but they're not Christians.

"Being a Christian requires that a person acknowledge sin in their life and then engage in a personal relationship with me. And while I know every infant and child by name, they cannot become a Christian until they reach an accountability that enables them to do that."

I questioned, "So, you're saying the number of Christians mentioned in the article I read is bogus?"

"Unfortunately, yes," he replied. "Prior to reaching the age of accountability, a child is under God's protection. But once they reach an age of accountability, they must make a personal and individual choice about their relationship with God."

"Well, J.C. or whoever you are, hope you don't mind the initials, because I don't feel comfortable calling you Jesus, I think you're as full of it as a Christmas turkey. And if people want to call themselves Christians, what's the harm?"

He shook his head in resignation said replied, "None, I suppose, until judgment day. That's when it's going to matter a whole lot.

"What do you mean?" I asked.

"Unfortunately, most people think of being a Christian in the same way they think of being a Democrat or Republican," he replied, then said, "No, that's not true. Being a Democrat, Republican or member of a country club is more important to them."

"Whoa," I said. "You sound a bit angry."

He smiled and said, "If you think I get angry, you should see God when He gets riled."

"I didn't know God got angry," I countered.

"That's because you don't know God," he said.

I laughed and said, "Anger and a sense of humor. I like that in a guy. You seem to know the Bible, and from the way you're dressed you're probably a country preacher, and not a very successful one. Not that I'm against country preachers. There was one that helped me out quite a bit."

"Yes, I know," he said. "God is a lot bigger than the Bible, the size of a church, or a person's clothes. What's unseen of God is greater than what's seen.

"But you, Mark, you've filed all the spiritual help you've received in your life away to where it's no bother to you. You don't want anything spiritual to interfere with the way you've chosen to live your life."

Luke, I admit that the guy was getting on my nerves a bit, so I responded, "I'll have you know that I'm not the worst guy around. And I do care about people and spiritual things. I've even been thinking about making a monthly commitment to Saint Jude's Hospital, or Shriners Hospital for Children. Maybe both."

He laughed and said, "Well, thinking about it won't cost you a dime."

It was a good shot, and it hurt, but I figured that I had been playing defense long enough. It was time to go on the offensive, so I asked, "Where were you before you came in here to interrupt my evening?"

"I went to church," he replied.

"Which one?" I asked. "Baptist, Catholic, Methodist? I've always wanted to know which church Jesus would choose."

"Denominations are an idea of people, not of God," he replied. "People should simply choose a church that coincides most with my way."

"You are one helluva an actor," I said, laughing. "So, you're not going to tell me where you went."

"No," he said, "but I will tell you that I was disappointed."

"If you're who you say you are, you must have known that you would be disappointed," I said.

"We won't get into that," he said, "but the building and many of the people were so ostentatious, the service such a production geared to stirring emotions totally unrelated to Christianity, that I almost puked."

I chucked and said, "I could have told you that most of the churches in Dallas are full of hypocrites."

He responded, "The hypocrites in the city's churches have a better chance of finding the truth than the hypocrites outside it."

I knew that I had been hit with another good shot, but undaunted asked, "Why didn't you cleanse the temple, toss all those ostentatious folks out of it?"

He gave me an indescribable look and said, "You probably won't understand this, but the building where I went to church has nothing to do with me or my way. In fact, this bar can be just as holy. My way has to do with where the Holy Spirit is, where He is welcomed.

"The buildings where people go to church, if they reject the presence of the Holy Spirit, they are nothing more than dead edifices. The elaborate furnishings, the stained-glass windows, they all belong to people and are for the glory of people. The only thing God is interested in and treasures are the souls of those committed to Him."

I agreed, saying, "Well, I've always said too much money is wasted on church buildings."

"Too much money is wasted on everything," he said, "like that margarita in front of you. Like most drunks, you want to find fault with all churches. They're not all bad. For all those that are rackets, with all assets vested in the name of the pastor, there are many more with members who are trying to do my work in the world. If you're searching for truth, not for people and doctrines to feed your prejudices.

"One of the great lies in the world is that one church is as good as another. Now that's true of bars, because you can get smashed in any bar, but you can't get the spiritual food you need in any church. It's okay to judge churches, like anything else, understanding that the judgment of all people is flawed."

To my way of thinking, J.C. had made a mistake when talking about judgment, so I was quick to correct him saying, "If you're who you say you are, correct me if I'm wrong but didn't you say something about not judging so you wouldn't be judged?"

"It's good to know that some of your days in church were not wasted," he said, "but, unfortunately, you retained just enough to be dangerous.

"The words Matthew attributed to me were, *'Judge not, that you be not judged. For with the judgment you pronounce you will be judged.'*

"Matthew recorded my words correctly, but what he didn't say was that I was using irony to get across my point. The intended implication is the exact opposite of the literal sense. I was not making a categorical command to never render judgment.

"If obeyed, a command like that would destroy all that is best in human life. I was warning that if you want to avoid judgment on yourself, you have to do the impossible, which is to refuse to engage in any judgment at all."

I peered at what was left of my margarita, and decided this guy was deep, even for me. You see, I kind of pride myself on my intelligence. I have a pretty high IQ, a few points higher than President Trump's, whose IQ is the second highest of all the American Presidents.

J.C. continued with "If you give up judgment, you give up almost everything that dignifies human life. You're forced to make judgments every day, and every moment of your life. I again stress that God gives you the opportunity to choose, to judge."

"If what you say is true," I said, "I've heard a lot of lying preachers over the years."

"Preachers do lie," he said. "A church operated by people is not necessarily my church. My church is spiritual, whereas human beings are incapable, because of their sinful natures, to keep materialism and their culture out of a church. The true church is an ideal for which committed people strive as a collective force."

The way you put it," I said, "it's impossible to have a true church. So, why try?"

"Why not?" he asked. "Impossible goals are what makes life worth living. If your only goals in life are easily attained, your missing out on the excitement and mystery of life. You shouldn't be content with imperfection just because you think perfection is unobtainable."

"I don't think many people are going to buy into that kind of deal," I said.

He agreed, saying, "You're right, not many people will make the commitment to follow me and my way."

The margaritas must have dulled my senses, because when the man said he had to find a room for the night, and that the motel next to the bar had no vacancies, I suddenly found myself inviting him to spend the night at my place.

The bartender, who had taken my car keys, helped him get me out to my car, a vintage BMW. If you lived in the Highland Park area, or in proximity to it, there was an unwritten law that you must drive a European-made foreign car. It was one of the ways you fit in, thus I had opted for a BMW that, granted, had some age on it.

My car had a missing back window that I had cleverly enclosed with cardboard and duct tape, the exterior paint had faded to another color, the windshield was cracked, the leather seats had tears in them, and you had to jiggle the ignition a certain way to get it to start, but it was a BMW, so I was proud of it.

When we walked outside the bar, the wind slapped me in the face like a woman reacting to an inappropriate remark. It was colder than the proverbial well digger's rear end.

However, the cold air was not strong enough to sober me.

"I'll drive," the man who called himself Jesus said.

I was about to give him directions, but he interrupted my thoughts with, "I know the way."

Because of my inebriated self, this did not seem strange to me at the time.

TWO

The following morning, I awoke to the smell of frying bacon and aroma of freshly brewed coffee, which was unusual. On the way to work, I usually grabbed a half dozen donuts and a coffee in a paper cup, some of which ended up on the front of my shirt because of braking in Dallas traffic.

After covering my undies with a robe and slipping my number tens into house slippers, I staggered into the master bathroom and, with cold water, washed the sleep from my eyes.

Unfortunately, cold water does nothing for an alcohol-induced headache. So, I popped a couple of aspirin in my mouth, hoping they would absorb some of the pain.

When I looked in the mirror to see if my head was as big as it felt, I was relieved to find that my face and head looked as normal as it always had. And as always, after a stupid bout with alcohol that can never be won, I mentally repented and was determined to change my ways.

Like most people, I have always done a lot of things mentally that I never followed through on.

When I entered the kitchen the man who called himself Jesus was sitting at the breakfast table reading the newspaper and nursing a cup of coffee. He glanced up from the paper and asked, "How do you want your eggs?"

I groaned and replied, "I don't," then asked, "What time is it?"

He answered, "It's six o'clock."

I exclaimed, "My god, it's still night."

He laughed and said, "You need to be up and about."

"Why?" I questioned.

He answered, "Getting started early in the morning is good for the soul."

I grunted and said, "Maybe that has been my problem all these years," then asked, "Anything interesting in the paper?"

I was still wondering why I had invited this guy to come home with me. I attributed it to my drinking, but also to the fact that for some reason I knew that I had nothing to fear from him, and that I am also more of a do-gooder than people give me credit for being.

"The city transit board is still bickering among themselves about the allocation of federal money," he said, "but you know that. You wrote the story."

He was referring to Dallas Area Rapid Transit (DART), a political group that was put together to allegedly solve the city's non-existent public transportation problem. Their bus and rail system cost taxpayers more than seventy dollars a ride per person, but hey, it was just taxpayer money.

I was investigating because I figured where money was concerned, you could always find an elected or appointed politician with their hand in the cookie jar. In this case, I was sure we had an entire DART Mafia, all of whom had both hands in the jar.

"That's really not news," I said. "They're always bickering, and for what? Dallas doesn't need mass transit. It's not New York City. But what do you think about my writing?"

"It's okay," he replied.

"Just okay?" I questioned.

"If you want a critique, don't look at me," he replied. "Besides, I'm not responsible for DART."

He got up from his chair, poured me a cup of coffee and set it down before me.

I laughed and questioned, "Are you telling me that God doesn't have anything to do with DART? That will make a great story. I can see the headline now; JESUS SAYS GOD DENIES RESPONSILITY FOR DART."

He smiled and said, "I have no problem with the content of the story or the headline."

"I meant to ask, but forgot," I said. "How did you get to the bar last night?"

"I rode a DART bus," he replied.

"Was it a lonely ride?" I asked.

He answered, "Well, I was the only one on the bus other than the driver."

I laughed and said, "A friend of mine recently saw four people on a DART bus and got excited about such a large crowd. However, he later found the driver was taking his family on an outing."

J.C., which is what I decided to call him, laughed and questioned, "This DART thing really irritates you, doesn't it?"

I replied, "I get angry at stupidity if that's what you mean."

The man shook his head in resignation and said, "Then you're going to be angry all the time. God didn't make people stupid; they've been able to do that on their own, especially in terms of right and wrong choices.

"Now, how about a couple of eggs with some bacon? I happen to know you like them over medium. I've also made some biscuits, just like your mother makes them."

"Oh, I doubt that you can make biscuits the way my mother makes them," I said. "No one can make better biscuits or cornbread than she does."

He laughed and responded, "I said my biscuits were like your mother's, not better."

Well, Luke, the guy did cook me a couple of eggs just like I like them, and the biscuits certainly tasted just like my mother's. The entire breakfast was better than what I normally got in a restaurant.

When he made himself a similar breakfast, I thought I had exposed him for the fraud he was. "You've been caught by bacon," I said. "The real Jesus is a Jew. He wouldn't eat pork."

"Why do you think Jesus was a Jew?" he asked.

"If you knew your Bible, you would know," I said. "The Bible says clear as day that he was a Jew."

"No, it doesn't," the man said. "Who does it identify as my father?"

I did not want to respond, but replied, "The Holy Spirit."

"That's right," he said. "Does the Bible say that God, His Son and the Holy Spirit are Jewish?"

Haltingly, I replied, "Well, I assumed…"

"Never assume," he said. "You should have learned that when you were in journalism school."

That hurt. But if he knew me, he would know that I had never learned anything in a journalism class, and am sure that the people in media today who pose as journalists did not, if any of them were ever in a real journalism class.

"So, you're telling me that people in heaven eat bacon and eggs?"

He sighed, laughed and replied, "No, what we have to eat in heaven is much better than what you called food here on earth."

He then questioned, "If you don't like the DART situation, why don't you do something about it?"

"Like what?" I asked.

"Well, you are an investigative reporter," he said, "and you do have the power of the press behind you."

I laughed and said, "To claim to be all-knowing, you have a very misguided view of the press."

He smiled and said, "You're referring, I suppose, to the fact that your superiors have swallowed the mass transportation lie being perpetrated by some politicians, those who will get rich off the lie, and who are buying media support by purchasing advertising from the media?"

I took a swig of my coffee and replied, "Well, yes. These clowns keep media from exposing them by purchasing advertising. Money talks."

He popped a piece of bacon in his mouth and said, "They do a lot more than that."

"What do you mean?" I asked.

He replied, "People are frustrated by traffic problems, many of which are caused by necessary road construction. Am I right?"

"That's not exactly some big revelation," I said.

"Offer some solutions," he said.

"What kind of solutions?" I asked.

He replied, "Well, most of the road construction that's causing problems could be done at night. That's when most cities do it, when there isn't as much traffic. And in the summer, it's easier on the workers, not so hot."

What the man said got my brain cranked up. He had given me an idea for an op-ed. I had been thinking about doing a series of editorials calling for nighttime road construction.

He interrupted my thinking and said, "As long as you just think about doing those editorials, it won't take much of your time."

The fact that he seemed to know what I was thinking irritated me.

"All this stuff you know about me and my attitude, there's no doubt in my mind that you've been talking to my friends," I said.

"Wrong, amigo," he said, I don't need to talk to your friends to know all about you. But since you've mentioned your friends, when are you going to introduce me to them?"

I questioned, "How am I going to introduce you, by what name?"

"Just introduce me as Jesus," he replied.

"Sure," I said, "and have the ones who aren't paying for this charade call me crazy."

He got up from the table, went to the kitchen counter where the coffee pot was busy staying hot, brought the pot over to the table and filled my cup, then returned it.

He then said, "Your friends might be more accepting of me than you are."

I laughed and said, "If you think that's a possibility, you don't know my friends. But if I do introduce you to one or more of my friends, I'll just call you J.C. Smith, unless you want to tell me your real name. J.C. Smith, that's a good name for you."

He smiled and responded, "You Southerners have always liked to use initials."

My guard went up immediately and I questioned, "You don't like the South?"

He chuckled and said, "I have nothing against the South. The South, and some Southerners have some redeeming qualities."

"I don't guess you would have been on our side during the Civil War," I said, "but most Southerners who fought in that war didn't own slaves. So, what are these redeeming qualities you're talking about?"

He replied, "Blackeye peas, fried okra, cold cantaloupe, cornbread, sweet tea, pork chops, chicken fried steak, fried chicken, brisket and barbecued pork ribs."

Luke, the man was now talking in a language I understood. And he had probably consumed a half dozen pieces of bacon. He chewed up bacon like a wood shredder chews up tree limbs, which gave me cause to question his authenticity. I was still clinging to the idea that the real Jesus would not eat pork.

"Now concerning all that good Southern food that you mentioned, it's not part of an Orthodox Jew's diet," I said.

"So?" he questioned.

"The real Jesus is an Orthodox Jew," I said, going back to my earlier contention.

"I'm not Jewish," he said.

"You probably aren't," I agreed, "but that's because you aren't the real Jesus. The real Jesus was a Jew, and the Jews are God's chosen people."

"That's ridiculous," he said. "God doesn't choose a people; a person has to choose God."

"You have some weird theology," I said.

He chop-blocked me with, "Any theology would be weird to you. You're like so many people who have a view of God that limits Him. You know a few Scriptures, but you can't think out of the little box that makes God no taller than you are."

Now, Luke, I do not know why I was taking it on the chin like this. You know me. I have never taken physical or verbal abuse from anyone. But for some reason I did not understand at the time, and still do not, I was letting this guy get in one punch after another without lifting a glove to defend myself.

"What about Moses?" I asked.

"What about him?" the man replied.

"God chose him to lead the Jews out of bondage," I said.

"God called him" the man said, "but he did not have to respond to the call. Following the call, Moses chose God, then sought and followed God's directives. Moses made a commitment to God's way. If he had refused God's call, God would have called someone else."

I argued, "When Jesus came to earth, He came as a Jew."

The man shrugged his shoulders and said, "It was a matter of coming into the most appropriate culture of the time. If at the time Ethiopians had been more in tune with the things of God than the Jews, the Father would have introduced me in that culture, and you would be saying that the real Jew was an Ethiopian. I'm universal, not ethnic."

Continuing to be argumentative, I asked, "So, what about prophecy that predicted Jesus coming as a Jew?"

"God knows prophecy before it is prophecy," he replied. "What I'm telling you is that I am every person, am every color, and speak every language of all humankind."

I thought about challenging him on the language thing but decided against it. In college, I learned one sentence in German and a couple of Latin words that I have since forgotten. On my own I had learned a couple of

Mexican words, which were and are taco and nachos.

"We could have a better conversation if you would dispense with the phony baloney," I said.

"You want me to lie about who I am, and I can't do that," he said.

I said, "It's just not right, a man claiming to be the Son of God to play a gag."

"I keep telling you it's not a gag," he said, "that I really am the Son of God. Why is it so hard for you to believe me?"

"Well, for one thing," I replied, "if you were real, it would mean that you're here in advance of what I've always been taught was your schedule. There's supposed to be a Rapture where all Christians are caught up in the air with you, then a seven-year tribulation period, and then you return to beat up on some clown called the Antichrist."

He questioned, "And you read all that in the Bible?"

"Well, not exactly," I replied. "I read some of it. Preachers and other people filled me in on the rest of it."

He asked, "Don't you think God is bigger than the Bible; that He can do whatever He chooses?"

"I suppose," I agreed, "but there's something else."

"I know what you're going to say, but go ahead and say it," he said.

I replied, "If Jesus was going to show up in Dallas, Texas, I don't think He would be hanging out with me."

"Why, because you're a far cry from being a righteous person?" he asked. "Prior to being crucified, I was accused of hanging out with a lot of bad characters, many of whom were worse than you.

"And if you recall any of your Sunday School lessons at all, you were taught that I came to bring salvation to sinners, not to the alleged righteous."

I shook my head in mock amazement and said, "I'll give you credit for this; you are one smooth talker. You seem to know the Bible backwards and forwards. But, of course, I'm not a theologian. You could pull the wool over my eyes and I wouldn't know it. But man, I get nervous about the way you're coming on. It has to be blasphemy."

He angrily questioned, "What do you really know about blasphemy? Most of those accusing others of blasphemy are themselves blasphemous to the core. So, I'm not surprised that you would accuse me of blasphemy against God, since I've always been accused of it."

"Don't get your panties in a wad," I said. "You're a great actor, and I mean that as a compliment. You never let your guard down, and your demeanor is truly genuine."

He responded, "You say I don't let my guard down. What about you, Mark? You keep your guard up constantly, so you won't betray to others what you really want in life. That's a tough sell, isn't it?

I asked, "How do you know what I want in life?"

"I know what you claim to want," he said "Claiming to want something, then working to achieve it are two different things. Why don't you tell me what you claim you want?"

"My wants are no secret," I replied. "I want a faithful wife, children, a nice home and a job making enough money to live comfortably on."

"How can you lie to me like that?" he asked.

Why this guy was not getting on my nerves, I do not know. For some reason, even when he was hitting me with one sucker punch after another, I seemed to be asking for more.

I argued, "I'm not lying."

"Mark, your entire purpose in life has been sex and money," he said. "You want more money because you think it will help you with your sex life."

I said, "I don't need any help with it."

"Well, that's debatable," he said. "You're not as much of a Romeo as you think you are, and most thinking women shun you like you're a transporter of the bubonic plague."

"I've been married," I said.

"I know, beautiful girl, too," he said. "And you were about as faithful to her as a feral male cat is to his nightly conquests. You couldn't even be faithful to her for a year."

Now, Luke, I do not mind telling you that the guy had pushed the wrong button. My ex-wife and her lawyer had a vendetta against me. And, so did the alleged Christian counselor that we were supposed to see together. The guy never took my side on anything.

The fact that I had been unfaithful to my ex-wife in our first year of marriage was something I was not proud of, and something I had not discussed with anyone.

So, where was this guy getting his information? Was he a friend of my ex-wife, her lawyer, or the alleged Christian counselor?

My response to him was, "I don't know where you get your material. but it's erroneous."

He asked, "Are you going to sit there and tell me you weren't unfaithful to your wife?"

"No, I'm not going to tell you anything," I replied. "I'm going to take a couple of Extra Strength Excedrin because I have a bad headache."

He laughed and said, "I told you what those margaritas would do."

I countered with, "Nobody likes an I told you so," got up from the table and obtained the bottle of pain killers that I kept in the kitchen for bad mornings. I popped a couple of those bad boys into my mouth and used a glass of water to aid me in swallowing them.

"What do you plan to do today?" I asked.

"Look for a job and a place to live," he replied.

I questioned, "What kind of job?"

"I've done a little carpentry," he said, but I'm willing to do any kind of work that's honorable. And money isn't important, I'm willing to work for room and board."

I said, "You're obviously an educated man. You can do better than just room and board."

He smiled and said, "I'm not educated in the sense that you're talking about. I never even went to what you call elementary school."

"You're putting me on," I said, then asked, "Where did you really go; Baylor, SMU, TCU?"

"Why do you think I would have gone to any of those schools?" he asked.

"Well, they're Christian schools," I said.

He gave a booming laugh and said, "If Christianity was shaped like a football, I might agree with you."

I questioned, "I take it you don't like football?"

"I didn't say that," he replied. "But if you prioritize and list what should be important in a person's life, football doesn't earn a place on page one of that list."

I questioned, "So, you're telling me that Baylor, SMU and TCU aren't Christian schools?"

"An entity like a school, even a church, can't be Christian," he replied. "Only an individual can be a Christian. It is an individual matter between each person and God."

The guy was taking me into some mine fields that I did not want to traverse, so I found myself saying something that I could not understand, which was, "You're welcome to stay here until you find a place."

He responded, "I don't want to be a bother."

"You won't be," I said. "There's just me and my dog, Cowboy. By the way, have you seen Cowboy?"

"He's asleep in the bedroom I used," the man said.

This was somewhat of a shock to me, Luke, because your grandad always slept in my bedroom, and he was very suspicious of strangers.

About that time Cowboy wandered into the kitchen, stretched, yawned and then went over and rubbed up against the man. The man got up from his chair, went to the cupboard, took out Cowboy's food and filled his bowl.

Cowboy gave the guy an appreciative wag of his tail and a grin. I was not sure of what to make of what was going on.

"If I stay, I'll do the housework and cooking," the man said. "I'll be your servant."

I protested, "Hold on now, I'm not in the market for a servant. I'm just saying that you can stay if you like, temporarily."

"We can try it," he said. "If you get uneasy with the situation, you can tell me, and I'll leave."

"You won't bother me," I said. "Just don't preach to me and everything will be okay."

"I'm afraid I can't make that promise," he said.

I sighed and said, "Okay, don't promise. Just don't expect me to listen to you. And I'm hoping you'll give up on this Jesus thing before long."

"I can't give up on the truth," he said.

I laughed and said, "I figure whoever is paying you will tire of doing it after a while."

"I keep telling you that no one is paying me to do anything," he said.

"And I keep telling you that I know when someone is putting me on," I said. "Nevertheless, if you're who you say you are, there's a lot of building going on this area. Maybe you can get a job as a carpenter. This is a right to work state. You don't need a union card."

"It might be a little more difficult than you think," he said, "since I don't have a Social Security card."

I questioned, "You don't have a Social Security card?"

He replied, "They're not required in heaven."

"The truth be known, if you're an illegal they're not required in Dallas, either," I said. "And, with the name you're using, you won't have a problem here. If you do, I'll loan you twenty bucks to buy a card."

He said, "The difference is that, unlike some of these illegals, I can't lie."

I disagreed, saying, "Everyone lies.

He countered, "Everyone but God."

There was something about his eyes that told me he was telling the truth about not being able to lie, but I did not want to believe it. So, I said, "If you can't lie, you're in for some tough sledding in this town."

"In any town," he said.

I suggested, "Maybe you could be a pastor. You seem to know quite a bit about the Bible."

He said, "I know everything about the Bible, and everything about God, and I can preach, which means I would be a problem for any church."

"If you were who you say you are, know what you say you know, I could see where that would be a problem," I said, laughing. "No church would want that much truth."

He smiled and said, "You're forgetting some of the other things modern day churches require of a pastor, like a college and seminary degree, a wife and a couple of kids, plus experience."

"If you think you would need a wife, I don't guess you're a Catholic."

"As far as man's religion is concerned, I'm not anything," he said. "There's a lot wrong with churches as a single entity, but not necessarily with specific churches.

"And, by the way, I consider myself more a teacher than a preacher. John the Baptist, now he was a preacher."

"Hey, I'm not the one who developed the system," I said. "It's my understanding that every church is built on God's word, or what people think is God's word."

"Every church should be built on God's word," he said, "but most try to improve on what God says and end up watering it down to fit their cultural criteria. The Son of God is the last person they want included in their chosen lifestyles."

I shrugged and said, "What you're talking about is a lot to think about, especially with a headache. And I need to shave and shower, so excuse me while I get ready for work."

I got up from the table and headed for the master bathroom, expecting Cowboy to follow me as he usually did. But his demeanor told me that he planned to hang with this guy who called himself Jesus. And since I considered him a roommate and never lorded it over him, I made the trip to my bedroom and bathroom on my own.

Once there I called Mary Lou Magruder and asked her to meet me for breakfast at a small deli on Preston Road, and she agreed. It was my favorite deli in Dallas, possibly because it did not smell of fish during the breakfast hours.

I do not know how anyone can handle fish for breakfast, and that alone could keep me from becoming a Jew.

Now, Luke, Mary Lou and I were once an item. She was one of the most beautiful women in Dallas and had hosiery advertising legs. Compared to her, Victoria Secret models were rejects.

Mary Lou and I came close to tying the knot, but as the last minute I got cold feet and told her I was going back to my ex-wife, which, of course, was a lie. Chances of my ex-wife taking me back were about as likely as an eco-environmentalist being right about one of their apocalyptic predictions for the country.

I considered Mary Lou a friend, even though she chopped my legs out from under me at every opportunity. Based on our history together, I could not blame her. So, she was a suspect when it came to who had sent the man who called himself Jesus, and no one could stand up to my interrogation methods.

I had a surefire technique for determining whether someone was lying to me, so simple that anyone can use it to determine whether there is an attempt to deceive them. You simply make a person look at your right thumb. If they can do it without laughing, they are telling the truth. If they laugh, they are lying.

I never wasted much time showering, shaving, brushing my teeth and dressing for the day, possibly because of my military background. My dress for the day was like for every workday; slacks, shirt, tie, sportscoat and loafers.

As I was going out the door, the man said, "Enjoy your breakfast with Mary Lou."

Now how did he know that I was meeting Mary Lou? I did not want to know, so said, "The meeting depends on me getting my car started."

He said, "If all else fails, pray."

Well, like the previous night it was still colder than the proverbial well digger's rear end. And when I put the key in the ignition of the BMW, there was not even a hum.

The battery was deader than the promise of a college president telling media that a coach's job was not in jeopardy following a losing season.

I remembered what the man had said, thought, "What the hell," then voiced aloud, "Lord, please start this card, in the name of Jesus. Amen."

When I turned the key again, the motor roared to life. I could not believe it. Of course, I was not foolish enough to attribute the car starting to prayer. Something just clicked.

The traffic flow was slow enough that I had plenty of time to think while on the way to my breakfast rendezvous. The guy who called himself Jesus was an enigma, but I figured whoever was paying him would soon tire of shelling out cash for a joke that was not working. Whoever it was, they must have thought I had fallen off a turnip truck.

I was a bit surprised at myself, that I had put up with the charade for as long as I had, and in some instances had enjoyed it. But enough was enough.

As I proceeded down Preston Road, several DART buses, all empty of passengers, got in my way. The buses made me angry because the city claimed to be having budget problems that made raises for police and fire-fighters problematic, but DART was siphoning money from the taxpayer tank like a thirsty bull at a waterhole.

Luke, I have always thought tax money ought to go for what our forefathers intended, protection of the citizenry; for military, police, fire-fighters and other essential services. Liberals want to use it for everything but, mostly to enrich themselves and tear down the government until there are no taxpayers. For some reason they want Communism, which they like to call Socialism.

Anyway, I figured that if mass transit was viable, private sources would fund and operate it. With the money DART had planned to spend back in the day, they could have for a century provided cab fare for everyone who needed a ride and had money left over.

I had entrenched myself in a booth and was working on a second cup of coffee when Mary Lou entered the deli. As previously mentioned, she was quite an eyeful; tall and willowy, with auburn hair hanging below her shoulders, a perfect complexion, dark penetrating eyes, a ready smile and a wit that was equal to that of anyone I have ever met. She could have walked away with both a Miss America and Miss Universe title.

There was a time in which I thought I was in love with her, but as I came to know myself better, I realized it was just lust. Of course, I have lusted after the thirty or so women that I have loved.

Mary Lou parked herself across from me and said, "This is quite a surprise. I haven't seen the great Mark Luther this early in the morning for quite some time."

I grinned and said, "Hey, I've decided to make early to bed and early to rise a regular habit. I've been told it's good for the soul."

"If that's the case, you should definitely do it," she said. "I don't know of anyone who needs more soul repair than you do."

I said, "Nice shot, Mary Lou. You're the kind of person who would pump a couple of rounds into a dead duck."

She laughed and said, "You kind of make yourself a sitting duck."

A waitress brought Mary Lou some coffee and took her order, which was hefty. She ordered everything but the kitchen sink, whereas I ordered only one scrambled egg and toast. Of course, I had already had a good breakfast.

Mary Lou's ex-husband reportedly said that she ate like a bird. If so, the man was talking about a very big bird, because Mary Lou could out-eat and out-drink anyone that I have ever known.

After the waitress was out of earshot, she asked, "To what do I owe this honor?"

I feigned hurt, asking, "Can't I just call and invite you to breakfast without wanting anything?"

She shrugged her shoulders and replied, "You could, but you never have."

I countered, "That's not true. We've shared a lot of mornings together when I didn't want anything."

"I thought we were going to share a lifetime of them," she said.

"Maybe we should have," I said, "but the timing was all wrong."

She asked, "How is Carole?"

Carole is my ex, who I told everyone I ever dated that I was going back to when things got too serious. And they had gotten very serious with Mary Lou.

It was a convenient lie, and it became very hard to sell when Carole remarried. And, of course, Mary Lou had seen through it long before Carole remarried.

"Carole's fine," I said.

"How's her husband?" she asked.

"He's fine, too," I replied.

I knew she was goading me. She knew Carole would rather talk to a couple of Mormon missionaries, or a Christian Scientist, before talking to me. It had been years since she had said a word to me, and on that occasion, it was in the presence of her lawyer.

While Mary Lou has nice eyes, a beautiful face and an innocent demeanor, she is more cunning than a fox in a hen house. At this time, she was in her mid-thirties, and she was convinced that our breakup was because of my desire for much younger women.

And maybe she was right. However, it was probably more my desire for numbers rather than youth that tolled the death knell for our relationship. I could not help but remember that the man who called himself Jesus made that observation.

But at the time I still liked Mary Lou a lot, maybe more than any other woman I had ever known. But there were times when I was in her presence that I felt that if we were together, she would have me goose-stepping like a World War II German soldier under her command.

I am not saying that she was a Nazi, but she had some serious control issues, along with an attitude about gender equality that kept her in hot water at her job.

So, attempting a counter-offensive in her blitzkrieg against me, I asked, "So, how's the job going, Mary Lou?"

She worked as a public relations flak for a major corporation, one that produced products that were unnecessary. There are a lot of corporations like that, all putting great emphasis on advertising and PR for obvious reasons.

Mary Lou sighed and replied, "It's a job. It pays the mortgage and car payments."

I knew she did not like the job, simply tolerated it. She worked with a lot of incompetent male bozos who spent all their time either kissing the chairman of the board's rear end or thinking up creative ways to kiss it. They were well-rewarded for the degrading act, which bothered Mary Lou a great deal. Intellect can be a burdensome and worrisome problem for a smart person trying to survive in the corporate world.

Faking sympathy, I said, "I was hoping you would have found something better by now."

"PR jobs aren't easy to come by," she lamented, "especially those that will pay a woman a living wage."

Mary Lou had graduated from SMU with a business degree in marketing. One of her professors had told her she should not take a job for less than sixty grand a year but was unwilling to help her find such a job.

College professors back then, Luke, were no different than they are now. They taught out-of-date stuff that was completely irrelevant for the real work.

Of course, they now teach a combination of Nazism/Communism and destruction of a system that has provided them status and financial security. But when you have poop for brains, as most of them do, you do not realize that you are destroying what has given you that status and security.

"Yeah, the job market took a big hit under that clown President Carter," I said, "along with everything else. I don't know anyone who could afford a home with the kind of interest rates being charged during his Presidency. But now that President Reagan has been elected, your job prospects will probably be better."

She shrugged and said, "Let's talk about something more pleasant than my job," he said, "like when you're going to take me on a cruise."

I feigned surprise and said, "I didn't know that I was," knowing she was going to blindside me with something from our checkered past.

"I figured you wouldn't remember," she said, "or, at least, claim you didn't."

"I have an unbelievable memory," I said.

"You have *unbelievable lots of stuff*, but remembering isn't included," she said. "You always attribute alcohol to your convenient loss of memory, and no one can argue with the fact that you're a ridiculous drunk.

"Would you like me to list all the other things you promised me?"

"That won't be necessary," I replied. "I probably don't have time to listen to all you say that I've promised you. I have to go to work this afternoon."

She laughed and said, "You're right. I would need a week or so to list them all."

Mary Lou likes a good joke as much as the next person, but I doubted that she was involved in the Jesus charade. When it came to money, she was tighter than a cap on what should have been, at the time, a producing oil rig. I use that analogy because back then phony patriot Jimmy Carter had again sold us out to the Arabs and curbed domestic oil production. The guy had about as much economic sense as Lyndon Johnson did when handing out welfare checks.

Still, although I doubted Mary Lou had anything to do with the man who called himself

Jesus, when investigating anything, I left no stone unturned. So, I asked, "Do you know a guy named Jesus?"

She looked at me as if I had finally gone over the edge and replied, "Are you asking me if I'm a Christian?"

"Oh, no, nothing like that," I replied.

She shook her head in mock dismay and said, "Since I haven't seen you in a few days, I thought that in that span of time you might have had an epiphany, or joined up with a fundamentalist church whose members go around asking everyone if they know Jesus."

"No," I said, "I'm asking if you know a real guy named Jesus, not the church Jesus."

"A guy named Hay-Seuss cuts my yard," she said. "He might use the name Jesus when he's speaking English, if he ever speaks English."

"The guy I'm talking about isn't Mexican," I said.

"Okay, so why are you asking me if I know this guy named Jesus?"

So, I told her the entire story of my encounter with Jesus, then asked, "It's not that I don't believe you, Mary Lou, but would you mind taking the test?"

She laughed and asked, "Are you talking about your stupid thumb test?"

"Yes, it will verify whether you're telling me the truth," I replied. "I'd like to wipe you off the suspect list."

"I refuse to submit to that kind of stupidity," she said.

I warned, "Then I can't take you off my suspect list."

"Like I could care," she said.

My uncle, who lived in Chicago, taught me the test when I was very young. He supposedly learned it from Al Capone, who he and my aunt partied with during prohibition and beyond. My uncle, who was an executive for a large meat packer, told me Capone used the thumb lie detector system exclusively and that it never let him down.

He could not, however, recall anyone ever telling Capone the truth, but said the man was not a killer. He let other people do the killing for him.

I knew Mary Lou well enough to know that if she refused to do something, all the solid reasoning in the world that I presented would not change her mind. So, when the waitress came with our orders, and filled our coffee cups, I asked, "Seen any of my pals lately."

"I saw Jimmy Joe Saturday night at Friday's," she replied. "He allegedly bought me a drink, wanted to talk, so bored me to death for almost an hour."

Her reference was to Jimmy Joe Johnson, a cowboy-booted compadre who sold oil deals. He was never able to sell me one, because I never had any money. I attributed that to my ex-wife and her lawyer, which, of course, was untrue. My shortage of funds was usually because of my addiction to drinking and gambling.

Anyway, Jimmy Joe was able to con enough people so that he always drove a new Cadillac, which was repossessed by the bank on a regular basis, but that never seemed to bother him.

Jimmy Joe always wore fashionable cowboy-style clothing and a white cowboy hat on his balding dome, although a black hat would have been more appropriate given his outlaw ways. It is probably enough to say that he was a fan of Willie Nelson and Wayland Jennings, neither of whom I thought could sing a lick.

My folks had visions of me becoming a country singer, and my paternal grandmother even bought me a high-dollar guitar. Unfortunately, the guy my parents were paying to give me guitar lessons retired from teaching rather than continue giving me lessons. But the truth is that my voice was too good to be a country singer. I could not sing through my nose, so did not have the right twang in my voice.

But getting back to Jimmy Joe, he ran up bills all over Dallas and never paid a dime on any of them, but I did not consider him a serious suspect regarding the man who called himself Jesus.

He was not the kind of guy to mock God. I am not sure he knew who God is, even though there was a time when he seriously considered becoming a preacher. Well, I might ought to rethink that word "seriously," because the word would probably have been alien to any of Jimmy Joe's thoughts.

"How's old Jimmy Joe doing?" I asked Mary Lou. "I haven't seen him in a couple of weeks."

"Count your blessings," she replied. "The man's more than a tad off center."

I said, "You shouldn't say things like that about Jimmy Joe. He always speaks very highly of you."

She popped a piece of bacon in her mouth, followed it up with a chunk of pancake saturated in syrup, and said, "He should. I'm certainly the classiest woman he has ever been around, and that probably includes his mother."

I responded, "That's a low blow, even for you, Mary Lou."

She shrugged her shoulders and said, "Truth is truth. You can't make a silk suit out of a sow's ear. You should have seen the slut he was with at Friday's when he allegedly bought me a drink."

I questioned, "What do you mean when you use the word allegedly?"

"He left before I did, and I got stuck with he and his date's bill," she said.

"He probably just forgot," I said.

She gave me a disbelieving look that was as icy as a December morning in a deer stand.

"Like he always forgets," she said.

Steering the conversation away from money to relationships, I agreed that, "Jimmy Joe's choice of women friends isn't always the best, but he's not one to think in terms of a meaningful long-term romance."

"He's not one to think, period," she said. "No self-respecting whore will have anything to do with him because he won't deal with them unless they give him credit."

I laughed and said, "I didn't know whores checked the credit reports of their customers."

She smiled and said, "They only check on slimeballs like Jimmy Joe."

Now, Luke, Mary Lou was never a Jimmy Joe Johnson fan, not from the first minute when I introduced them. She has always considered Jimmy Joe in the same category as the lowest criminal on earth, which I, of course, think is a child sex trafficker or pedophile.

Jimmy Joe was a conniver, someone who would rather make a dollar dishonestly than ten dollars honestly. As for me, I always liked old Jimmy Joe because what you saw was what you got.

I first met him when he was a ministerial student at Baylor. That lasted for one semester, the same length of time Willie Nelson was a ministerial student at Baylor before playing dominos took precedence over religion classes.

Jimmy Joe lasted a full year at Baylor, and only rejected the faith after twice flunking the first semester of freshman English. He prayed to God for help in his classes but got no help.

He flunked everything, including chapel attendance and physical education. He loaded up on PE classes because even athletes could pass them, but badminton and ping pong proved too challenging for him.

Jimmy Joe had this idea that if God wanted him in the ministry, God would do the studying for him. When God failed to get him passing grades, he decided that it was a sign that God did not want him to be a preacher.

"Best thing that ever happened to me," he once told me when explaining why he forsook the ministry. "I misread the call. From the get-go, God was calling me to help people by selling them oil leases."

I did not argue with Jimmy Joe about the logic he applied to his calling, because it would have been like debating a turnip. If deep thought was like water, he would never have gotten his feet wet.

Mary Lou and I talked for a good hour. I grilled her and she grilled me. After a game of cat and mouse, I concluded that she had nothing to do with the man who called himself Jesus.

But the entire scenario was making me a bit shaky. My nerves were like a ball of worms all tangled together and wiggling to get free. And I was thinking that it would just be my luck to not know the real Jesus when he came back to earth.

Before we parted company, Mary Lou asked me, "What are you going to get me for Christmas?"

"It's a surprise," I said.

She laughed and said, "I'm sure it is, since you've never before gotten me anything."

THREE

Billy Bob Raintree is not one of Dallas' premiere lawyers. To the contrary, Billy Bob is to the legal profession what a shade tree mechanic is to the automotive industry. Those of us who knew him well wondered how he was able to escape with a degree from Baylor Law School, or how he was able to pass the bar.

We figured it was because he faked being a liberal, all the while being a closet conservative, although he really did not know the difference. There was also the possibility that he got on the nerves of his law school professors to the extent that they passed him rather than have him repeat their class, and that the people giving the bar exam did the same.

Billy Bob was admitted to law school by breaking into the administration building and changing his undergraduate C and D transcript to one with nothing but A's. Since Baylor accepted transfers from Texas A&M and the University of Texas, changing the grades on your Baylor transcript was considered acceptable behavior.

Practically every male student in Baylor's infamous "Nose Brotherhood" did it.

Billy Bob was very good at breaking into buildings, which, I suppose, was an asset to his legal career. He once stole a small camel from a circus and put it in the school's Armstrong Browning Library, possibly the most expensive building on campus at the time. It was built to hold a handkerchief that allegedly belonged to Elizabeth Barrett Browning, and people from all over the world came to view it.

Some people got a spiritual high from viewing the hanky, which was, and I suppose still is, in a glass case, but I once checked it out and did not feel anything.

A man once told me that if he gave a billion dollars to a university, within a year the school would not know where any of the money went. I figured the Armstrong Browning Library was a testimony to what the man told me.

Now, Billy Bob did not have anything against the Armstrong Browning Library. He just figured it was a good place to keep a camel, just like he thought a particular English professor's office was the best place to leave a boa constrictor, or that a particular math professor's desk drawer was the best place to leave a sack of dog dung.

But lest you get the wrong idea, Billy Bob did not spend all his time in college and law school placing camels, snakes and dog dung in specific places. Practically every night he went on one-man panty raids. And not one time during all those years did any girl, even a real bow wow, toss him a pair of panties. The girls in dorms did look out their windows and echo the common refrain, "It's just Billy Bob."

Attempting to turn a negative into a positive as he always did, Billy Bob contacted *The Guinness World Book of Records*, hoping to get a listing for conducting the most unsuccessful one-man panty raids in history. He, unfortunately, received a rejection letter from one of the editors. An A&M student had beaten him by several raids. Billy Bob argued, to no avail, that the Aggie student had been tossed, and had received, some male underwear.

That was the basis for the lawsuit he brought against the book of records, threatening to take his case all the way to the Supreme Court.

It is my understanding that the Guinness people settled out of court.

Despite that most people felt they needed a shower after a few minutes around Billy Bob, he made a decent living as a lawyer. Some said it was because neither judges nor other lawyers wanted to be in the same room with him. Even when it was detrimental to their clients, other lawyers were anxious to settle out of court.

Billy Bob never bothered me that much, because when I was around him, I practiced disassociation from my surroundings.

So, it was because of the man who called himself Jesus that I invited Billy Bob to lunch. And just to make things interesting, I also invited the guy I had named J.C. Smith.

When J.C. asked about transportation, I suggested he take a DART bus, have the person who was paying him provide a ride, or transport himself supernaturally.

I was pleased with my suggestions, because I have always thought that I had the makings of a comedian. The man did not seem in the least bit offended by my suggestions, laughed and simply said, "I'll see you there."

"And your transportation?" I asked.

He said, joking I think, "I'll take a DART bus, if I can find a driver who is awake at eleven in the morning."

I wished him luck and said, "If you can find a driver who's awake, that will be supernatural enough for me."

Our lunch meeting was scheduled for eleven forty-five at Raphael's Restaurant on McKinney Avenue. It was, obviously, a Mexican place, and I chose it because Billy Bob liked alleged Mexican food.

The truth is that Tex-Mex, which was what Raphael's served, was not real Mexican. Texans and everyone else would gag on real Mexican food. It is as bland and boring as a wishbone offense in football.

I have never liked Tex-Mex food, and I certainly have never liked real Mexican food. I will eat beef nachos on occasion, if I am convinced the restaurant is not substituting dog or cat for beef.

I worry about any liquid product produced in Mexico, because of what might float to the surface of the country's water supply. I do drink margaritas on occasion because I like salt and ice, but I have always shunned Mexican-made beer.

I feel it is important that I share this with you, Luke, so you will not think that I am contradicting myself. And, of course, I think you share my concerns, which is why I never feed you food canned in Mexico.

Now, granted, I have considered opening a Mexican restaurant, because where else can you get away with a menu of bad ground beef, rice, refried beans, cheese, tortillas, weird salsa and chips served in nine hundred different ways? Except for USDA grade nachos, it is difficult to have any respect for Mexican food.

Anyway, the man who called himself Jesus was already at the restaurant when I arrived.

He was wearing a nondescript sport coat, slacks that really did not go with it, and what looked like an old pair of Hush Puppy shoes. He had on a button-down collared white shirt, no tie, and his hair was mussed from the icy wind that was battering the area. I did not bother to offer him a comb.

We were shown to a table and asked if we wanted a drink. I opted for a margarita and he asked for a water with lemon. I informed the waiter that we had another guest coming, so would delay ordering a meal.

The waiter was a Mexican, so the man who called himself Jesus talked to him in what I assumed was Mexican. It could have been Greek for all I knew.

"What have you been doing all morning?" I asked.

He replied, "I've been cleaning the house. It was a real mess."

I shrugged my shoulders and said, "I have a maid service come in every other week."

"They obviously don't do windows, clean behind furniture or scrub the kitchen floors," he said.

"I've always thought they did a good job," I said, "but, of course, I don't check everything out that thoroughly."

The way he talked about housework you would have thought it was the most important thing in the world. It really kind of irritated me, even though I have always thought housework was the most important thing a woman can do. Unfortunately, most women do not share my enthusiasm for their importance.

The waiter brought my margarita and the man's water, and he asked, "So, how has your morning been?"

"Well," I replied, "my editor almost had a heart attack seeing me at work so early."

"And how did your breakfast with Mary Lou Magruder go?"

Before I could answer, Billy Bob showed up and said, "I hope I didn't keep you guys waiting."

Discussing my breakfast with Mary Lou would have to wait. Billy Bob had appeared, seemingly on cue, and he was dressed as dapper as ever. He was wearing an odd colored designer suit, a stranger than fiction colored tie, and Nike running shoes.

This, of course, was before the clown of all NFL clowns, Colin Kaepernick, became the face of Nike for refusing to stand for the National Anthem, and before Nike was exposed for using slave labor in China to make its products. When the choice was alleged social justice or millions of dollars, you can guess which the clown Kaepernick chose.

Back then Billy Bob had given up sharp-toed wingtips that could crush a roach in a corner for running shoes, although he did not run or jog. In fact, he often commented that he had never seen a jogger smile. Billy Bob was of all men most observant.

He once told me that a high dollar suit with running shoes made a fashion statement, although he did not explain what kind. I did read somewhere that annually each person in America bought eight pair of athletic shoes, which means I have not been keeping up with the trend. Somewhere, someone is wearing athletic shoes that I should have bought.

Now the article I read only talked about the purchase of athletic shoes. It did not account for the shoes stolen by peaceful protesting social justice warriors who, after smashing the windows of shoe shores, helped themselves to such products.

Thus, it is today impossible to know how many pair of athletic shoes are owned by members of Antifa and Black Lives Matter.

But as some sage said, "It takes a lot of shoes to destroy a country."

I said, "Have a seat, Billy Bob. I think you know J.C., don't you?"

Cool as a cucumber, he replied, "Can't say that I do," taking the extended hand of the man who called himself Jesus.

"My name is Jesus," the man said.

"The name's familiar," Billy Bob said. "Have we met before."

"Unfortunately, no," the man said.

Exasperated, I said, "Oh, for crying out loud, you guys need to can the crap and the sacrilege."

You could almost see the light click on in Billy Bob's brain, which was for the most part a big empty space. "Now I remember," he said. "Your name came up in one of my classes at Baylor."

The man laughed and said, "I'm surprised."

Billy Bob was playing his role to the hilt. He questioned, "So, you're Jesus Christ? I'm surprised to meet you."

The man smiled and said, "I'm a bit surprised myself."

J.C., obviously, was being facetious. I had to admit, he was one cool character.

Where Billy Bob was concerned, I took nothing for granted. He may not have recognized the name Jesus Christ but being a lawyer, he acted as if he knew the name. It was what lawyers and politicians did. It was in their DNA.

"Did you hear that, Mark?" Billy Bob asked a bit too loudly. "We're having lunch with Jesus Christ. You've outdone yourself this time."

"This guy is not the real Jesus Christ," I said. "He is a very good actor. And you know it. You probably put him up to it."

You could look Billy Bob square in the eyes, ask him a question, and still not know whether his answer was a lie or if he was telling the truth. He was gifted in that way even before he became a lawyer. But his ability to lie with a straight face was always a tremendous asset in his profession.

Now, Luke, I had given Billy Bob the thumb truth-test many times, and he always passed. I attributed that to him not knowing the difference between the truth and a lie, which is learned behavior for lawyers and most preachers. So, I gave him the test to see if he knew the man who called himself Jesus and it showed that he did not.

The man said, "Billy Bob doesn't know me and never has. Hopefully, he will. I'm praying that he will."

"You are one cool customer," I said. "Since I can't get the truth out of you or Billy Bob, we might as well change the subject. What do you think about how Dallas decorates for Christmas to honor Jesus?"

He laughed and replied, "Do you really think all the decorating is to honor me?"

"What else could it be for?" I asked.

Billy Bob chimed in with, "I thought we decorated because everybody else decorated."

Both the man who called himself Jesus and I gave him an incredulous look.

If Billy Bob was putting on an act, about not knowing the man who called himself Jesus or not knowing the reason for the season, he was going one whale of a job. I could not think of a better job of acting.

Well, John Wayne or Jack Elam might have done a better job. But I was beginning to believe that Billy Bob honestly did not know.

The man who called himself Jesus seemed bemused by the entire scenario, but before I could respond to his look or level any type accusation the waiter came to take our order. Since all Mexican food other than nachos tastes the same to me, I ordered another margarita and whatever he could bring me without onions, garlic, tomatoes and Pico De Gallo, which was limiting.

My companions ordered big Mexican dinners with all the trimmings. The man who called himself Jesus asked for another glass of water and Billy Bob ordered a Mexican beer.

I noticed that Billy Bob looked a little green around the gills but did not give it much more than a glance since he often looked that way. He did keep taking quick nervous looks at J.C., then just as quickly looking away. This was unusual behavior on his part since he normally acted as if he did not know where he was, and probably did not.

Being tacky was one of my best attributes, so I asked, "Lawyers don't have much of a shot at heaven, do they?"

The man smiled and replied, "Just as much as reporters and preachers. Heaven isn't denied because of a person's profession. Only the individual can deny Heaven for themself, and that only because of what they have in their heart. God's laws and man's laws can't be equated on the same basis. God is about forgiving, and people are about condemning."

"You didn't answer my question," I said.

He countered, "I answered. You simply weren't listening. If a person refuses to accept God's way for their salvation, it doesn't matter if they're a preacher, priest the Pope, or morally a saint by man's standards. There is only one way to spend eternity in the presence of God. The truth is, unfortunately, that most people who claim to be Christian talk a good game but really don't want to spend an eternity with God. They prefer what they have right here on earth."

Billy Bob squirmed and said, "That's right, Mark. You need to quit putting me down in front of Jesus."

I could not believe what I was hearing. I gave him an incredulous look and said, "That does it. Now I know you're in on this so-called joke."

"I don't know what you're talking about," he said, "but for the sake of our friendship, I would appreciate it if you wouldn't try to belittle me in front of Jesus."

I asked, "Are you kidding me? A few minutes ago, you claimed you couldn't even remember the name Jesus."

He said, "Well, my cognitive ability caught up with my other abilities."

"Whew!" I exclaimed. "I figured that happening was about as likely as me running a four-minute mile."

"Billy Bob really doesn't know anything about what you think is a joke," the man who called himself Jesus said. "And I told you that some of your friends would accept me before you did. And you now have evidence of that in Billy Bob."

"You have to be kidding," I said. "We're talking about Billy Bob Raintree here, a man who in college set a bridge on fire, stole a bulldozer and ran it into a creek, put a camel in the Armstrong Browning Library and spent years going on one-man panty raids."

"I'll try to make this simple for you," the man said. "When a person accepts me, their past is forgiven. You tend to underestimate God's grace and mercy."

"C'mon," I said, "enough is enough. Drop the Jesus act and we'll all have a good laugh. I can handle being the butt of a good joke."

"I'm no joke," he said.

Then Billy Bob piped up with, "Mark, you had better wake up. This man is the Son of God."

He was acting so serious that I had to laugh. "You've outdone yourself on this one, Billy Bob. To tell you the truth, I'm a bit in awe of your acting ability. It's no wonder that most people want to settle their lawsuits with your clients out of court."

The man who called himself Jesus looked at me somberly and said, "If you think this is an act, I pray that you will remember the Scripture stating that God once overlooked ignorance, but that He now expects repentance from all people."

The way he spoke caused a tingle to run down my spine, along with a few goose bumps, the kind you get when the *Star-Spangled Banner* is played at a ball game.

Some people, obviously, do not get those feelings but, instead, belittle everything patriotic.

Fortunately, the waiter arrived with our food about that time, giving me a chance to regroup, order another margarita and tell J.C. and Billy Bob to get serious.

As I recall, the man who called himself Jesus started talking to Billy Bob about spiritual things during the meal. I do not remember much about the conversation but had never seen Billy Bob listen so intently to anyone. Up until then, I had always though his maximum attention span was five seconds, ten at the most. But he seemed to be taking in everything the man who called himself Jesus said, nodding his head in the affirmative and listening like his life depended on it.

That puzzled me because Billy Bob normally argued with everyone about everything. I figured he was argumentative because he was a lawyer, and because he did not know much about anything.

Like I said, about the spiritual stuff the guy told him, I do not remember much of it. And I do not think I can be faulted for not remembering. Even the disciples did not remember all that Jesus said and did.

At least they did not write everything He said and did down for us to read, which is a good thing since most people have enough trouble reading what they did write down for us to read. My guess is that the New Testament is like the Reader's Digest, a condensed version of what Jesus said and did.

The situation was this: I had invited one of my Looney Tunes friends to lunch to find out if he was in on the Jesus gag being played on me, and he had ended up falling under the spell of the man who called himself Jesus.

So, the joke was on Billy Bob, not me.

After Billy Bob had been brainwashed, which took very little water, I wanted to know more about what the charlatan Jesus thought about Christmas.

"Have you had a chance to see how some of the mansions in Highland Park are decorated for Christmas?" I asked.

He shrugged and said, "I doubt that any mansion on earth would impress me all that much."

"Every year these people spend thousands on Christmas decorations to honor who you say you are," I said.

"That's not true," he said. "They spend thousands to impress each other. Do you really think Christmas is about me?"

"Not about you," I said, "but about the real Jesus."

He laughed and said, "The real Jesus disappeared from Christmas a long time ago."

FOUR

After determining that Billy Bob Raintree was not responsible for sending the man who called himself Jesus into my life, I became irritated that he had fallen under the spell of the charlatan. Even Billy Bob, not the sharpest knife in the drawer, should have had better sense than that. He should not have been so easily duped.

Granted, the man's knowledge of the New Testament, the entire Bible for that matter, was incredible. I had initially pegged him for a seminary student but was beginning to rethink that assessment.

He knew too much Scripture to have gone to a Bible college or seminary, which are very much like schools of education where students are taught how to teach but nothing about the subject they will be teaching. People learn that by osmosis or on their own.

Over the years, I have known many college and university professors with doctorates who never reached the intellectual level of a moron when it came to subject matter or anything else.

And, of course, there must be rejoicing in Heaven when any media person today achieves moron status, which, of course, is as rare as a nun riding a donkey western style.

It irritated me that the man who called himself Jesus could make what was biblically implausible, plausible even to me. And he did it with a common-sense approach that made me feel a little stupid and wondering why I had not comprehended what was so obvious.

Still, I was not ready to believe the man who called himself Jesus was anything other than a charlatan, an exceptionally gifted actor who had been employed to toy with my mind, which was already a junkyard of wrecked matchbox cars.

However, I could not even explain my own actions regarding the guy. After all, I had invited him to be a permanent house guest after knowing him for less than twenty-four hours. As you know, Luke, I like my privacy, which was always the case. My ex-wife would readily attest to this, if she had been willing to speak to any of my friends.

Forgive me for belaboring a point, but my primary point is that around this guy I was reacting to and saying stuff completely contrary to my normal behavior.

And, as for Billy Bob, I did not consider him a bad person back then, but as a candidate for Heaven, I figured I was a couples of notches ahead of him.

I have always had a problem getting things out of my mind, so I could not get out of my mind what Billy Bob said to me after lunch. The man who called himself Jesus had already left, presumably to catch a DART bus back to the vicinity of my house.

He asked, "Can't you see it, Mark? That man really is the real Jesus."

"You're as full of crap as a Christmas turkey," I replied, "and if I find you're in on this gag, I'll nail your ass if it's the last thing I ever do."

But Billy Bob was as serious as lip cancer when he said, "I can't believe you're so blind."

Although Billy Bob was as hard to read as the small print on an eye chart in an optometrist's office, I was beginning to believe that he was not putting me on, that he really believed what he was saying.

So, while at the newspaper writing a couple of meaningless stories for the following morning's edition, I pondered how this man who called himself Jesus could exercise such power over the mind of an individual in so short a time. I was willing to admit that he had my mind going around like a NASCAR vehicle on a track but figured he had put a clamp on Billy Bob's brain.

The situation was as tough to figure as was how the State of Texas could trim millions and millions of dollars from its budget, unless, of course, there was a lot of pork in the budget. But who would ever believe that politicians wasted money foolishly?

I finished my assignments about midafternoon and decided to see if my best friend at the paper, Bobo Harrison, wanted to join me for a cup of coffee.

Bobo was an alleged sportswriter at the paper, which he vehemently denied. Because he was a sportswriter, he wrote in clichés and often spoke in clichés. He covered college basketball, even though he did not consider basketball a real sport.

He wanted to write about the outdoors, fishing and hunting, but another guy had that job. He tried to sabotage the paper's outdoor editor at every occasion, even to the point of accusing him of being a transgender.

Someone at the paper must have believed Bobo, because the paper, which was big on diversity, gave the outdoor editor a big raise in pay.

Bobo often complained to me about having to spend so much time with tall boys in short pants and attributed his fate to previous sins. He had achieved a somewhat dubious reputation among basketball's elites when he authored a book titled *The Best One Thousand Basketball Cliché's I Can Remember While Canoeing Down the Brazos River and Fishing for Whatever I could catch.*

Despite the rather lengthy title, Bobo thought the book would be a *New York Times* number one bestseller but did not account for the fact that most basketball fans cannot read. Still, the *Times* was willing to make his book a number one on their list if he had been able to come up with the required money for advertising.

That has always been the beauty of media. If you want to find the source of criminal activity, follow the money. And if you want to be on the *Times* bestseller list, you must come up with the money.

Bobo, of course, had no money, and what money he did have he spent on beer, paying his mortgage and groceries.

What I liked most about Bobo was that he usually agreed with me, even when he did not know what we were talking about. That is why I usually sprang for his beer.

Also, in addition to speaking good cliché, which was ideal for taking about sports, Bobo was supportive of my ideas about DART and all things derogatory about city government. He, of course, did not know much about world affairs and thought Philadelphia was another country.

Bobo was six feet, six inches tall and weighed in at two hundred sixty pounds. His college days were spent playing defensive tackle for the University of Texas at El Paso, drinking beer and visiting Boys Town in Juarez, Mexico. For those unfamiliar with Boys Town, it is the equivalent of an entire city of brothels, the difference being that there is no beginning or end to it.

Bobo had not changed all that much in the couple of decades that I had known him. He had played defensive tackle for UT-El Paso because he did not want to bother learning offensive plays, was the center for my touch football team, still ate everything in sight, was probably responsible for the song *Ninety-nine Bottles of Empty Beer Bottles on the Wall*, and would still have been visiting Boys Town if it had not been six hundred miles west of Dallas.

At the time Bobo was married and had a couple of kids. He was serious about his kids, not so serious about his marriage. He was always looking for a woman who shared his attitude about his wife, but never found one.

Cocktail waitresses familiar with his drinking habits usually served him three glasses of beer at a time. By the time I finished one margarita, he could put away a half dozen glasses of beer.

I found Bobo in his usual working position, leaned back in his chair with his feet on his desk. To my invitation he responded, "Hell, yes, I'd like a cup of coffee. Are you buying?"

"Yeah, it's on me," I replied, "and I'll even buy you a package of Twinkies."

He rubbed his belly and said, "No Twinkies. I'm on a diet."

Bobo was always on a diet, but they never lasted more than a day. "Where do you want coffee?" I asked.

"They have good coffee down in the pressroom," he replied.

The coffee in the pressroom was about what you would expect. It was blacker than black and had enough ink in it to stain your teeth to the color of twilight on a cloudy day. So, that is where we got our coffee and where Bobo found six stale donuts left by the crew that had come on at midnight.

We took the coffee and donuts to the newspaper's recreation room, which was furnished like an abandoned restaurant from the nineteen fifties, found wobbly chairs at an ink-stained table, and sat.

"This diet you're on, have you quit drinking beer," I asked.

He gave me an incredulous look, bit a stale donut in half, slightly chewed it before swallowing and replied, "It's not that strict of a diet. I'm just trying to eat a lot of fish."

"That's not for me," I said. "I don't particularly like fish."

"I like them," he said, "especially with lots of fried potatoes and hushpuppies."

"Well, I was going to invite you over to Joe Miller's after work for a few brews, but I don't want to screw up your diet," I said.

Back then, Luke, Joe Miller's was a bar where quite a few journalism types hung out.

"I'm not going to turn down a brew," Bobo said. "What time are we talking about?"

"About five-thirty," I replied.

"I'll have my column done by then," he said, "and that should put me home for supper by ten."

"What are you writing about?" I asked.

Bobo shrugged his shoulders and replied, "Hell, I don't know. I've been thinking about a piece about the correlation between free throw shooting and whether a player wears or doesn't wear a jockey strap."

"Sounds interesting," I said.

"A column like that takes a lot of research," Bobo said.

I questioned, "Don't you have some sources?"

"Of course, but most want to remain anonymous," he said. "They afraid that if they're wrong it would ruin their credibility as an anonymous source."

Sometimes it's important to just go with your gut feeling," I said. "And when push comes to shove, you can't have too many anonymous sources. *The New York Times* and *Washington Post* only use anonymous sources."

Bobo took on a puzzled look and said, "I assume you're talking about newspapers. Where are they located?"

Because of his lack of geographical knowledge, the newspaper handled all of Bobo's travel arrangements. And he had trouble both reading and spelling, but, of course, neither are requirements for being a sportswriter.

Realizing it was time to change the subject, I said. "I see where Hop Baymore is again pushing for Dallas Cowboys players to receive more money."

Just mentioning Hop's name got Bobo all riled up. Hop had been a sportswriter for the *Los Angeles Times* that our paper had hired to be a columnist. He wrote the kind of slop that any self-respecting pig would refuse to eat, but management at our paper introduced him to Dallas as if he was the Second Coming.

Hop was paid a six-figure salary, which none of our people approached, and the paper spent millions in media space and time to establish him as the guru of the sports world. It was a job that Bobo thought he should have had, because Hop had never authored a book as he had and was unknown to people in Frisco, Texas.

At the time, prior to hiring lawyers as journalists, we had several sportswriters who could put together better clichés than Hop, but he must have had a picture of someone in management hugging or kissing the proverbial goat, which resulted in his huge contract.

Upon arrival in Dallas, Hop immediately began attacking the Dallas Cowboys salary structure, as if they were being brutalized by the team's ownership. He was queer for jocks, no doubt about it.

Anyway, after our paper had established Hop as the premiere sports voice in Dallas, he jumped ship and went to our rival paper for even more money.

Like Howard Cosell, he had never played the game, but with no writing talent was able to milk it for more money than most players.

"Anything I say about Hop sounds like sour grapes," Bobo said, "so I don't say anything about the prissy little asshole."

I laughed and questioned, "Why don't you tell me how you really feel about him?"

Bobo grunted, smiled and replied, "All I can tell you is that management isn't planning to replace him with me. I'm going to be stuck chasing tall boys in short pants for as long as I work at this rag."

"I don't think any of us can count on a lengthy career here," I said. "Almost everyone will be illiterate and unable to read within a few years. There won't be any need for newspapers."

"What do you plan to do when that happens?" he asked.

I answered, "Fish, I guess."

"You don't like fish," he said.

"I like to catch them," I said. "I just don't like to clean them or eat them."

"What do you think about Hop's future?" Bobo asked.

"It's probably pretty good," I replied. "He's a Nazi/Communist, and the country's going in that direction."

"Do you have any proof?" Bobo asked.

In response, I questioned, "Since when has anyone with my perceptive ability needed proof?"

"That's true," he replied. "You've never needed any basis for making an accusation."

I said, "One of the reasons I want you to show up at Joe Miller's today is that I want to introduce you to a guy who claims to be the real Jesus."

Bobo gave me a disbelieving look, chuckled and said, "You're putting me on."

Again, obviously, I did not suspect Bobo of being responsible for the Jesus joke. He liked a good joke as much as the next guy, but rarely understood what was or was not a joke, and he could never remember the punch line when trying to tell a joke. He could not focus on anything for more than a few seconds. His comprehension level was the equivalent of that of a fly landing in front of a guy with a swatter.

So, he was not one for pranks. He was more likely to be the butt of a joke than the instigator of one, and since he rarely understood when a joke was being played on him, very few people bothered trying.

Bobo was the kind of guy who when someone told a joke on Monday might take on a puzzled look, then break out laughing on Wednesday when he seemingly, but not necessarily, understood it. However, if after a couple of days, he did not catch on to a joke, he forgot about it. That, I thought, was one of his redeeming qualities. After all, why spend time contemplating something you do not understand?

Now do not get the idea that Bobo was dense or anything like that. He simply was not a deep thinker, but being a sportswriter, or any kind of journalist for that matter, does not require a mind like that of an Aristotle or Plato.

So, I shared with Bobo all that had happened the previous evening, including breakfast with Mary Lou and lunch with Billy Bob.

After he had seemingly comprehended what I told him, he grinned and said, "It's that Mary Lou. You know how much she likes a practical joke. She's one fine looking woman, too. I don't know why you're not more interested in her."

I did not bother to tell him that interest was a two-way street. Everyone assumed that all I had to do was holler and Mary Lou would come running. I figured she would run all right, but in the opposite direction.

Bobo's smile turned into a frown an he said, "Of course, the clown behind the joke might be that little asshole Billy Bob."

Bobo is not one of Billy Bob's fans, the primary reason being that during one of our football practices, even though it was just touch, Billy Bob used his head to butt Bobo in the crotch. It was the first and last time I had ever seen Bobo cry.

It was my pleading and Billy Bob's speed that saved him from certain death at Bobo's hands.

I said, "For some reason, I don't think Billy Bob is behind it. I could be wrong, although I rarely am, but I don't think he really knew the man until lunch today."

Snarling, Bobo said, "He's a devious, shifty little bastard."

Nodding agreement, I responded, "Well, he is a lawyer."

"That doesn't give him a pass with me," Bobo said.

Trying to calm Bobo's mental anguish, for which I was responsible, I said, "That reminds me of a new lawyer joke."

"Let's hear it," Bobo said.

I asked, "Did you know that scientists are now using lawyers instead of white mice for their experiments?"

Serious, Bobo said, "No, I didn't know that."

I did not tell him it was not true, simply continued with, "There are three reasons, the first being that there is a shortage of white mice. The second is that scientists don't get attached to lawyers like they do to white mice, and the third is that there are certain things white mice won't do."

When Bobo realized that I had finished the joke, he chuckled, but it was obvious he did not comprehend it. I understood. Maybe he would get it later.

After finishing our coffee, and after Bobo had consumed all the stale donuts, we went back to our respective desks to finish out the day. There I called the man who called himself Jesus and asked him to meet us at Joe Millers. And I also called Jimmy Joe Johnson and invited him.

Joe Miller's was kind of dark and had a distinctive smell about it, which was a combination of beer and food. The place made a decent burger.

There was a table in the place that I particularly liked, which I commandeered. From it you could see all that was going on in the place. That was where I usually sat with my back to the wall, something I learned from reading about the life and death of Wild Bill Hickok.

I had gotten to the bar a little earlier than the after-five crowd to make sure I got the table but found the man who called himself Jesus already sitting at it. He greeted me with, "I figured this is where you would want to sit."

I do not mind telling you, Luke, the guy was a little spooky, but I said, "Yeah, this table is fine." Then I took my normal seat.

"Been here long?" I asked.

"Not that long," he said.

The waitress came and took our orders. I ordered my usual margarita and he had a Diet Coke.

The guy was dressed just as he had been at noon, which did not surprise me. In the short time I had known him, he had not shown me much when it came to style.

We chatted for a while about nothing that I can remember, then Jimmy Joe arrived. Before anyone else could speak, I said, "Jimmy Joe, I'd like you to meet J.C. Smith."

But before my words had time to sink in, the man extended his hand to Jimmy Joe and said, "Just call me Jesus."

Jimmy Joe did not say anything for a few seconds, then responded, "That name's familiar."

Now even though Jimmy Joe had been a ministerial student at Baylor, he had been away from the faith for some time. And because I knew how his mind worked, when it worked at all, I was not surprised by his response. I knew he was sizing the man who called himself Jesus up as a prospect for an oil deal.

Jimmy Joe questioned, "You're not from Amarillo, are you? I seem to recall meeting a Jesus family out around Amarillo, or was it in Lubbock?"

The man laughed and replied, "I can assure you that we've never me, and that you don't know me or my family."

Jimmy Joe, whose attention span rivaled that of Bobo's, turned to me and asked, "How's it going, hoss? It's been a while. What are you drinking nowadays?"

The waitress appeared with my margarita and the man's Diet Coke, Jimmy Joe made note and told her, "Bourbon and Dr Pepper for me."

I grimaced at his selection, but the waitress was undaunted. A lot of Jimmy Joes hung out Joe Miller's.

Turning his attention to the man who called himself Jesus, Jimmy Joe asked, "What line of work are you in, Jesus? Do you want me to call you Jesus or J.C.?"

The man shrugged his shoulders and replied, "Whatever is most comfortable for you. And as for my line of work, I'm a servant."

"Is that profitable," Jimmy Joe asked.

"I guess that depends on what you call profitable," the man said. "And I think Mark would be more comfortable is you called me J.C."

Jimmy Joe questioned, "What the hell has Mark's comfort got to do with anything? If Mark calls you J.C., I'll call you Jesus. He needs to quit bossing everyone around."

The waitress brought Jimmy Joe's drink. He downed it in one gulp before she could leave the table and told her, "Bring me a bottle of bourbon, a big glass, a bucket of ice and a six-pack of Dr Pepper."

"That's going to be a pretty big bill," she said.

"And you're going to get a pretty big tip," he said.

Since Jimmy Joe had never paid a bill, I knew where this was headed. But the waitress dutifully left to fill his order.

After she left, Jimmy Joe seemed to be thinking, which meant he had all kinds of veins popping up, and he looked as if he was having an attack of constipation. "Now I remember," he said. "There's a guy in the Bible named Jesus. Are you that Jesus?"

"Oh, c'mon, this has gone far enough," I said, groaning. "Please let it lie. How much did you pay this guy for the Jesus joke, and does he know he has as much chance of you paying him for his performance as a feral cat has of making friends with a coyote?"

Jimmy Joe gave me a blank look, which is normal for him, and questioned, "What are you talking about?"

The man who called himself Jesus laughed and said, "He really doesn't know what you're talking about, Mark."

Addressing Jimmy Joe, I said, "You know damned well what I'm talking about. You hired this guy to play like he's Jesus."

Jimmy Joe replied, a bit angrily, "I ain't hired nobody to do nothing. And with Jesus right here at the table, I'd be careful about what I said. I'm scared poopless, and you should be, too."

Then turning to the man who called himself Jesus and said, "Sorry, Jesus, I don't know if poopless is a word. It's not what I would usually say."

"I know," the man said

"This man is not the real Jesus," I told Jimmy Joe.

"I'm not taking any chances," Jimmy Joe said.

Fortunately, about that time Bobo made his entrance. He saw me waving at him, came in the direction of our table, encountered our waitress and ordered three glasses of beer. He really did not have to say anything. She knew him.

When he arrived at our table, I introduced him to the man who called himself Jesus, but he seemed more interested in questioning Jimmy Joe. "How's our oil well doing?" he asked.

Jimmy Joe had talked Bobo into borrowing money from the newspaper's credit union to invest in an oil deal. That had been months earlier, and thus far there had been no report on the well, if, indeed, there was a well.

"It's coming," Jimmy Joe assured Bobo. "These things take time. We'll be hearing something any day now."

Bobo warned, "We'd better. If we don't, I'm going to put on of my size fourteen boots so far up your ass that it will clog your throat."

Jimmy Joe laughed uneasily and said, "Patience, patience. When that black gold starts flowing, you'll be neck deep in money."

The waitress brought Bobo's beer, and with one suck a glass was empty. "You interested in football?" he asked the man.

Before the man could respond, Jimmy Joe replied, "Of course, he's interested in football, especially the Cowboys. Bobo, Mark introduced this man to me as J.C. Smith, but he's really Jesus. You know, the one in the Bible."

Bobo grunted and said, "The Bible isn't on the UT-El Paso reading list, but I remember we had one at home when I was growing up. My dad stole it out of a motel. I think it had belonged to a guy named Gideon, who must have forgotten it when he stayed at the motel.

"But I asked Jesus if he liked football. I didn't ask you to answer for him."

"It's okay," the man who called himself Jesus replied. "Of course, I don't have much tolerance for highly paid, sinful-living and sniveling athletes, but there's nothing wrong with the game."

"Well, hallelujah," Bobo said. "It's good to know that someone else doesn't appreciate the seven-figure salaries being paid to a bunch of cry baby jocks. When I was playing college football, I never received more than a five-figure salary."

The man laughed and said, "I knew you would like my answer, as does Mark."

I grumbled, "Everyone knows how I feel. But are you going to sit there and tell me that Jimmy Joe didn't put you up to the game you're playing?"

"I am because it's the truth," the man replied. "No one, and certainly not your friends, has put me up to anything. And I'm not playing a game."

"Speaking of games," Bobo said, "if you are who you say you are, who is going to win the Cowboys and Eagles game on Sunday, and what is the score going to be?"

"That's way down on my list of priorities," the man said.

Bobo persisted, "If you were going to bet, who would you bet on?"

"First of all, I don't have to bet," the man replied. "What you need to understand, Bobo, is that God in His infinite wisdom and knowledge knows who is going to win the game but doesn't care.

"It may be hard to understand, but while God does know who the winner will be, He doesn't determine the winner. In his infinite wisdom, He knows what plays the coaches will call, and He knows the physical and mental abilities of each player, but because of free choice each coach and player makes the choice as to how he uses the abilities that God has given him.

"When man makes the right choices, he most often credits himself. When he makes the wrong choices, he blames God."

The man's explanation was a bit too deep for Jimmy Joe, who smiling questioned, "But God does favor the Cowboys, doesn't He?"

The man shook his head in resignation and replied, "If every Cowboys player was a Christian, and every Eagles player was an atheist, God still wouldn't reward the Cowboys with a victory. When I say God gives every person freedom of choice, I mean that He gives every person freedom of choice, whether they're a Christian or an atheist.

"Thinking that God determines the outcome of something as unimportant as a football game trivializes God."

Bobo grumbled, "I figure God favors the Cowboys because Coach Landry is a good Christian."

The man said, "Tom Landry did not become a Christian to win football games. That would be a pretty shallow reason. He became a Christian to serve both God and his fellow man."

I questioned, "If being a Christian isn't going to help you win in life, what's the point?"

"I could say the alternative isn't all that great," the man said, "but if you think winning or losing a football game is all there is to life, Mark, life isn't worth living. Winning in anything isn't all there is to life. Life is a continuing problem that must be solved by every individual every second of every day. Being a Christian helps you endure losing and serving God and other human beings makes you humble and appreciative when you're victorious."

I grumbled, "You have an answer for everything, don't you?"

"God has an answer," he said, "and the answer isn't always going to be to your satisfaction."

Jimmy Joe filled a large glass half full of bourbon, half full of Dr Pepper and added a few ice cubes. The man observed what he was doing but did not say anything.

Then Bobo said, "What you're saying makes a lot of sense. When I was playing college ball, we had a team prayer before every game, but didn't win many games. I figured the reason why was that the other team prayed longer and harder."

The man took a sip of his Diet Coke and said, "What coaches and teams call prayer falls way short of what prayer really is. Prayer should be meaningful, not a formality, and not a request for something as trivial as victory in a football game. And it certainly shouldn't be for show."

Jimmy Joe said, "I figured you were honoring God when you prayed."

"You don't honor God when you pray," the man said, "you honor yourself. When you acknowledge God, you make yourself better than the beasts of the field and the animal-like criminal humans who seek to destroy others. When you pray, it's not necessary that you request anything from God other than simply conversation with your Heavenly Father. But if you do request something, pray for something worthwhile, not that the jocks you like beat the jocks that someone else likes."

I laughed and said, "Jimmy Joe should be praying that some of the oil deals he's sold come in."

The man smiled and said, "That happens only when you drill in the right places."

Jimmy Joe asked, "What if I pray that God will have us drill in the right places?"

The man replied, "I hope you won't do that, Jimmy Joe, because that means you'll blame God when you drill in the wrong places. Hiring a good geologist is a much better bet than a selfish prayer."

"So," I asked, "what are we supposed to pray for, just that God's will be done?"

"Do you have a problem with God's will?" the man questioned.

"My only problem is knowing what God's will is," I replied.

He looked at me with those piercing eyes and said, "The Bible reveals everything about God's will that you need to know."

I was in an arguing mood and said, "According to you, if we were in a war with the Russians or Iranians, God wouldn't be on either side."

He countered, "I did not say that. But wars are fought by men, not by God. If such a war was being fought, I think you will agree that Christian men would fight harder than men with no faith, or those whose faith was evil. And, obviously, there are many faiths or ideologies that are pure evil. people who fight for what is righteous most often overcome those who fight for evil."

I continued being belligerent, and questioned, "Then calling on God for help is a waste of time?"

He looked at me with resignation and replied with the question, "Has it ever occurred to you that people who truly believe in God have the ability to use their intellect to a far greater extent than those who don't believe in God? And has it ever occurred to you that a country where Christianity is freely practiced is normally a country where a person's mind is not handicapped, where because of free choice that they can reach inside themselves for answers and solutions to life's most perplexing problems?"

The guy was a deep thinker. I gave him credit for that. The way I read what he was saying was that because of freedom of choice, a country that espoused Christianity had more going for it technologically, which included production of war materials, than one that did not have those same freedoms.

In other words, freedom encouraged thought and creativity, whereas a lack of freedom stifled thought and creativity.

I hated to admit it, but the guy made sense, so I spoke truth as a question. "What you're saying is that while God may not fight a battle for you, the very fact that you believe in and trust God might decide the battle in your favor?"

"God has never lost a battle," he replied, and neither has any Christian when you think about the eternal and not just the present. Belief in what is right is a strong motivator, and belief in God most often enables the weak to overcome the strong."

We ordered another round of drinks; a margarita for me, three beers for Bobo and a Diet Coke for the man. Jimmy Joe still had plenty of bourbon, Dr Pepper and ice.

I could not help noticing that quite a few people whom I did not know had crowded close to our table to listen in on our conversation. The fact that the man was talking all this God stuff kind of embarrassed me, but it did not seem to bother Bobo or Jimmy Joe. And, of course, more listeners certainly did not bother the man who called himself Jesus.

I questioned, "You say that God is just, so how does that fit into the Hitler narrative?"

You could see the man's eyes sadden, even in the semi-darkness of the bar, then he replied, "I have already told you that God has given all people the freedom to choose good or evil. It is a personal choice. Hitler chose evil, which means he is spending an eternity in hell. And, unfortunately, many people chose to follow him there."

Someone in the crowd asked, "Was Hitler the Antichrist?"

The man who called himself Jesus replied, "There have been many Antichrists in the past, there are several in today's world, and there will be many in the future."

Someone asked, "Do you think Hitler killed all those Jews because their forefathers rejected Christ?"

He did not reply that he had been crucified, but answered, "They died because of where they were when one of the evilest men in history chose absolute evil over God. Satan is absolute evil. Hitler was responsible for murdering many more people than the six million Jews attributed to him.

"And you have people today in this country who are responsible for murdering more people than the most ruthless dictators the world has ever known."

"What do you mean?" someone asked.

"Abortion," he replied. "Thousands of little children to whom my Father gave souls are being murdered in the wombs of their mothers every day."

I noticed that people who had inched closer to our table to hear the man began to back away. He had touched on something that most people did not want to talk about. I was one of them.

Another someone did try to steer the conversation back to Hitler, asking, "How do you think God will judge Hitler? What kind of punishment will he receive?"

The man took a sip of Coke and paused momentarily before answering. He then replied, "God does not have to judge Hitler, or any like him. Men like Hitler judge themselves, just as each of you will judge yourselves."

I questioned, "What do you mean, that we will judge ourselves?"

"You have access to the truth, to the way," he replied. "It is strictly up to you as to whether you choose the way of God or the way of Satan. Therefore, you judge yourself."

I argued, "There are a lot of things in the Bible that I just can't justify."

He responded, "It isn't your place to try to justify God's method and means of salvation. Your only option in the matter is to choose or not choose it."

The conversation continued for two or three more hours, maybe more. I cannot tell you how many margaritas I consumed, or how many beers Bobo stowed away in the reservoir he called a stomach.

And I do not recall much of the dialogue that took place, only that there was a lot of heavy stuff from the man who called himself Jesus. What I do recall was that my mind was like a windmill that is unable to determine from which direction the wind is blowing.

It was Bobo who finally broke the seriousness of the conversation when he asked,

"I'd still like to know how the game is going to turn out Sunday."

Almost everyone laughed, including the guy who called himself Jesus. Jimmy Joe did not laugh. He was more serious than a tightlipped frog waiting for a fly to get within a tongue's length.

That worried me, along with the fact that everyone other than me seemed to be accepting the man who called himself Jesus as the real thing.

FIVE

Joe Don Barnes joined the police department right after graduation from Howard Payne University, which is a small Baptist school in Brownwood, Texas. Brownwood is a two- to four-hour drive from Dallas, depending on how fast you want to drive.

Now it may seem ridiculously obvious to say that driving time depends on the speed at which you drive, but redundancy and obvious symbolize the way things are in Brownwood. This is not to say that Joe Don is redundant or obvious, only that he did spend a couple of years in Brownwood where he was a running back on Howard Payne's football team.

The truth be told, Joe Don was a city boy, if someone wants to call Dallas a city. Most people familiar with Dallas see it as just a town where Texas farm and ranch kids go after they allegedly grow up and graduate from high school or college.

Illegal aliens from Mexico, California and New York all come to Dallas to allegedly work, but only a few ever do any. Californians and New Yorkers mostly spend their time trying to get people to think they are smarter than the locals, which is harder to do than getting someone to take a feral cat.

Anyway, Joe Don grew up in a Dallas suburb before going to college in the country. And when I talk about country, I am not talking about Brownwood. He first went to Fayetteville, Arkansas to play for the Arkansas Razorbacks, which at the time was a remedial learning center in the Southwest Conference.

If someone thinks Brownwood is country, they should have spent time in Fayetteville back then. It made Waco seem metropolitan. The only culture you could find was a churn full of buttermilk gone bad.

Today Fayetteville is much more a haven for culture than New York City, but what city or town is not? After all, New York City culturally even lags far behind Mount Ida, Arkansas, which does not have a shoe store.

Football was the reason Joe Don ended up at a university where people sing out "Soohey Pig," with the same reverence with which they sing "Amazing Grace."

The coach who recruited Joe Don was considered a champion for the alleged "student athlete," and to his credit there were a few of his recruits on the team who could read. The coach later went on to become an unemployed TV network commentator. But while a commentator he often lectured the audience about the importance of education, the integrity of college football, the pureness of University of Arkansas athletes, and so on.

This is the same guy who, when Joe Don got teed off, left the team and went home to mama, showed up at his parents' house with fifty shiny hundred-dollar bills and enticed him to return to Fayetteville.

This was simply bonus money. Joe Don was already making a pretty good salary, although the Southwest Conference schools did not pay as much as the Big Ten and Southeastern Conference.

As for the coach, he was a real "holier than thou." He might even have been able to spell "integrity," but never practiced it. He had all the makings of a politician and might have become governor of Arkansas had it not been for Bill Clinton's accusations against him.

Anyway, Joe Don got tired of the coach's sermonizing without substance and used his substantial laundry money to move to Brownwood. There Howard Payne enabled him to play a little football, ride bulls in a few rodeos and get his degree in whatever the school offered.

Joe Don liked to play cowboy and thought about making a career of it, but he was never able to keep a pinch of snuff between his cheek and gums. The fact that he kept swallowing his snuff caused him to realize that it was not God's will for him to be a rodeo cowboy.

Even though Joe Don was quick to give God credit for his demise as a bull rider, if any Baptist doctrine was ever instilled in him at Howard Payne, I never witnessed it. I am sure that he believed in God, like almost everybody in the Lone Star State says they do, but he never let that belief keep him from doing what he wanted to do.

Doing what he wanted to do was why he was divorced. I could empathize with him because my ex-wife accused me of the same thing.

Joe Don was a little over six feet tall and weighed in at slightly over two hundred pounds. He was square-jawed, had brown eyes and he had a military-style haircut. he looked like the exact prototype of a police detective portrayed by the movies, although he was not a Clint Eastwood or Gene Hackman lookalike.

The only other thing I might add is that Joe Don never heeded the surgeon general's warning about smoking. More smoke came out of him than comes out of a dying diesel engine. Despite this character flaw, which is as offensive as onions, garlic and tomatoes, Joe Don and I maintained a strong friendship over the years.

There are advantages to having a friend who is a police captain, not the least of which is that he has access to certain information that is unavailable to most citizens. Because Joe Don had computerized information on much of the criminal element in Dallas and the rest of the country, I asked him to run a check on the man who called himself Jesus.

"I don't think we're going to have much luck chasing someone with a Jesus alias," he said. "About half the illegal Mexican males in Dallas claim to be named Hay-Seuss."

"This guy isn't Mexican," I said. "At least I don't think he is. Anyway, I brought you a glass with his fingerprints on it."

He laughed and questioned, "Damn, you're really out to get this guy, aren't you?"

Denying the accusation, I replied, "Not really. I'm out to get whoever hired him for this charade."

Joe Don said, "With all the sources you have at the paper, I would think you could get a line on him there."

Although I had not tried all that hard, I said, "I've tried, but I've gotten nowhere."

He grinned and questioned, "Has it occurred to you that the taxpayers might not approve of me checking things out for you?"

With irritation in my voice, I asked, "Damn it, Joe Don, are you going to do this for me or not?"

He chided, "Don't get your ass in an uproar, pal. It'll take my guys a while. In the meantime, you can bribe me with a little lunch."

I laughed and said, "You don't know the meaning of a little lunch."

Joe Don used a police car with flashing lights and a siren to transport us to the Highland Park Cafeteria, which has since closed. Luke, it was one of my favorite places to eat in all of Dallas, and one of Joe Don's, too.

I do not understand why the place closed but think it may have had something to do with too many Communists moving into the area, and as an aftermath to SMU's football team receiving the death penalty from the NCAA. The place had a sterling reputation and was written up in national magazines as one of the best places to eat in Dallas. The only negative to the place was that it did not serve alcoholic beverages, which resulted in some locals bringing their own bottles.

Since I was buying, Joe Don opted for the upstairs buffet, which was much more expensive than going through the cafeteria line. "Have the paper pick up the tab," he suggested. "Tell them you were interviewing me for a breaking story, a raid on the home of a Dallas Cowboys player who is a closet drug dealer."

"Is that true?" I asked.

"Do you want it to be?" he questioned.

"I'm not going to use our lunch for something untrue," I replied.

He rolled his eyes and loaded a plate with beef brisket, barbecued ribs, smothered steak and friend chicken.

"Are you going to eat any vegetables?" I asked.

"I'm putting those on a separate plate," he replied.

The buffet was a pitch until you won deal, meaning you could eat all you wanted, even to the point of not being able to waddle out of the place. And there was no time limit.

I laughed and said, "You know, of course, that you can come back for seconds, thirds and fourths."

"I intend to," he said.

By the time Joe Don loaded other plates with vegetables, desserts and breads, our table resembled the spread the Pilgrims and Indians combined on for the first Thanksgiving. As for me, I was content with some chicken fried steak, fried chicken and a couple of vegetables.

By the time I had polished off one drumstick and a glass of sweet tea, Joe Don was back loading up on more meat. Of course, he had to smoke a cigarette while he was filling a plate. I had encouraged him to quit smoking, but worried that if he did his appetite might increase and jeopardize the city's food supply.

"I haven't been eating well lately," he said while wolfing down some brisket. "You know how it is when you get a divorce."

I reminded him that he had been divorced for three years, and that during that time he had eaten a herd of cattle.

He grumbled, "I don't care what you say, Mark, "it's obvious that you're just not as sensitive as I am."

As to why Joe Don did not gain weight, I am at a loss to say. My knowledge about such things ranks right up there with my interpretation of the Book of Revelation, so I simply attributed it to his metabolism and his DNA.

After polishing off a couple of pieces of chocolate cake and a piece of pecan pie, Joe Don mellowed out and seemed ready to talk about the man who called himself Jesus. He agreed that the man was probably the hairbrained idea of one of our mutual friends. However. he did not have a clue as to who it might be since all were candidates for the funny farm.

I had dismissed Joe Don as a suspect because he spent all his money on child support, rent, cigarettes and food. He did not have a dime left to use on a joke.

By the time we got back to the police station, some of the officers Joe Don had assigned to check on the man who called himself Jesus were ready to report their findings.

They discovered that the FBI had more than a dozen people on file who claimed to be the real Jesus, all of whom were politicians. I checked out the mugshots and he was not among them. And a check of his fingerprint on the glass turned up nothing.

"Sorry, pal," Joe Don said. "You say this guy exists, but there is no evidence that he does. But there are still a few people out there who aren't in a law enforcement file."

"That's very comforting and reassuring," I said, sarcastically.

Joe Don laughed and said, "That's just like you, complaining about Big Brother but using Big Brother to check out this guy. You're a real piece of work, Mark."

I was teed off by his statement. I have never liked being trapped by my own reasoning. So, I changed the subject and asked Joe Don if he was planning to be at my house on Sunday for food, a touch football game and the Cowboys' game.

"Who's going to be there?" he asked.

I told him it would be the usual crowd, the same people who always showed up for these events.

"I'll be there if you don't invite Sue Beth," he said.

The reference was to Sue Beth Larsen, a realtor by profession who had once had the hots for Joe Don. He thought she was still after him, so I assured him that she had met her true love and was no longer interested in him.

"Who told you that?" he asked.

"Mary Lou," I replied.

He came back with a sarcastic, "And who's the lucky guy?"

"Just be assured that she no longer gives a damn about you," I replied. "As for the guy, he's a professional jockey that she met at Louisiana Downs."

Louisiana Downs was a horse racing track near Shreveport.

Joe Don laughed and questioned, "Sue Beth and a jockey? You have to be kidding me."

I assured him that I was serious, to which he responded, "Mark, the woman weighs in at more than two hundred pounds. How much does the jockey weigh?"

I argued, "Sue Beth doesn't weigh all that much over two hundred pounds, and she's tall."

He questioned, "You call five feet, two inches tall? How tall is this jockey?"

"I understand that he's at least five feet tall," I replied.

"And how much does he weigh?" Joe Don asked.

"At least one hundred ten pounds," I replied.

He laughed and said, "So, Sue Beth outweighs him by a good hundred pounds, and towers over him by a couple of inches."

While agreeing that Sue Beth and the jockey might look a bit comical together, I admitted, "Well, I haven't met him. I'm just going by what Mary Lou said."

Smiling, Joe Don said, "If she suffocates the little rascal, I might be investigating her for homicide."

I reminded him that Sue Beth furnished him a room for a couple of months after his wife booted him out of the house.

"I'm not saying she isn't a good-hearted woman," he said. "I just don't want her smothering me with affection."

"She's not going to bother you," I assured him. "I think she and the jockey plan to go into business together."

"What kind of business?" he asked.

"They're planning on building a racetrack right here in Dallas," I replied.

"Isn't gambling on horses illegal in Texas?" he asked.

I shrugged and replied, "You know more about that kind of stuff than I do. I know that pigeon shoots and cock fighting are illegal, but that doesn't keep people from having pigeon shoots and cock fights, and from betting on them."

"Where do they want to build this racetrack?" he asked.

"On the SMU campus," I replied.

Joe Don guffawed and sarcastically questioned, "A horse racing track in Highland Park? That will be the day. I grew up Methodist and know how goofy some Methodists are, but even I know there will never be a horse racing track on the SMU campus. People have been trying without success to get a decent football stadium on the campus for years."

I countered, "From what I understand, Sue Beth has talked to the dean of the business school and is willing to underwrite the cost of a master's program in horse racing."

Joe Don shook his head in mock resignation and said, "The woman must have more money than the Federal Reserve."

"She has plenty," I agreed, grinning. "If you had shown more interest in her, maybe even married her, you would have been set for life."

He countered, "Money isn't everything." He then turned somber and said, "A lot of our legislatures want pari-mutuel betting in Texas. They also think a lottery will fill the state's coffers with money.

"But look how much horse racing has helped Arkansas and Louisiana. Now there are a couple of profitable states for you."

I was not interested in getting into an argument with Joe Don about all the ill effects horse racing and other forms of gambling would allegedly bring to our state. That was an area where he was pure Baptist, although I do not know if he had ever darkened the door of a Baptist church.

However, I think most of his negative feelings about gambling had to do with the fact that when he was in high school his dad lost every asset the family had betting on the Cowboys.

When he got started on the subject, it was hard to turn him off, so he ranted, "Look how profitable gambling is for Atlantic City and New Mexico. That's another couple of real winners for you."

All that I knew about Atlantic City at the time was what I had learned in a movie titled *King of Marvin Gardens*, which starred Jack Nicolson and Bruce Dern.

Joe Don's contention was that no matter how allegedly well-regulated gambling was in the state, it would still be run by organized crime. When I felt like arguing about it, I contended that organized crime was better equipped to run the state than state government. Organized crime would show a profit, something state government never did. Government, I contended, simply squandered taxpayer money and taxed for more.

Of course, I could have cared less about horse racing. And I really agreed that it would cost the state more money than it brought in. I also agreed with him that it would increase the crime rate substantially.

As you know, Luke, people say marijuana is harmless. But if that is the case, how come it seems that the perpetrator of every heinous crime is said to be under the influence of marijuana or some other drug?

"So," I asked Joe Don, "will you be at the house on Sunday."

"What are you fixing?" he asked.

"I'm thinking about brisket and spareribs," I replied.

"Well, if you'll do more than think about it, I'll be there," he said.

I joked, "You just have to promise me that you won't go into a jealous rage when you see Sue Beth with her new jockey love."

Joe Don laughed and said, "I think I can promise you that I'll be good."

I was thinking, of course, that with all my friends in one place, I could give them the thumb test, which would tell me which one of them was responsible for the man who called himself Jesus.

SIX

Ribs Davis was a man with a message, which he usually wore emblazoned on the front of his T-shirt or cap. Some of those messages I remember, like WHEN WATERMELONS ARE OUTLAWED, WHITE CRIMINALS WILL STEAL THEM FROM BLACK FARMERS. Another was MUHAMMAD ALI WAS A SISSY and still another was ALL OLDER MEN CAN DRIBBLE.

One of my all-time favorites was IF YOU INTEGRATE YOU WILL END UP GOING TO A WHITE CHURCH WHERE EVERY SERVICE IS LIKE A FUNERAL.

Ribs was not my only black friend, but he was the only one who loved to make fun of alleged racism. He refused to let anyone call him an African-American because, he said, "I've never even been to Africa. And I thank God for slavery, because if my ancestors hadn't been slaves, I wouldn't have been born here.

"So, I'm just a plain old patriotic American," he would say. "If you insist on giving me a double identity, you can call me a

Dallas-American because I was born in South Dallas."

No one knew whether Ribs was serious, because he had the ability to be as straight-faced as Mother Teresa.

Ribs operated in a different mental sphere than most people, and the fact that I thought I understood it frightened me. It made me think that my ex-wife was right about me needing psychiatric help and medication.

There was a radio station in Dallas that was always running contests where winners received substantial cash prizes. Ribs had entered those contests for several years, but never won.

Finally, after years of frustration, he sued the station for discrimination, claiming it was racist. His lawyer, of course, was Billy Bob Raintree, a champion of frivolous lawsuits.

Both Ribs and Billy Bob raised such a fuss that they got a lot of media attention. And even though the station disproved their charges, Ribs became somewhat of a celebrity as a media justice warrior.

The word "warrior" got him to thinking that he might be both an American Indian as well as a black man. He thought he might be a Choctaw Indian, since some other tribes looked down on Choctaws.

It soon became evident that all ethnic groups paled in comparison to Ribs when it came to racism. Ribs prided himself on not liking white people, black people, brown people, yellow people, red people or people of any combination of colors. He even tried to start a colorless people movement but could never come up with a colorless color.

Even more baffling, Ribs did not like pork chops, watermelon or soul food but would have eaten escargot and caviar every day if he could have afforded it.

Everything in the food world that Ribs disliked, I craved. But it will be a cold day in hell before I ever eat snails and fish eggs.

Ribs always said the reason there were so few black quarterbacks in the NFL was that no black man wanted to pass something that looked like a watermelon to someone else.

Ribs never paid any attention to my complaints about his racism. He, instead, flaunted it at every opportunity.

When Ribs tried to join the Ku Klux Klan because he liked their uniforms, no one gave him much of a chance. That did not deter him. When the Klan turned down his membership application, he had Billy Bob sue the organization for discrimination. And they promised, if necessary, to take his fight for membership all the way to the Supreme Court.

When Ribs lied and said he was a Democrat, the entire East and West Coast media took up the fight with him. He even threatened to move to Harrison, Arkansas, if the Klan did not approve his membership application.

Ribs became so angry about being rejected by the Klan that he refused to buy anything at a department store WHITE SALE.

As previously mentioned, some of Ribs' more intelligent communication was on his T-shirts, but his caps had some great messages, too. They advertised everything from cow manure to artificial insemination.

I was always appreciative that he wore the caps backward, as if he was a baseball catcher. If you wanted to read what the cap advertised, you had to stand behind him. The caps were as much a part of his wardrobe as the T-shirts.

You would have thought that he would have accessorized the T-shirts and caps with jeans and running shoes, but his other attire always consisted of brightly colored and expensive pegged slacks, wing tip pointed toed lace shoes and ultra-suede sports coats. Like many of my friends, he made a fashion statement that defied the norm.

Before you get the wrong idea, I have never been one of those people who goes around bragging about how many black and Mexican friends I have. This is something Democrats do to cover up their history of racism.

My relationship with Ribs came about because of his touch football abilities and had absolutely nothing to do with politics. I had met Ribs year earlier while playing a serious game of touch football.

My team was short a man and I noticed Ribs standing on our imaginary sideline looking baleful, whatever that means. But whatever the meaning he did it better than anyone I have ever known. Anyway, I invited him to play with us and he agreed.

I recall saying to him, "You look like a split end to me."

That drew a suspicious look and the question, "What do you mean?"

"Split end is a position in football," I replied. "You're kind of tall and lanky. Most split ends are tall and lanky."

Ribs was five feet eight inches tall and he was skinny, but most short people like to be perceived as tall. So, tall was just a suggestion on my part.

"Oh," he responded, "I kind of wanted to play center."

"I'm the center," Bobo Harrison snarled. "Want to make something of it?"

Ribs looked at Bobo and replied, "Like you say, I'm a split end."

Bobo always played center because it required little, if any, running. At least, that is the way Bobo played the position. And because he always had a bottle or can of beer in his hand, he was a one-handed snapper.

We ran every play from what some might think was a punt formation. It was really a spread formation and everyone in the backfield had to be alert because Bobo's snaps were most often erratic.

On that day we were using Bobo's ball, so if Ribs had insisted on playing center, Bobo would have taken his ball and gone home. Fortunately, being a good teammate overrode Ribs' selfish ambition to play center.

Anyway, when we were in the huddle, I told Ribs to run a fly pattern. He glanced down at his crotch and with obvious suspicion in his voice questioned, "Say what?"

"No, no," I said, then patiently with an index finger drew the play on the ground. Ribs nodded as if he understood, but when I looked into his eyes my observation was that there was no one home.

When Bobo snapped the ball back to me, I was able to field it despite that it bounced a couple of feet to my left. Ribs sprinted downfield and I lofted a pass in his direction. He caught the ball in full stride, but instead of tucking it away and running for the goal line, he started trying to dribble it.

At the time I thought Ribs might be putting me on, mixing basketball and football into one sport. But as I got to know him better, I realized that Ribs danced to a different drummer than most people.

Nothing brought that home better than learning he was taking accordion lessons and that his dream was to become the next Lawrence Welk. He was a pioneer in what would become *Polka Rap*.

When I told him that it was strange that a black man would want to play the accordion and dance the polka, he reminded me that people looked at black country singer Charley Pride with a jaundiced eye when he integrated country music. I did not quite understand the connection, but there was a lot about Ribs that I did not understand.

Once trained not to dribble the football, Ribs became one of my team's best pass receivers. And for a man who wore wingtip, lace-up shoes on the football field, he was amazingly fast and agile. He made cuts that would be the envy of any NFL receiver.

When I met Ribs, he lived in a North Dallas apartment complex several miles beyond prestigious Highland Park and several blocks from me. Although he had lived there for some time, he was always threatening to move because there were no other blacks in the complex, something he attributed to discrimination. Therefore, he filed a lawsuit against the owner.

In an obvious attempt to appease him, the owner offered him a substantial decrease in rent if he could get other black tenants to move in. He refused the offer, saying he would move out if other blacks moved in because they would trash the place.

Ribs, who used the N-word liberally, told me that if a bunch of N*****s moved into the complex, nothing he had would be safe. "You know how they are," he said. "It's just natural for them to lie and steal."

I told Ribs quite often that if that was the case, you did not have to be black to be a N*****.

For a while Ribs got on a kick where he wanted to date a white girl. He kept asking white girls out but was turned down more than sheets on a hotel bed. But finally, one agreed to a date.

He broke the date, he said, because he had no respect for a white woman who would go out with a black man.

Ribs was, indeed, difficult to figure out.

When I first met Ribs, he was trying to make it as a stockbroker. The word minimal would best describe his success, which he attributed to the fact that no white man would ever trust a black man with his money.

And he also added that no black man would ever trust another black man with his money. He said black people would not even buy watermelon futures from him.

If a college education means anything, Ribs had one. He had a degree from an all-black college, but said it was worth less than a roll of good toilet paper.

Ribs often laughed at TV commercials promoting all black colleges, and especially their theme that "A mind is a terrible thing to waste." He said the easiest place to waste your mind was at an all-black school. I argued that no effort on your part was required to waste your mind at any school.

Once I mentioned the names of some of the people who had graduated from alleged prestigious Ivy League schools, he decided that he was a genius.

Ribs often asked me how I felt about "Black Privilege," the fact that the government allowed all-black schools, but not all-white schools.

"I think we ought to call a spade a spade," he often said. "Black Privilege is racism, pure and simple, and it's destroying America. Black schools promote racism, and any black person with a severe learning disability has a good chance of graduating with honors."

When he went on one of his rants, I simply pointed to most of the people in Congress as proof that stupidity is colorblind. I would follow that up with, "Besides, I thought you were an Indian?"

"I applied for membership in the Choctaw Tribe," he told me, "but they made membership contingent on establishing a residence in Oklahoma. Can you imagine a Texan doing that?"

I told him I could not, but that rules on ethnicity were rules; that if he wanted to be an Indian it would require that he both sacrifice his status as a black man and as a Texan.

While awaiting his shot at becoming the new polka king, and after leaving his role as a stockbroker, for a short time Ribs became a DART bus driver. He said the test for being a bus driver was much harder than that for being a stockbroker. In addition to a written and driving test, he was required to go through Dallas Police Academy training, since as a DART driver he would have more contact with criminals than did the police.

He was fired from that job for driving with one hand and playing the accordion with the other. However, I always thought there was more to it than that. I think some of his polka rap offended some of the DART management. It called for them to face a firing squad or be shipped to Cuba.

Following his tenure with DART, which he said was one of the loneliest periods in his life (he averaged three passengers a month), Ribs became an automobile broker. He told me it was easy to unload old Cadillacs, Buicks and Pontiacs on the brothers, and to unload Chevrolets on illegal Mexicans.

He was doing quite well in the car business, but it still was not fulfilling his entrepreneurial dreams. He was still driving a Volkswagen that was several years old.

If I recall correctly, it was a Wednesday afternoon, eight days before Christmas, when I found Ribs walking his dog in my neighborhood. He always drove over to my neighborhood to walk the dog because he did not want dog poop in his neighborhood. And he always ate supper at my house on Wednesdays.

Ribs' dog was a white German Shepherd named Blackie. Ribs explained that he had named the dog Blackie because he did not want to name him Indian. I acted as if I understood his reasoning, which was that the dog, being very sensitive, was embarrassed by his color.

Although Blackie was seemingly oblivious to the world around him, he always seemed a bit bemused by Ribs' comments about him. Anyway, Blackie was a friend of my dog, Cowboy, and when Blackie was at my house the two of them cruised the neighborhood together looking for female dogs.

From shortly after we first met, Ribs had supper with me every Wednesday. However, when I suggested that we make it a standing invitation, he said he did not want to tie himself down.

On the Wednesday that I have in mind, the man who called himself Jesus had gone to church and I was out retrieving the mail when Ribs and Blackie showed up. And, as always, I issued my usual invite, asking, "Do you and Blackie want to have supper with Cowboy and me?"

And, of course, Ribs asked Blackie, "Do you want to have supper with Mark and Cowboy?" You may not believe this, Luke, but Blackie always shook his head yes.

Then Ribs would ask, "What are we having, Mark?"

"Fried chicken, mac and cheese, blackeye peas, cornbread and sweet tea," I replied, which is what we had every Wednesday night. Of course, Blackie and Cowboy each had a can of Alpo, which they preferred to our table food. Because they always chose Alpo over what we ate, I was tempted to taste it to see what we were missing, but never did.

While we were gorging ourselves, I told Ribs about the man who called himself Jesus.

"Where is he now?" Ribs asked.

"It being Wednesday, he's in church," I replied.

"Well, if he's Jesus, I guess church is as good a place as any for him," Ribs said.

"He isn't Jesus," I said, "but you can meet him on Sunday."

"Blackie and I are going coon hunting Saturday night, so I might not be as sharp as I usually am," Ribs said.

Ribs' affinity for hunting racoons all night was something I never quite understood, but it was one of the most serious things in his life. He was the only black member of the Dallas Chapter of the American Coon Hunters Association, and through intensive study had achieved thirty-third degree status.

He had an American Coon Hunters (ACH) belt buckle, jacket patch and membership card. And, of course, he had decals on his car that promoted the organizations.

I had even helped him with a couple of articles that he wrote for *Coon Masters* magazine.

I reminded him, "You know we have a big game scheduled on Sunday, plus the Cowboys are playing the Eagles."

"Yeah, I know," he said, "but I should be home no later than four o'clock in the morning. A couple of hours of sleep and I'll be good as new. By the way, I have big news for you."

"What kind of news?" I asked.

He asked, "You know that T-shirt shop I've been eyeing in the mall?"

"Yeah, what about it?" I questioned.

"I'm buying it," he replied.

"Where did you get the money?" I asked.

"SBA," he answered. "I'm borrowing a quarter million from the Small Business Administration."

"The T-shirt shop isn't that profitable," I said. "How are you going to pay it back?"

"I'm not," he replied. "It's part of Black Privilege being promoted by the government. I met this black dude who is getting his eighth SBA loan. He defaulted on the other seven and filed bankruptcies. So,

I'm not worried about paying back the T-shirt shop loan."

"Wow!" I exclaimed. "Things really are changing."

"You know that you can now choose your color and gender," Ribs said. "If you want to be black, I'll sponsor you."

"Maybe later," I said.

Ribs questioned, "This guy who calls himself Jesus, is he black."

"No," I replied.

"Then he's probably not the real thing," Ribs said.

SEVEN

Mary Lou Magruder and Sue Beth Larsen were good friends, which was why I did not trust either of them. It was an unusual relationship since Mary Lou for the most part detested female realtors.

She still pictured women realtors as trying to look somewhat like Dallas Cowboys Cheerleaders, primarily because they all wore white mid-calf cowboy boots. Any other similarity was purely coincidental.

Most female realtors accessorized the boots with short shirts, lowcut sweaters and flashy jewelry. But that had been the trend years earlier. Unfortunately, the look had fossilized in Mary Lou's mind.

Of course, Sue Beth did not look like a realtor. She wore expensive dresses that looked like sacks, and physically looked more like a mud wrestler than a realtor.

However, she might well have been the most successful realtor in Dallas, possibly because clients were afraid of her. She was a millionaire several times over, owned a mansion in Highland Park that was valued in eight figures and always drove a new Rolls Royce with a new Cadillac and Mercedes for backup.

Sue Beth never took much pains with her wardrobe or appearance, and thought diet was a four-letter word for whatever she wanted to eat, and she ate plenty.

She could down a two-pound Porterhouse steak with all the trimmings before a thoroughbred could run a quarter mile, and a gallon of ice cream was child's play for her.

Obviously, I could not fault her for the ice cream, especially if it was Blue Bell, which was manufactured in Brenham, Texas.

Sue Beth never saw herself as fat, just big boned, which was like saying that an elephant had the same bone structure as an antelope.

Someone once told me that most fat people are jovial, and Sue Beth was certainly that. She seemed to find the entire world amusing, whereas skinnier people that I knew had those phony laughs, indicating to me that they were hungry.

I figure it is hard to be happy when you are dieting and doing a lot of exercise to be skinny. I preferred Sue Beth's idea of exercise, which was steering one of her cars through the drive-through of a Kentucky Fried Chicken or Church's to buy a family-size bucket of fried chicken for a bedtime snack.

Someone once told me that rich people are never happy, but I have also never seen poor people jump up and down with joy because of their poverty. So, I have always been willing to risk being rich and unhappy.

Being rich did not seem to make Sue Beth a bit unhappy.

I should mention that in addition to selling real estate, Sue Beth was also a half-assed psychic, or claimed to be. She made a ton reading tea leaves, although she never achieved the fame of California psychics who receive a dollar for every telephone minute that they can keep you on the line.

Hundreds, if not thousands, of divorced female realtors in the Dallas area worshipped at Sue Beth's feet, paying her big bucks to tell them that they would soon meet *Mister Right*.

I figured Sue Beth had as much, or more, insight than the preacher-prophets on TV who were always predicting the date of the Rapture, the end of the world, or the Second Coming.

There are some things that I would just as soon not know.

If Sue Beth wanted to practice Voodoo or witchcraft, it was okay with me. Even though I have never been a fan of weirdness, I liked her. And I also knew she liked a good joke, so figured she could very well be the one responsible for the Jesus joke, probably with the help of the devious Mary Lou.

So, on Thursday evening, seven days before Christmas, we met at Andrew's, a nice little spot on McKinney Avenue that offered a unique ambiance.

We arrived simultaneously and Mary Lou asked, "Where's Jesus?"

"He and Cowboy are watching TV," I replied. The truth was that I did not know what my dog and the man who called himself Jesus were doing, just gave a convenient answer.

I had become a bit irritated with Cowboy's attitude. He seemed to be more interested in hanging with the Jesus character than with me.

Mary Lou was her usual charming and sarcastic self, saying how privileged she felt to be in my company twice in one week.

I reminded the two women to be at my house on Sunday for the touch football game, the Cowboys and Eagles game, and a wagonload of unhealthy food and drink.

"I'll be there," Sue Beth said, "and you two should get back together. You attack each other better than any married couple I've ever known."

"I've already been through Marine boot camp once," I said. "And I didn't have to pay for it."

After being shown to a table, we all ordered our favorite libations. I had my usual margarita, Mary Lou ordered a screwdriver, and Sue Beth, who was not pretentious, ordered a longneck brew. She also ordered four all the way half-pound burgers with a quadruple order of fries.

Mary Lou asked Sue Beth, "Has Mark told you about his house guest?"

"No," she replied, "I haven't seen Mark for a while. So, who is your house guest, Mark?"

I answered, "He claims to be Jesus Christ."

Sue Beth guffawed, gulped down some beer, and said questioningly, "Jesus Christ at your house and hanging out with you? That will be the day."

"You're acting as if the guy were the real Jesus Christ, he wouldn't have anything to do with me," I said, irritated.

"There's no act to it," Mary Lou said. "I can't understand why anyone who even poses as Jesus Christ would want to hang out with you."

"You weren't quite so sarcastic when we were having breakfast Monday morning," I said.

"That's because you caught me on a bad day," she said. "I was feeling melancholy."

"You should try melancholy more often," I said. "It's more becoming."

"About this guy who claims to be Jesus, fill me in on what's going on," Sue Beth said.

"I figured the mouth here had already told you," I said. "Or, I figured you already knew everything because you had sent him my way."

"Not guilty," she said. "Why would I do that?"

"It beats the hell out of me," I said. "Are you ready to prove your innocence by taking the thumb test?"

"Sure," she replied, but you already know I can't look at your thumb without laughing."

"And why is that," I questioned.

"Because the thumb test is the stupidest excuse for a truth test that anyone has ever come up with," she replied.

"You're admitting that you can't pass it," I said.

"In all seriousness, Mark, I swear that I know nothing about your house guest," she said. "And Mary Lou hasn't told me about him because we haven't talked this week. I just got back from Louisiana."

I questioned, "Over seeing your jockey friend?"

"Yes," she replied.

"And, how is he?" I asked.

She responded, "He's wonderful."

Now, Luke, I have to say that Sue Beth was as hard to read as Billy Bob Raintree, but for a different reason. Billy Bob was just flat cunning, what you would expect from a lawyer. Sue Beth, though, had laughing eyes that made her difficult to read. Her eyes laughed all the time, so you did not know when she was playing a joke or when she was not.

"What has Chigger been up to?" I asked. Chigger Dodgen, Sue Beth's boyfriend, was not exactly a household name among horse racing fans. "I hope he'll show up at the house on Sunday."

"He can't," she said. "He has the children for the weekend and has to stay in Louisiana. They're going to pick up aluminum cans along the highway to earn Christmas money."

The waiter came and filled our table with Sue Beth's order, which gave us a chance to order more drinks.

From what I had learned from various sources, Chigger had conned Sue Beth out of several hundred thousand dollars, much of which was used to bet on whatever nag he was riding at Louisiana Downs. And while Chigger thought of himself as one of the top jockeys in all of horse racing, you could count the number of his wins on one finger.

But it was not my place to rain on Sue Beth's parade, so I said, "Chigger sounds like a wonderful man, a real Fred Crachet."

Out of the corner of one eye, I saw Mary Lou's eyes spin like a roulette wheel.

While chomping down on one of her burgers, Sue Beth agreed that Chigger was, indeed, the Lone Ranger and Zorro all rolled into one small package.

"How many children does Chigger have?" I asked.

"Twelve," she replied.

I laughed and said, "Man, he has been busy. He must have worn his ex-wife out."

"Not really," she said. "He has twelve ex-wives. He had a child with each of them."

"Are you going to be wife number thirteen?" I asked.

"I hope so," she said.

"I don't think there's any doubt about it," I said. "And I hope you have a long and happy marriage."

Sue Beth smiled and said, "I know you think it's funny, the fact that Chigger has been married twelves times."

I questioned, "Now why would you think that, Sue Beth?"

"I know you too well," she replied, "and you seem to forget that I'm a psychic. You can make fun all you want, but I think Chigger is now ready to settle down for good."

"Hey, I'm envious of old Chigger's record," I said.

"You should be," Mary Lou said. "You couldn't get twelve women to agree to a second date with you."

I gave her a hard look and asked, "What's the longest Chigger has been married to any of these women?"

"He was married to his last wife for fourteen months," she said.

I questioned, "And that's the longest he has been married?"

"Yes," she replied, "but he has been on the road a lot."

I was not sure that had anything to do with the length of Chigger's marriages but was afraid to request an explanation. I had this funny feeling that Mary Lou and Sue Beth were about to gang up on me.

I figured Chigger needed a purse or briefcase in which to carry the pictures of his children. A wallet would have to be the size of a big pillow.

I questioned, "I don't mean to be nosy, Sue Beth, but have you and Chigger talked about having children?"

"We've talked about it," she replied, "but only if it doesn't interfere with his career."

I wanted to say, "It hasn't thus far," but, instead, said to Mary Lou, "You're awfully quiet."

"There's nothing to say," she said. "I already knew everything Sue Beth told you. So, why don't you tell her the story you told me about this guy named Jesus?"

"She probably already knows it," I replied.

"No, I don't," Sue Beth said.

I was reluctant to go over the same ground that I had covered with some other people, but thought, "What the hell?" So, I began telling Sue Beth every stinking detail of my encounter with the man who called himself Jesus.

She seemed genuinely fascinated with my story, interrupting only long enough to order two more burgers, a double order of fries, and a couple of longnecks.

I finished the story saying, "Being a psychic and all, you should be able to tell me who the man is. I already know he's not the real Jesus."

She shook her head in resignation, reached in her purse and took out a pair of dark glasses that she normally put on for her psychic readings. She covered her eyes with the glasses and said, "If I had something belonging to the man, I could probably help you, and if you believed in psychic phenomena. But because of your skepticism, I don't know that I can help you."

I responded, "If it helps, Sue Beth, I believe in BS, so why don't you think I believe in psychic phenomenon?"

Mary Lou attacked with, "That's the problem with you, Mark. You think you're so damned smart."

I nailed her saying, "Hey, cut me some slack, Sugar. I'm just kidding."

Mary Lou hates being called Sugar, which, of course, I knew.

While Mary Lou seethed, Sue Beth pondered and then acted as if she was in a trance. Her ruse might have worked if the waiter had not arrived with the burgers and fries.

The smell of the food broke whatever trance she was in. She was soon chomping down on a burger, popping a fry loaded with catsup in her mouth, and taking a swig of beer from the longneck bottle.

Sue Beth explained, "The setting is all wrong here and I don't have anything belonging to the man. I can give you a reading when I get to your house on Sunday."

"If he's still there, you can touch the man himself," I said.

"Who else is going to be there?" she asked.

"The usual bunch," I replied.

"Including Joe Don?" she asked.

"Yeah, he'll be there," I said.

"That presents a problem," she said.

"How's that?" I asked.

She replied, "You know he's crazy about me. And Chigger is the jealous type."

I knew Joe Don thought Sue Beth was crazy about him, but her revelation that he was crazy about her was news to me.

"Since Chigger isn't going to be there, I'm sure you can handle it," I said.

"Oh, I know I can handle it," she said. "But even though I'm committed to Chigger, I don't want to hurt Joe Don."

"Hey," I said, suddenly enjoying the dialogue. "Joe Don's a big boy. He's going to have to learn to deal with heartache and rejection sooner or later. And you owe it to him to explain your feelings for Chigger. He'll understand."

Mary Lou, I knew was angry at me for my teasing, but Sue Beth was as serious as a DART bus driver who had been awakened from his afternoon nap.

Sue Beth questioned, "So, you think I should talk to Joe Don?"

"Definitely," I replied. "Just let him down easy."

EIGHT

Chico Neiman-Marcus was one hundred percent Mexican, but like Ribs Davis was willing to become all things to all men if there was the possibility of a buck in it.

Chico's Mexican name was Sergio Vincente Martinez Dominguez, thus the name Chico.

He was very image-conscious, which was why he attempted to tie the name of his used hubcap shop to the famous Neiman-Marcus department stores. He was a well-educated and prideful man who had a degree in hubcap identification from a Dallas community college.

I often asked Chico where he obtained the "new" used hubcaps that he sold, and he always told me that people just brought them in. When all four of the hubcaps for my BMW came up missing, he was able to replace them with the car's original hubcaps. And he was Johnny on the spot. He had a set just like those missing off my BMW in the trunk of his car.

He explained to me that like a person's fingerprints, every hubcap is unique, and that if it is in the National Hubcap Database, he can find it.

He also told me that a used hubcap shop was like a pawn shop. I asked if that meant he made loans on hubcaps and he quickly replied, "No, no loans."

When I persisted and asked him to explain how a used hubcap shop was like a pawn shop, he replied, "Just trust me on this."

Chico is another guy who just showed up one day and started playing touch football with us. He lived in the same apartment complex that Ribs Davis lived in, which had more reported hubcap theft than any other apartment complex in Dallas.

Chico's business was operated out of an old building on Harry Hines Boulevard, a section of Dallas where there were a lot of porno shops, men's clubs and photography studios where you could rent a camera and model for thirty minutes to an hour. The area attracted a lot of aspiring artists and ladies in tight, short skirts who did a lot of walking along the street in spike heel shoes.

The building where Chico displayed his hubcaps had at one time been a Texaco service station, and the last time the restroom had been cleaned was several years earlier when it was a service station.

If you wanted to use the restroom you had to ask Chico for a key, and you had to have your own toilet paper.

Paint on the building was weathered, yellow-stained and peeling. I recall that Chico had started painting the building pink and chartreuse but saw no need in rushing the project. So, after five years it was about a fourth done, and the initial paint had cracked and weathered.

During this time, he expanded his product line to include velvet paintings, pottery, blankets, serapes, sombreros and Mexican dresses. In Mexico he never paid more than three dollars each for any of these products but sold them for thirty to forty dollars. He bought cheap, sold high.

The Mexican he hired to paint the sign for his store had a little trouble with his spelling, so the sign read KNEEMANO MARCOSO HUBCAPO. I suggested that Chico have the guy redo the sign, but he said, "What is written is written."

It was a brilliant response to my suggestion, causing me to drop the subject.

As for Chico's appearance, he was a short, wiry man who used his Mexican accent only when he thought it would benefit him. He spoke English better than most people, but he could lapse into an almost indistinguishable Mexican dialect if he was trying to con someone.

He, of course, was born in Dallas, went to Dallas public schools and then to El Centro Community College. He spent four years in the Army in a supply company, so was well trained in missing goods.

No one in Dallas was more anti-immigration than Chico. He claimed that if he had been alive at the time, he would have fought alongside General Travis at the Alamo, and he thought General Sam Houston should have executed Santa Ana and the entire Mexican army when they surrendered to the Texans at San Jacinto, which, of course, was what Santa Ana did at Goliad and the Alamo.

Bobo loved to pull Chico's chain and often agitated him, saying no Texas general would have wanted him in their command. Bobo could turn Chico's brown face red.

Anyway, when the man who called himself Jesus had come home from church the previous evening, I could tell he was a little downcast. Wednesday night church services affect people in that way.

Baptist churches vote on whether to have such services and most do if a meal is provided. So much for feasting on the word. Mama just does not want to cook.

Every Baptist feels obligated to vote for Wednesday night services, but no one wants to attend them. It is a little like people voting for a Nazi or Communist if they are on the Democrat ticket, for no other reason than that their parents or grandparents always voted a Democrat ticket.

I wanted to encourage the man who called himself Jesus, so engaged him about his future. I figured that he would appreciate my interest in helping him with his job prospects. Although, he was doing a heckuva job cleaning the house, everything cleaner than a hospital and almost as spit clean as a Marine barracks, I did not think housework was all that fulfilling.

The man seemed a bit amused about my interest in his future, but listened while I made several suggestions, including that he be tested to determine the kind of work for which he was best suited.

Ribs had told me during our Wednesday evening supper that Chico was looking for some help. And, since I usually had breakfast with Chico every Friday morning, I invited the man who called himself Jesus to join us.

I was busy talking to anonymous sources all day Thursday and met with Mary Lou and Sue Beth that evening, so had no idea what he had done that day.

At eight o'clock Friday morning the phony Jesus and I met Chico at the Mecca Café, one of the more famous eating places on Harry Hines Boulevard. If you are wondering about what time Chico opened the hubcap store, it was whenever he got there. He did not think time was important, and simply wanted to make sure he opened in time to close for his afternoon siesta.

The Mecca Café was decorated in a lot of University of Oklahoma and University of Texas stuff, along with a Texas A&M decal that someone had tried to peel off the wall. The waitresses were forever apologizing for it, and many Mecca employees had without success attempted to remove it. The decal was thought to be made of some secret formula concocted in an A&M lab.

There was nothing pretentious about the café. It specialized in some of the best down-home cooking in Dallas, food that put some of the city's more pretentious restaurants, of which there were many and probably still are, to shame.

Most of the Mecca's customers were male. You did not take a date to the Mecca unless you were about to propose marriage.

After introducing the man who called himself Jesus to Chico, we entrenched ourselves in a booth.

With his over medium eggs, the man ordered bacon, grits and a side of gravy for his biscuits. This made me feel better about him. It indicated that he had southern DNA.

While the three of us were sipping our coffee, Chico said, "Mark tells me you call yourself Jesus."

"That's my name," the man said.

Chico, who was about as tactful as a pig being slopped, asked, "You're not illegal, are you?"

"If you're asking if I can prove U.S. citizenship, I can't," the man said. "I don't have a driver's license, Social Security or voter ID cards."

"No problem," Chico said. "I sell all three. I just don't need some greaser coming in and stealing from me. I have hubcap insurance, but still have to pay the deductible."

The and laughed and said, "That's a bummer."

Chico questioned, "So, you're not from Mexico? A lot of Mexicans are named Jesus, although they pronounce it Hay-Seuss."

"My residence is Heaven," the man said.

"Mark told me you claim to be the real Jesus," Chico said, "but you'll understand that I find that hard to believe. I sell velvet paintings of the real Jesus, and I've seen pictures of him in my mother's Bible. You just don't look like Him."

"Sorry to be a disappointment to you," the man said, "but artists have always been strange."

Fortunately, breakfast arrived, and I had the opportunity to work on some ham, biscuits and gravy, but even with his mouth full Chico continued questioning the man. I recalled what Ribs had told me on Wednesday evening when he told me Chico was looking for help.

"Of course, you can never tell about the little spic, whether he's lying or not," Ribs had said. "He likes to act as if he's running some big conglomerate instead of something several notches below a Goodwill store."

So, I should not have been surprised when Chico asked the man, "Do you have any hubcap experience?"

The man laughed and replied, "I can't say that I do."

I questioned, "Experience? Just how many people in the world do you think have experience in hubcap sales?"

Chico shrugged his shoulders and replied, "How should I know? And if you're so damned smart, Mark, what kind of questions would you ask someone that you might hire to sell hubcaps?"

He had me there. "I can't answer that," I said, "because you're the only one I know in the hubcap business."

"Well, until you can come up with some better questions," he said, "don't be criticizing me for the ones I ask."

Then, addressing the man who called himself Jesus, he asked, "What do you consider your major strength?"

"Honesty," the man said. "I can't and won't lie."

Chico gave a negative shake of the head and said, "That's not really an asset in hubcap sales."

I questioned, "You don't want to hire someone who will steal from you, do you?"

Chico gave his classic shrug of the shoulders and replied, "It doesn't matter. I've got that built into my price structure."

I insisted, "Still, even if you do, it's more profitable if you don't have theft."

"Maybe you're right," he said, "but I've never worried much about employee theft since I'm my only employee. And it's okay if I steal from me."

You can imagine what it was like when Chico and Ribs got together. Their perceived logic spewed forth like the geyser erupting in Yellowstone Park. Both Aristotle and Plato would have been overwhelmed by it.

The conversation that Friday was not that memorable. We did talk about Sunday's game and the meal at my house. Chico said he would be there if I did not serve Mexican food. But he knew I disliked Mexican food and never served it, other than chips and salsa. I also suggested that the man who called himself Jesus catch an early church service so as not to miss anything. I was still planning to use the truth thumb test on everyone present.

The several cups of coffee I had drunk were begging for release, so I excused myself and went to the john. When I was returning to the table, I noted that the man and Chico were engaged in heavy conversation, which diminished when I returned and sat down.

I asked, "Well, have you decided whether you're going to hire J.C. or not?"

Chico gave me a distasteful look and said, "I'm not sure it's proper to use initials for Jesus Christ."

I gave him an incredulous look and attempted to respond, but the man beat me to the punch saying, "It doesn't matter."

I felt that Chico was attempting to berate me, when he said, "It matters to me. And yes, Mark, I have hired Jesus. I think he will be a natural in hubcap sales."

"Great," I said, "when does he start?"

"As soon as you pay the check and we get to the store," Chico replied.

"How are you going to get home this evening?" I asked the man.

"I'll give him a ride to your house," Chico said. "Don't worry about it."

Outside the café it was still blue blizzard cold, which I figured would not be that great for the hubcap business. Chico seemed to read my mind and said, "With Christmas just six days away, today and tomorrow we should be busier than a couple of beavers felling a tree."

Puzzled, I questioned, "Are used hubcaps a big Christmas gift?"

"Oh, yeah," Chico replied, "especially American-made used hubcaps. In recent years the Chinese have increased production of used hubcaps, so a lot of what you see on the road today are cheap imitations of the real thing. I don't handle any stinking Chinese imitations of the real thing."

"It sounds like something the paper ought to do an expose on," I said.

"Good luck," he said. "The Chinese used hubcap lobby is one of the most powerful in Washington."

I expected a reaction from the man who called himself Jesus when he saw Chico's car, but he was as expressionless as a smooth Brazos River rock. You see, while Chico was anti-Mexican, it did not extend to cars. He had an old Chevrolet he had purchased from Ribs that had a jacked up rear end and radio amplifiers that spilled out music that was loud enough to raise the dead.

In the sale Ribs had included tapes of his accordion polka rap, which had become some of Chico's favorite music.

The car's exterior had a custom purple and yellow paint job. The interior had red shag carpet, chartreuse vinyl seats, and was trimmed in fake wood. There was a plastic Jesus on the dashboard, big cloth dice hanging off the rearview mirror, and a Dallas Cowboy doll with a wagging head in the space behind the back seat. The doll seemed to be looking out the back window, but it was hard to tell.

The car had not come with an ignition key, so Chico had to hotwire it every time he drove it. I watched as he herded it out of the café parking lot, with the man who called himself Jesus riding shotgun.

NINE

It never occurred to me that Chico could have been the brains, or lack of brains, behind the man who called himself Jesus. He was capable of a practical joke, but he was so obsessed with hubcaps that he did not have time to think of anything else.

After breakfast I spent a little time at the paper, then called Bobby Jack Lewis and asked him to meet me for lunch. I suggested the Point After, a bar/restaurant that served burgers with a pound of meat. I am, as you know Luke, a carnivore.

Bobby Jack owned the Apocalypse Now Dating Service, but never seemed to be able to get a date. He lied well, though, always telling me that he was with the hottest chick in Dallas. He had names for all these phantom women, so I played the game with him.

He was always able to break away from any fictional girlfriend and join me for breakfast, lunch, dinner or happy hour. He was the most "always available" busy person that I have ever known.

He always had a silly grin on his face and a story about how he almost had to get a wrecker to pull his date off him. I went along with his stories and always suggested that he bring his date with him when we were getting together. He always said he did not want a bimbo hanging on him while he was talking to a pal.

To hear him tell it, all his fictional girlfriends were bimbos. But then, as far as he was concerned, all women were bimbos. That is why he did not like to be around Mary Lou Magruder. Her IQ was so much higher than his that it intimidated him.

Looking at the man who called himself Jesus from a religious perspective, Bobby Jack had to rank as a prime suspect. He had been born to people of the cloth. His father had been a Jewish rabbi who had fallen in love with and married a Catholic nun.

Both would have had to reject their callings for their love affair to continue, but they ended up having no choice. Bobby Jack was on the way.

With rejection by Judaism sure to come, Bobby Jack's dad turned to Christianity, changed his name and became a Pentecostal evangelist.

And he was immediately a hit on the sawdust trail. Pentecostals turned out in drove to see this man who had seen the light and rejected Judaism. He became as popular as an athlete who, after losing his athletic skills and the money to fund his drug habit, turns to God and starts going to church to lift weights for Jesus.

Bobby Jack's mother experienced an epiphany equal to that of his father, giving up nun-hood to speak in Pentecostal churches about the evils of Rome.

The couple did quite well financially, but never achieved the financial success of today's mega-church charlatans. They never had mansions in the twenty-five thousand square foot range, but they did have a modest home that in their senior years was seized by the IRS for failure to pay taxes.

With such a dynamic mother and father, both religious zealots, it seemed normal enough that Bobby Jack would follow in their footsteps. And he did for a time.

By the time he was two years old, Bobby Jack was standing on a stool behind a pulpit sharing his testimony about giving up sin. While speech was difficult for him at the time, the more religious folk identified it as the unknown tongue.

This charismatic outpouring abandoned him when he entered kindergarten, but he continued to be a much sought-after preacher of the word. *Time* magazine, in fact, named him the "The Comeback Kid" and "The Five-Year-Old Kid Most likely to Become President."

With his father on the road evangelizing for days on end, the burden of bringing Bobby Jack up right fell heavily on his mother's shoulders. And she was equal to the task. For eighteen years she never let Bobby Jack miss a church service of any kind, except for those months he was in the closet.

Bobby Jack and his parents made their home in a small, forgettable Texas town, the name of which he could never remember. In fact, when he went off to college, he never returned home for holidays because he could not remember the name of the town or in what part of the state it was located.

Anyway, Bobby Jack was somewhat of a celebrity in that town, him being a boy charismatic preacher who at one time spoke a language that no one understood.

His mother added to his celebrity status. She, being a frugal woman, still wore the habits that she had worn when a nun at a convent.

Bobby Jack vaguely remembered that there was a lawsuit against his mother, the plaintiff being the Pope and the entire Catholic Church. Her crime was that of posing as a nun in nuns clothing. The church wanted the garments back and accused her of theft.

She was supposedly vindicated and cleared of the charges by one of those TV judges, but Bobby Jack said for as long as he could remember a couple of men in black from the Vatican watched their house from a black Chevrolet hoping his mother would hang her habits on the clothesline so they could steal them back for the church.

Unlike Dallas, Bobby Jack's hometown did not have a store that specialized in used religious clothing.

He said his mother was too smart for the Vatican guys, that she handwashed her old habits and dried them inside the house.

Bobby Jack said one of the sure signs of your popularity in school was how often your classmates beat you up. He said he was beat up daily, so was pictured in the high school annual as the "Most Popular Boy."

Bobby Jack said he was never into drugs when in high school but was often stoned with real rocks. He figured it was just part of the burden of being popular.

The town where Bobby Jack was raised was farming country, the primary crop being oil. In fact, there were oil wells pumping at each end of the school's football field.

The first time he saw the field, it clicked in his mind that something was wrong. You see, Bobby Jack was somewhat of a proportional genius. He was always measuring stuff in his mind, which might have had something to do with him being a charismatic.

One moonlit night, he took his slide rule out to the field and measured it. And sure enough, he discovered the field was only ninety yards long. He also found that the yard markers on the field were only nine yards apart. That prompted him to break into the athletic fieldhouse where the chain marking first downs was kept, which revealed that it was only nine yards long.

His school's football team was undefeated and on the way to a possible state championship so, armed with this information and with hopes of ingratiating himself with the coach and getting a good grade in physical education, he took his findings to the coach.

But instead of being grateful, the coach became angry, and told him his slide rule was ten yards short, and that the field was exactly one hundred yards long.

Because he was a proportional genius, Bobby Jack begged to disagree. Furthermore, because he was scheduled to preach at the local Pentecostal church on the following

Sunday, he told the coach his message would be about the short field.

He had already preached damning sermons on the evils associated with the school's PTA carnival, and about the pros and cons of a catcher wearing a plastic cup inside his jockey strap.

The coach became irate at Bobby Jack's threats, locked him in a gym closet, and told him he would have to stay there until the team's ten-game season was over, or for fifteen weeks if the team went to state.

This all happened before the first game of the season, which is why the team was undefeated. Timing was always one of Bobby Jack's problems.

As for his folks worrying about him, the coach simply called them and said their son would be going on a ten- to fifteen-week field trip. And because people in small towns never question a high school football coach, his mother said "Fine" and continued counting her beads, which the Vatican had placed a lien on.

For Bobby Jack, life inside the closet was not all that bad. He initially complained about the bowl of gruel the coach brought him every day, so the coach began bringing him a tray of food from the school cafeteria.

After a couple of days, he asked the coach to bring the gruel again.

Thanks to the coach, Bobby Jack made better grades in the closet than he would have if he had gone to class. The coach ordered all the teachers to give him a passing grade, and that was a first for him.

Although he had never played football, the coach got him a football scholarship to Texas A&M, which enabled him to graduate from college without ever attending a football practice or a class.

Bobby Jack was not alone during his tenure in the closet. He made friends with an old football, an old basketball, two roaches and a spider. While at A&M, and before he forgot the name of his hometown, He corresponded weekly with the old football.

He had what you might call a forgettable college education, which he attributed to forgetting the name and location of his hometown.

Timing is everything, and Bobby Jack never had any. The year the coach put him in the closet, his high school team won the state championship, which meant sixteen weeks in the closet.

The coach forgot to call Bobby Jack's mother to tell her his field trip had been extended, but it did not matter. She did not remember that he had called in the first place.

His parents never worried when they did not see their son for weeks at a time. They simply thought of it as an answer to prayer. And his teachers were happy to pass him, because they did not want to put themselves in the position of having him in their class for another year.

The time Bobby Jack spent in the closet was a period of reflection and deep meditation. It was there that he pondered all the deep mysteries of life, such as why a man could purse his lips and tongue a certain way to emit a whistle. He figured that most people had ignored the subject, so prepared a series of sermons for a book titled *Will There Be a Whistle Before the Second Coming?*

Several televangelists offered the book free to their viewers for a two-hundred-dollar contribution.

He even wrote articles for the *American Journal of Medicine*, delving into taboo subjects like "How Many Pairs of Shoes and Purses Does a Woman Really Need?"

Bobby Jack did think about trying out for ministry at Baylor but accepted the football scholarship to A&M because he felt that proportional evangelism was the greater calling. Because of some Baylor professors who had become rogue liberals, the subject had been dropped from the school's curriculum.

He also thought he could be more of a missionary at A&M than at Baylor. So, dressed in sackcloth, and with ashes on his head, he beseeched the A&M study body to lay aside their tall boots with spurs, beat their whips and swords into plowshares, and give up their relationships with animals.

Deep down, I think Bobby Jack always regretted not going to Baylor. I know he liked Waco and a place there that served barbecued baloney.

After graduation from A&M, Bobby Jack kind of lost his way. He could not get a job in proportions, which he blamed on the state's disproportionate lack of concern with numbers. He thought too many people, namely Yankees and Californians, had been allowed to cross the Red River and come into the state. Of course, he preferred Californians and New Yorkers to Iranians, but that was a no brainer.

Bobby Jack was always willing to take on the tough questions, like why is it that sex education and driver education cannot be taught on the same day in Iran? The answer, obviously, is that it is too hard on the camel.

The real tragedy of Bobby Jack not being able to find a job in the ever-expanding field of proportions was that he lost his confidence in God. Now, Luke, I want you to know that he did not get mad at God, or at the fact that the billionaires in the Proportional Valley and insisted on bringing in people from Bangladesh and paying them more than American workers. No, it was nothing like that. He just figured that asking God to favor an Aggie was too much to ask.

Another problem for Bobby Jack was that there were no time slots available on TV for another televangelist, which would have been very lucrative for someone with as little theological understanding as Bobby Jack possessed.

So, somewhere along the line, he gave up preaching, simply because no one would listen to him. I encouraged him, told him that no one listened to any preacher, especially those who insisted on telling the truth.

He would not listen to me, although I believe he continued to be a closet preacher, sneaking out to speak in Pentecostal churches to supplement his income.

As for his dating service, it was a living. He ran specials from time to time, giving preachers a fifty percent discount, and priests a thirty-five percent discount. He told me that most of them stiffed him, which also did not surprise me.

If Bobby Jack had been a foot taller and handsome, he might have passed for Robert Redford. Unfortunately, he looked more like Elmer Fudd.

And although he had the perfect background to initiate the Jesus joke, I did not consider him a prime suspect. He was a guy who, when he said "darn," looked up expecting to be hit with lightning.

I should mention that after the IRS seized their house, Bobby Jack's parents moved to New York. His mother became a professional dancer and his father became a politician, primarily because he had heard that if he could prove minority status as a politician, he would never have to pay taxes.

While the Point After served exceptional burgers, it was primarily a drinking establishment. And Bobby Jack did not drink. So, when he met me for lunch or drinks, he brought his own bottle, or I should say a half dozen bottles. The man never went anywhere without a six-pack of Dr Pepper, all of which he carried in an Igloo cooler.

When he arrived, he asked, "How have you been?"

"So, so," I replied. "How about you?"

"I couldn't be better," he replied.

The waitress came over to take his order and he asked me, "What are you having?

"An Irish coffee," I replied. "With the weather outside being frightful, I figured by choice of drinks was a perfect prelude to a big burger."

"I brought my own liqueur," he told the waitress. "Just bring me a pot of coffee and some Miracle Whip and I'll mix my own drink."

Since she was used to dealing with drunks, she was unfazed by the request and said, "We only have Hellman's Mayonnaise."

"I'll have to do," he said.

She scurried off muttering under her breath. Sniffing the air, I said, "Something smells fishy."

Bobby Jack smiled and said, "That's me. I've been fishing out at Lake Ray Hubbard and I cleaned my catch out in the parking lot before coming in."

"My gosh," I said, "the temperature is in the thirties and the chill factor must be zero."

"When you have love to keep you warm, you don't notice the cold," Bobby Jack said.

"What do you mean?" I asked.

He gave me a poop-eating grin and replied, "This young lass named Patricia has been bugging me to take her fishing, so this was as good a day as any. First date fishing has always been very effective in all my more serious relationships."

I knew Patricia was as much an apparition as Casper the friendly ghost, and that Bobby Jack's fishing partners, especially women partners, were as imaginary as most of his big catches. But what was not imaginary was the fact that he would fish in any weather.

"Why don't you bring her with you the next time we meet?" I asked.

"Oh, because of her professional status, she would never come in a place like this," he replied.

"And just what is her professional status?" I asked.

"She's a topless dancer in a very high-class gentleman's club," he replied.

I nodded understanding and steered the conversation in another direction. "Bobby Jack, do you know a guy named Jesus?"

"What kind of question is that?" he asked. "Of course, I know Jesus."

I said, "I mean literally."

"Well, I suppose it's what you literally mean by literal," he said.

It is my understanding, Luke, that several years later Bill Clinton would use what he learned at one of Bobby Jack's relationship seminars to answer questions about his relationship with Monica Lewinsky.

The waitress brought the pot of coffee, a cup and jar of mayonnaise to our table. Bobby Jack poured the cup half full of coffee, popped the tab on a Dr Pepper can and added soft drink to the cup, and then a tablespoon full of mayonnaise. After that he added two teaspoons of sugar.

"What do you call that?" I asked.

"It's a Waco latte," he replied. "It was developed in a Baylor chemistry lab."

"Strange that I've never heard about it," I said.

"Just because you went to Baylor, Mark, doesn't mean you're privy to all that's going on there," he said.

"No doubt about that," I agreed.

After sipping his coffee and grimacing, he asked, "Have you finished your Christmas shopping?"

"Yeah," I replied. "Something wrong with your drink?"

"It's the mayonnaise," he replied. It's a lot stronger than Miracle Whip. So, mind telling me what major gifts you're giving this year?"

I replied, "I'm giving everyone a nice picture frame with an autographed photo of me."

He asked, "Isn't that what you gave everyone last year?"

"It's what I've given everyone for the past ten years," I replied, then said, "I don't know how you can drink that concoction."

"Don't knock it until you've tried it," he said.

I said, "Well, I won't knock it then. But I think it would gag a maggot."

Then out of the blue he asked, "Did you know that I used to raise maggots?"

I confessed, "No, I didn't."

"Yeah," he said, "but they preferred red soda pop to other soft drinks."

"Why were you raising maggots?" I asked.

"They make great fish bait," he replied.

I shook my head in dismay and said, "I had no idea."

"Oh, yeah," he said. "European larvae make great fish bait. Unfortunately, American larvae does not."

"I assume you have quit the business," I said.

"I quit when several manufacturers here in the U.S. started making artificial maggots," he said. "People prefer artificial everything to the real thing.

"Another factor was that the European Union authorized the controversial Maggot Artificial Insemination Act, which undermined the traditional methods of American producers. European producers flooded the American market with maggots conceived through artificial insemination, making it impossible for American maggot growers to compete."

This, of course, was all news to me, but Bobby Jack often provided me the raw material needed for my investigative reporting.

I never sought to question anything Bobby Jack said about fishing. The man was a member of U.S. Bass, Pro Bass and Bass Angler's

Sportsman Society, which goes by the unique acronym BASS.

If a fish was important enough to have an association built around it, Bobby Jack was a member of the organization. Almost every doctor's office and oil change center in Dallas had at least one used fishing magazine in its waiting room with Bobby Jack's name and address on it.

The waitress came back to our table and asked, "Are you ready to order?"

"I'll have the double meat burger," I replied, "cut the onion and tomato."

She questioned, "You know that's two pounds of meat, don't you?"

I replied, "I know. I usually order the triple meat burger, but I had a late breakfast. And no fries with that. Bring me a bag of Lay's potato chips with my burger, not one of those sissy bags but a family-size bag. I'll also have a Diet Coke."

"Just the one pound of meat burger for me," Bobby Jack said, "and a double order of fries. I'm on a diet."

While she was writing down our order, Bobby Jack thrust his hands in front of her and asked, "Don't my hands smell great."

She recoiled like a bungy cord, gagged and said, "I don't need to know where they've been."

"Cleaning bass," he said, "I cleaned a limit this morning."

The waitress hurried away from the table, and Bobby Jack questioned, "What's wrong with her?"

"Most women don't like fish smell on a man's hands," I explained. "And to tell you the truth, my feminine side doesn't like it either. Why don't you wash your hands after cleaning fish?"

He grumbled, "If a woman can't handle a little fish smell, she's not much of a woman. Besides, what can you use to get fish smell off your hands."

"Boraxo Powdered Hand Soap works just fine," I replied. "It's what I use."

"When was the last time you cleaned any fish?" he asked.

"It hasn't been that long," I replied.

"Tell the truth," he said.

"Well, it has been a few years," I said, "but I remember that my hands smelled fine after using Boraxo hand soap."

"Maybe I'll try it," he said, "but it's not on my list of priorities."

Rather than become more frustrated with Bobby Jack's reasoning, I began telling him about the man who called himself Jesus. When I told him that the man claimed to be the Son of God, he said, "I sort of doubt it."

"Well, I hope you don't think I believed him," I said.

He shrugged and said, "Well, you are pretty gullible."

I could not believe what I had just heard. Bobby Jack, a man who sprays crawfish scent on an artificial bait and thinks it attracts bass from a mile away was accusing me of being gullible.

"Where do you come up with this gullible crap?" I asked.

Raising his hands in a defensive position, he said, "Now don't get huffy. You don't know the Bible all that well, so you can be easily deceived."

I said, "I know a lot more Bible than I'm given credit for knowing."

"I'm not going to argue with you," he said, "but if I meet the man on Sunday, I can tell you right off if he's the real thing."

"Well," I said, "if you're coming to the house for food, the touch football game against our toughest opponent, and to watch the Cowboys on TV, you will meet him."

"Let's withhold judgment until then," he said.

I asked, "How are you going to determine if he's the real thing, which he isn't?"

"I have my ways," Bobby Jack said.

"Mary Lou is going to be there," I said, "so I suggest you wash the fish smell off your hands."

"I'll bathe in tomato juice," he said.

About that time a booming voice rang out in the semi-darkness. The good lungs belonged to Bum Criswell, who was polo coach for one of the more affluent private high schools in Dallas. He had at one time been a football coach, but decided the game moved too slowly and offered no future.

He then considered becoming a baseball coach, but after much consideration settled on polo because he saw it as the game of the future. In fact, he was sure it would in time become the national pastime.

Arguing with Bum on this subject was like challenging the heavyweight boxing champion of the world, whoever that is, to a few rounds. It is a no-win situation. The man is totally committed to polo, even plans to write a series of children's books on the sport.

He was forever writing letters to the editor of both papers, criticizing their sports pages for lack of high school polo coverage.

Bum got this burr under his saddle about the lack of respect for polo and threatened a boycott of all sporting goods stores that did not handle polo clothing and equipment, which included the sale of horses, saddles and bridles. Obviously, this did not go well.

However, there were enough peaceful protesters burning, looting and killing sporting goods store employees over failure of the stores to stock horses, saddles and bridles that Congress had legislation on the table requiring that every American family purchase a horse, saddle bridle, Colt forty-five pistol and Winchester rifle.

Before this legislation could become law, Bum testified before Congress and a compromise was reached. Polo horses would be replaced with riding lawnmowers. All horses were content with the compromise. Their new role would be to hang out in fields and barns, eat hay and oats, and make occasional appearances in western and Hallmark movies.

Bum was born and raised in the affluent Highland Park area of Dallas. He was a trust fund baby, whose grandfather at one time owned an oil field. Bum still had a room in his grandparents' mansion, which was ostentatious to the point of having gold-inlaid everything.

Although Bum had money out the kazoo, he petitioned Congress to enact a national sales tax to pay for his extensive polo initiative, which in addition to Little League included Babe Ruth, Connie Mack, Stan Musial and American Legion leagues.

I argued that Ruth, Mack and Musial were baseball people, but Bum's retort that all would have been polo people if given the opportunity. He told me Connie Mack was a great horseman, with which I could not argue.

I just knew he wore double-breasted suits and a fedora when managing the Philadelphia Athletics.

Bum always had a plan. He knew that a national sales tax for polo was unlikely, but that he might be able to get his leagues funded by United Way. "If you don't buy anything, you don't pay a sales tax," he explained. "But you can't escape paying United Way. All employers pressure their employees to give to United Way."

Bum further explained that he was trying to get his polo leagues accepted as part of United Way's administration, since ninety percent of its funds were for administration and only ten percent for charity.

"You never want to be on the charity end of one of these charity organizations," he said.

One of Bum's virtues, possibly his only one, was to be fashionably late. I had invited him to join Bobby Jack and me at the Point After, knowing he would be late arriving. I did not tell either man the other would be there because they did not like each other, although neither would admit to that truth.

Because Bum always wore his polo outfit, he stood out from the crowd. Because Bum was short and fat, with the funny little polo hat, along with the riding pants and tall boots, he looked somewhat comical.

He plopped himself down at our table and Bobby Jack said, "I didn't know you were coming."

Bum responded, "I didn't know you would be here either."

There was no animosity. Bobby Jack thought it was his Christian duty to love everyone, and Bum thought it unsportsmanlike to dislike an opponent.

Bum asked Bobby Jack, "What are you drinking?"

"It's called a Waco latte," Bobby Jack replied.

"Looks good," Bum said.

"It's a little flat because of the mayonnaise," Bobby Jack said. "The genuine article calls for Miracle Whip. Want me to fix you one."

"Yeah, I need something to warm me up," Bum said. "It's cold enough out there to freeze your balls off."

Noticing the icicles hanging out of his nose, I questioned, "You don't have a heater in your car?"

"I rode over on a lawnmower," he said, "been at polo practice."

Now one of the reasons Bum was always late was to avoid buying anything. He had the annoying habit of eating off your plate and drinking out of your cup or glass. He would often ask a waiter or waitress to bring him a clean plate, utensils, glass or cup, then take some of your food or drink. He explained that this was because he was never hungry or that he was on a diet. Even though he was rich, he did not like to spend money.

After Bobby Jack had fixed him a Waco latte, he took a swallow and said, "Man's that's good."

"It was discovered at Baylor," Bobby Jack explained. "The combination of ingredients was discovered by the psychology department back when the school was training chimpanzees for space travel."

Bum, an SMU graduate, said, "I never thought anything good could come out of Baylor."

That irritated me, Luke, because I came out of Baylor. At the time of this meeting lawnmower polo was still in its infancy. People in Stephenville, Texas were still experimenting with bull riding polo, and in Oklahoma cow chip tossing was still the number one sport.

That, of course, went down the tube when it was learned that artificial cow chips were being manufactured in China and sold in the United States, putting a lot of cows out of business.

Lawnmower polo has, as you know, now become the number one college and pro sport, fulfilling Bum's dream. It went through some shaky periods before blades were removed from lawnmowers. But that cut down on quite a few injuries.

Despite my reservations about the sport, it thrived, and Bum ended up in the Lawnmower Polo Hall of Fame, which is on the Harvard campus. The National Lawnmower Polo League draft is very cutthroat every year, but the College of William and Mary has dominated the college game for several years, this despite ESPN's efforts to always make Ohio State or Notre Dame number one.

The College of William and Mary was unrecognized for a time, but then joined the Southeastern Conference and began beating Big Ten opponents like a drum.

On this day we talked about nothing of importance, which was what we talked about most days when we got together. We did discuss our Sunday get together, playing our archrival, eating and watching the Cowboys play the Eagles.

With his chubby, short physique, Bum was built for comfort rather than athletic achievement. Although he had been a sixth team quarterback for the SMU Mustangs in his seventh year of college, thanks to a ten million-dollar gift to the athletic department from his grandfather, he had pretty much lost interest in football.

In his seven-year college career, Bum never ran a play for the varsity, but lettered all seven years. He was even named All-America by a couple of sports magazines.

By the time of this meeting, Bum preferred watching reruns of high school lawnmower polo on TV to watching the Cowboys. So, rather than have him become sullen like an old opossum unable to find a ripe persimmon, I always made my bedroom and second TV set available to him for watching reruns of high school polo while the rest of us watched the Cowboys on the TV set in my den.

I did not, of course, know how tasteless Bum had become until that day when he became a connoisseur of Waco latte. He had by this time acquired a larger collection of riding lawnmowers than Jay Leno has cars, but still had a few polo horses. Why he kept the horses, I do not know. He would ride one occasionally and explained to me that horses liked to be ridden. Where this tidbit of information came from, I do not know. I do not recall any horse saying it enjoyed being ridden.

Because of his grandfather's ten-million-dollar gift to SMU, there was a plaque in a in trophy case somewhere on the campus that read *Bum Criswell, the kid who would not give up.*

However, Bum waved the white flag of surrender numerous times while in college. He dropped out of freshman English fourteen consecutive semesters when attending SMU and never received a degree. He kept getting the same professor from India, who could not speak English. SMU prided itself on diversity, which meant hiring a lot of faculty members who did not speak English.

After Bum had eaten all the fries off Bobby Jack's plate, even took about half his burger, and tried to get his hand into my bag of potato chips, we talked about the man who called himself Jesus. He claimed no knowledge of him, as did Bobby Jack, and I believed them.

Bobby Jack had his mind on fishing and imaginary women, and Bum was too busy promoting lawnmower polo, to spend their time playing a joke on me.

I said, "Bobby Jack says he has a test for the man who claims to be Jesus, which he will spring on Sunday."

"What kind of test?" Bum asked.

"Just be at Mark's house on Sunday and you'll find out," Bobby Jack said.

"I'll be there," Bum said, "if there's no objection to parking my horse in the back yard."

I questioned, "You're not coming on one of your riding mowers?"

"I don't want Cowboy or Blackie urinating on one of my mowers," he replied.

When I got home the man who called himself Jesus was there. He had cleaned everything to perfection. No germ had escaped his scrutiny. He had also prepared a nice dinner, making me feel a little guilty about talking behind his back. I attributed this feeling of guilt to too much booze, and especially to questioning the possibility that he might be real.

"Sell any hubcaps today?" I asked.

"Quite a few," he replied, "even sold a set to your friend Ribs."

I questioned, "Ribs bought a set of hubcaps?"

"Yes, and he invited me to go coon hunting tomorrow night," the man replied. "I think he's planning to invite you and Joe Don, too."

"Are you going?" I asked.

He replied, "I thought it might be enjoyable."

I laughed and said, "Jesus on a coon hunt. "That might be entertaining."

TEN

Ribs' Volkswagen was more than a little crowded. Ribs was driving, the man who called himself Jesus was in the front passenger seat, and Joe Don and I were sharing the back seat with Blackie and Cowboy. Both dogs took turns licking my face, and because of the crowded conditions it was impossible to fight them off.

Knowing some of the things that you dogs will eat, Luke, I have never been one to enjoy kissing a dog or the slurp of a dog's tongue. Do not be offended, Luke. There have been some women in my life that I felt the same way about.

Going on a coon hunt on a Saturday night was not high on my list of priorities, and it certainly was not my number one choice of things to do. There was a pretty female reporter at the paper who I had invited to spend Saturday evening with me. She had told me where I could stick my invitation, which is why I had opted for the coon hunt.

So, I was reluctantly going on a coon hunt, and knew that if I acted disgruntled about sharing the back seat with two dogs that Ribs would use my complaint as a springboard for one of his tirades on prejudice. And he was a lot more vehement about prejudice against dogs, and specifically coon dogs, than people. He thought coon dogs represented the last great bastion of truth in our society.

"How far is it to this coon hunting place?" I asked.

"About a hundred miles," Ribs answered. "We'll be there before you know it."

With his accelerator all the way to the floorboard, Ribs' Volkswagen sliced through the cold, windy weather at about forty-five miles per hour. I was not sure I could survive Blackie's halitosis for more than two hours but thought his fetid breath might be much better than what Joe Don was having to endure. Blackie's rear end kept bumping his nose.

Although Blackie and Cowboy were good friends, they were as different as night and day when it came to personal hygiene. Cowboy showered regularly and brushed his teeth in both the morning and evening. Blackie did not. He preferred rolling around in a dead cat carcass to bathing.

For some unexplained reason, Ribs was ecstatic about us going coon hunting with him. I was lamenting my decision, and Joe Don was in the car because I had convinced him it would be a fun way to spend a Saturday night. Unfortunately, his fun had been limited to viewing Blackie's rear end.

Things were not great, but they were peaceful until Joe Don did what I should have anticipated him doing. He lit up a cigarette.

Ribs exclaimed, "Hey, man, that smoke is going to mess up Blackie's nose!"

"From where I'm sitting, I didn't know he had a nose," Joe Don said.

I complained, "You're going to choke all of us to death. And it's too cold to open a window."

Joe Don grunted and said, "I guess all of you think a little cigarette smoke is going to give you lung cancer. What do you think about smoking, Jesus?"

"Nothing you do that hurts your body is smart," he replied.

The calm way in which he responded took all of us off-guard and caused Ribs and me to laugh. Joe Don did not laugh, but he did not get mad either. At least I could not see any anger on that part of his face that was not hidden by Blackie's rear end.

"Why don't you tell us the difference between a Christian smoker and a non-Christian smoker?" I asked.

He sighed as if exasperated with me and did not respond. One of my more irritating habits, or so I have been told, is that I will not let go of a subject even when everyone else is through dealing with it.

"What about smokers in Heaven?" I asked.

He forced a smile and replied, "People won't be bringing their addictions and habits to Heaven with them. I know you're just trying to start an argument. But if you're concerned about smoking, alcoholism or drug addiction, sex addition or any other kind of addiction in Heaven, forget it. They don't exist and they won't exist."

He then spoke directly to Joe Don and said, "It bothers me that people abuse their bodies with cigarette smoke and then want to blame God for their health problems. However, the cigarette smoker doesn't just abuse his or her body, they abuse everyone's health with their smoke."

"Right on," Ribs said.

The man continued, "This is no parable, Joe Don, but what would happen if you took four puffs off the tailpipe of this car while it was running?"

"I'd die of carbon monoxide poisoning," Joe Don replied.

"That's right," the man said. "And it's something that every sane informed person knows. If you inhaled what the tailpipe is emitting, it would go into your system and convert to carboxy hemoglobin, which would shut off the oxygen supply to the heart muscle and vein wall, causing a brain problem and death.

"Carbon monoxide is so bad that persons working in plants that produce it are restricted by this country's government health standards to breathing no more than four hundred parts at any one time. That's the limit. But when you take a puff off a cigarette, you breathe in twenty-eight hundred to three thousand parts with every breath. Of course, you don't keep it all. You blow about half of it out on the people around you, exposing them, too."

Carboxy? Hemoglobin? Heart muscle and vein wall? Who was this guy anyway? Was there anything that he did not know? He was not arrogant or patronizing. He spoke matter-of-factly.

Joe Don argued, "A cigarette isn't going to kill you, not like sucking in carbon monoxide from the tailpipe of a car."

"Not just one cigarette, and not as quickly," the man agreed. "Cigarette smoking over time causes emphysema, lung cancer, stroke and heart disease. Smoking causes these diseases not only in the smoker but in those around him or her."

Priding myself on being a master antagonist, I saw an opening and took it. I said, "Then cigarette smokers are murderers, and murderers can't enter the Kingdom of Heaven. Isn't that right?"

The man who called himself Jesus sighed and said, "I am salvation, the way, the truth and the life. Only through acceptance and belief in me can anyone enter the Kingdom of Heaven."

The way he said it, the calmness and sincerity in his voice, stunned and shocked me. I believe that Joe Don and Ribs reacted in the same way. Of course, I still could not see Joe Don's face because Blackie's rear end was covering more than half of it.

It was mystifying to me as to how the man who called himself Jesus was affecting my friends. The guy was obviously a charlatan. Why was I able to see it and no one else? Why were my friends giving the guy a pass?

I said, "I know a couple who are chain smokers and their kid have all sorts of respiratory problems."

The man said, "Children all over the world suffer because of the decisions their parents make. Some are aborted, some suffer malnutrition, and some suffer because their parents refuse to give up harmful substances. People tend blame God for their bad decisions.

They want the freedom to make their own decisions, but not the consequences for making them."

"I can agree with that," I said. "I'm aware of a couple who bought their sixteen-year-old son a hot car. He decided to see how fast it would go, crashed and was killed. At his funeral they wore T-shirts with the words 'Screw God'."

The eyes of the man who called himself Jesus took on a weary look, and he said, "I repeat, God gives people freedom of choice, they abuse it, then blame God for their wrong choices. When the driver of an automobile tries to take a thirty-mile per hour curve at ninety miles per hour, loses control of the car and crashes, is the choice he or she made God's fault?"

Ribs chimed in with, "Of course not. A black man wouldn't be blaming God for something like that. It's these uncolored folks who blame God for something that stupid."

I reminded him, "I don't know if you've noticed, Ribs, but the person you're agreeing with is one of those uncolored folks."

The man who called himself Jesus continued, "When a person chooses to drink alcohol and drive is killed in an automobile accident, or kills or injures another human being, is that God's fault. Is God responsible for every irrational act of people? Is it God's fault that in this country seventy-five to eighty people are killed every day in alcohol-related automobile accidents? Is it God's fault that in this country more than a thousand people are permanently injured every day as a result of alcohol related automobile accidents?"

The man presented his case calmly, but I think I recognized a tinge of anger in his voice. From what I knew of the New Testament, the real Jesus could get a little worked up over stuff that was stupid. Not that I thought the guy was the real thing or anything like that, but if he was playing the role accurately, there would have been nothing wrong with him displaying a little anger.

Joe Don, anxious to keep the conversation off cigarettes, said, "It sounds to me like Mark's drinking is a bigger threat to society than my smoking."

I said, "I don't drink that much."

The other three people in the car, along with both dogs, gave me these incredulous looks. "C'mon," I said, "you guys will have J.C. here thinking that I'm a drunkard."

"They don't have to tell me who you are," the man said. "I know you better than you know yourself."

There was a hushed silence, except for the hum of the car's engine, if you could call it that, and heavy breathing by both Blackie and Cowboy. I wanted to direct the conversation in a different direction, so asked Ribs how he liked his new hubcaps.

"They're okay," he said, "but you know how it is. The car ran better with the originals. I was attached to them, hated to give them up."

"Yeah, I know what you mean," I said. "My BMW hasn't driven the same since I replaced the hubcaps."

I was lying, of course, because I was pretty sure the hubcaps I purchased from Chico after mine were stolen were those that had been stolen off my car. But I figured that empathizing with Ribs might get the conversation off my drinking and back to discussing something more relevant.

"I have to say that the hubcaps I bought from Chico's store look original," Ribs said.

I said, "I'm sure they do. J.C., that was your first sale, wasn't it?"

"Not my first," he replied. "I had sold a couple of Jesus paintings on black velvet, plus one of Elvis, before selling the hubcaps to Ribs."

"How's Chico's business going?" I asked.

Ribs answered, "Great. There must have been a hundred people there, but not all of them were buying stuff. Most of them were just listening to Jesus talk."

Speaking to the man who called himself Jesus, I said, "It looks like a few people are interested in your act."

"There have always been a few people interested in truth," he said.

I laughed and said, "I wouldn't think you would draw a very elite crowd down on Harry Hines."

He laughed, too, but not in a humorous way and questioned, "Wouldn't you expect me to draw the poor, the prostitutes and people who live without much hope?"

He had me there. From my days in Sunday School and church, I recalled the New Testament record of the kind of people Jesus attracted. But my learning about Him had been done in a clean and sanitized building with well-dressed people who were outwardly clean and sanitized.

My fellow church attenders, many dressed in the latest fashionable clothing, did speak about how Jesus loved the poor and downtrodden. And preachers also asked us to give our money to pay someone to present Jesus to these people so that we did not have to deal with them. I even gave a little money for that purpose

I asked, "Did Chico have much business today?"

"Business was brisk," the man said. "A lot of people bought hubcaps as stocking stuffers."

I do not know if he was joking or not, but he seemed to be amused.

I questioned, "You said you sold some paintings of Jesus on velvet, which certainly don't look like you. Didn't that bother you?"

"How someone perceives me with their eyes isn't important," he replied. "It's how they perceive me in their heart, mind and soul that's important."

There it was again; this claim he made that he was the real Jesus. It made my mind race in directions I did not know it could go. I felt a confusion that I did not understand.

Joe Don interrupted my thoughts with a question for Ribs. "Are we going to shoot these coons that Blackie trees."

"What kind of question is that?" Ribs asked, sarcastically. "Of course, we're going to shoot the coons, and we might get lucky and get a possum, too.

"Then, like all black men, I'm going to skin the coons and possums we kill and cook them along with sweet potatoes and collard greens. It's that kind of diet that enables us to dunk and dribble a basketball better than you white boys."

"Hey, it was a simple question," Joe Don said. "I didn't mean to pull your chain."

"Have you ever had coon or possum?" Ribs asked.

"Can't say that I have," Joe Don replied, "and not sure that I ever want to."

"Well, you're missing a treat," Ribs said. "Coon is as good as dog or cat and it's not as greasy as possum. Throw in the collards and sweet potatoes and you have a meal fit for a king."

"I can't say I like collard greens or sweet potatoes either," Joe Don said.

Ribs, who was on one of his teasing tears, questioned, "Lord help, you don't like collards and sweet potatoes? That's a slap in the face to every black man who ever walked on the face of this earth. I wouldn't want my sister marrying someone who didn't like coon, collards and sweet potatoes."

I reminded him, "You don't have a sister."

He feigned hurt and said, "I was just trying to make a point."

"Well, I'm just hoping to bring down a ferocious coon with my three fifty-seven magnum," Joe Don said.

"I was just putting you on, Joe Don," Ribs said, "but we coon hunters do have an unwritten rule, which is that if you kill it, you eat it."

"If I had known I wasn't going to kill anything, I wouldn't have come," Joe Don said.

I responded, "You also wouldn't have come in you had known we were going to bitch and moan about you smoking in the car."

"Smoking isn't that important to me," he said. "I can quit smoking anytime I want to."

Since being ostracized for lighting up, Joe Don had gone to his backup Copenhagen tin of snuff. He had a Styrofoam spit cup, which was pressed up again Blackie's rear end.

I asked Ribs, "You weren't really planning to cook coon, possum, sweet potatoes and collard greens, were you?"

"I would if I had them," he answered, "along with some cornbread and buttermilk. I like a variety of food, not just fried chicken, jalapeno blackeye peas, mac and cheese and cornbread."

"That's what you've always wanted for supper every Wednesday," I said.

"What I've wanted is escargot and caviar with cornbread and buttermilk," he said. "You just assumed that a black man would want fried chicken."

"Well, I'm not black and fried chicken is one of my favorites," I said. "Escargot and caviar are out, but what would you like other than fried chicken next Wednesday?"

"What's Wednesday?" he questioned.

"It's the night you and Blackie always have supper with Cowboy and me," I replied.

Ribs pondered for a full minute and then said, "I can't make plans that far in advance. and next Wednesday is Christmas Eve."

I sighed and said, "Okay, if you can clear your busy schedule and have supper with me next Wednesday, what would you like me to fix?"

"I wouldn't mind having fried chicken," he replied. "And since it's Christmas Eve, how about some cranberry sauce and dressing with the jalapeno blackeye peas and cornbread?"

I reminded him that we always had supper at Sue Beth's house on Christmas Eve.

The conversation continued at an inane clip for the rest of the trip. We finally turned off Interstate Forty-five near Centerville, Texas and traveled a back road that led us deep into a wooded area. We eventually arrived at what was, obviously, a large campsite. What looked like a bonfire lit up the area.

Ribs' Volkswagen was the lone car in the area. Pickups with camper tops were parked in helter-skelter fashion, along with a few old school buses and other vehicles that defied description. Dogs were everywhere, along with many overall-clad men in a variety of lumberjack flannel shirts, and coats and hats of every possible description.

Banjo music filled the air and memories of the movie *Deliverance* played tricks with my mind. We had stepped back in time to a place where a full set of teeth and a sound mind was a rarity.

When we exited the VW, I jokingly told Joe Don that he had something brown on his nose. He did not appreciate the humor and said Blackie's rear end could ride on my nose on the way home.

Although I had very little experience in coon hunting, meaning none, the cold air had possibly frozen my brain because I was beginning to think that the evening might be enjoyable. I could not help but take note of the fact that I was the best dressed of all the hunters. When I learned that I would be going on the hunt, I had gone by an Abercrombie and Fitch and purchased a complete safari outfit.

Ribs had outfitted the man who called himself Jesus with Army Surplus store clothing, except for the REBEL LURES cap on his head. He was only slightly better dressed than most of the coon hunters, although he did have all his teeth.

Joe Don was wearing stuff that looked as if it had been stolen from the police SWAT team, and Ribs was dressed much like his fellow coon hunters.

I soon learned that Ribs not only knew coon hunting thoroughly, but he knew coon hunting talk. Since he was the only black coon hunter among more than a hundred men, he was easily identifiable. I mention this only because it became obvious that all the other coon hunters knew him. It was at this gathering that I realized all white coon hunters look alike.

Ribs insisted on introducing each of us to every coon hunter there and would have introduced us to the five hundred or so dogs that were present if Beep Jenkins had not stopped him.

When Beep was introduced to the man who called himself Jesus, he said, "That name is familiar to me. Do you have family in Oklahoma, somewhere up around Tulsa?"

The man denied having relatives in Oklahoma, but I think Beep hit a nerve.

From the get-go it was obvious that Beep was one of the nation's most important and scholarly coon hunters. We would learn that he was from Oklahoma and that he had taught law at Harvard for a time but resigned because he was too ethical to teach students who planned to go into politics or work for mainstream media.

He produced a tin cup for each of us, then filled them with syrupy thick black coffee from a pot on a campfire apart from the big fire. It was the kind of coffee coon hunters drink, which I appreciated, but I did have a problem with the grounds I kept getting between my teeth.

Beep then produced a tin plate for each of us, wiped them with the sleeve of his jacket, and commanded, "You boys have some vittles. There's not much coon left, but we still have plenty of beans, ham and cornbread."

Then he turned the man who called himself Jesus and said, "Sorry, Jesus, I know you Jews don't eat pork. I've got a few cans of tuna on my bus that you're welcome to."

The man who called himself Jesus sighed and said, "I have no problem with eating pork."

"Oh, I don't guess you're orthodox," Beep said, "or you would be wearing a funny hat, funny clothes and have a beard."

I must say that Beep's beans, ham and cornbread were the best I have ever eaten. And we did get a smidgen of barbecued coon, which also was good. We also had a little bobcat, which tasted a lot like coon.

We were experiencing a scene right out of a Norman Rockwell painting, sopping bean juice from tin plates with cornbread, drinking coffee from tin cups, and sitting on a log before a blazing fire with the most knowledgeable coon hunter in the country.

Beep, of course, was not sitting on the log but in his lawn chair, which was much like a throne. Powerful and important men have an aura about them that is difficult to explain, but I recall Ribs making a statement that I will never forget. It was, "It doesn't get any better than this."

And he was right. I sensed, and would before the night was over, know for certain that I was in the presence of greatness.

All the hunters were gathered around Beep as closely as they could get without being ignited by the fire. And all the dogs were walking around sniffing each other and the filtered results of beans and cornbread.

Then out of the blue, Beep said, "There's nothing comparable to a cold-nosed hound."

There was a rumble of appreciation from both men and dogs, along with nods of appreciation for such valuable information. The exception was the man who called himself Jesus. He seemed amused, but I figured that was because he did not know that much about coon hunting. I, on the other hand, was beginning to get a real feel for the sport.

It became obvious to me that all the coon hunters looked to Beep for direction because they hung on his every word.

There was a lot of chewing, dipping, spitting, crotch scratching and bragging about dogs, but no cigarette smoking. I would later learn that every coon hunter who was a member of the American Coon Hunters Association was required to recite by memory the surgeon general's statement on cigarette smoking that is found on every pack of cigarettes.

A couple of guys got into an argument about whether Beechnut chewing tobacco was softer or moister, which resulted in a fistfight, but the highlight of the evening was when Beep agreed to give his personal coon hunting testimony.

He agreed to give that testimony after someone asked him what he would do if he had a million dollars. He straightened up his wiry body in his chair, with the sleeve of his jacket wiped some tobacco juice off his chin that had a three-day growth of beard, and said, "I'd buy some more coon dogs."

A rumble of appreciation went up from the men, all good and true to their calling. They understood Beep and his commitment to the sacredness of coon hunting.

Beep's thin red hair was beginning to gray up in spots, his face had more lines than a Dallas city map, there were sunspots on his crepe-like skin, and his ears were more prominent than a donkey's. Beep's Purina Feeds cap was splotched with grease and sweat, his overalls faded, his brogans scuffed and his brown coat tattered and stained with coon blood and who knows what else, but despite all this he was a kingly man with a kingly bearing.

Beep's poignant story brought tears to the eyes of everyone around the bonfire except the man who called himself Jesus. In fact, I thought I saw him chuckle, and did not understand how anyone could be so coldhearted.

Beep had been an oil man and banker early on and had made and lost several fortunes over the years. He had made wise investments, purchasing land, banks and coon dogs. "I always thought my strength was love of the land, the people of Oklahoma and coon dogs."

But Beep's weakness, like many of us, was his choice of women. He had married seven women, and all those marriages had ended in divorce because of incompatibility. It was not incompatibility with Beep, but with his coon dogs.

Beep said a few of his coon dogs slept with him, and every wife complained of fleas and ticks. Beep suffered their complaints, but what he would not tolerate was a woman raising her voice to one of his dogs.

He explained, "A coon dog's psyche is a fragile thing. If you let a woman yell at and boss a coon dog around, the first thing you know that dog won't be worth a damn."

His profound statement elicited a chorus of "amen."

Following their divorce from Beep, each of his former wives had married their divorce attorney, each of whom then retired from their law practice and moved to Maui with their new bride. According to Beep, none of the seven lawyers had ever been on a coon hunt, which meant they had a limited understanding of truth, if any understanding at all.

Beep said all seven wives attempted to get him committed to a mental institution, but when each judge learned that he had taught at Harvard they decided he had already served enough time in the cuckoo's nest.

Beep spit out his wad of chewing tobacco, having sucked all the juice out of it. Everyone else did the same. He took his Beechnut pouch out of his coat pocket and reloaded his cheek. And everyone did the same.

The man was a spellbinder, using every technique of a great orator. After his Beechnut was properly situated, he continued with his powerful commentary.

"Coon hunters are what this great country is all about. Without the truth and logic of the coon hunter, there would be no such thing as real freedom. The coon hunter has been the fiber that has kept America great through all its trials and tribulations.

"My last wife claimed she had all the evidence she needed to have me committed, the fact that I paid a million dollars for a champion coon dog, Oklahoma Crude. But, boys, that dog is still with me and my ex-wife is in Hawaii living off my dime. I've been getting five thousand a pop for that coon dog's pups, and I can't think of a damn thing that any woman has ever done for me that was worth five thousand dollars. So, you tell me, what's more valuable, a good coon dog or a woman?"

There was a crescendo of hooting and clapping that lasted until Beep held up a hand for quiet. And until Ribs yelled out, "Right on."

Beep turned to the man who called himself Jesus and said, "You were wise not to marry."

The phony Jesus shrugged his shoulders and said, "Thanks," but I do not think he really meant to express gratitude. I think he rolled his eyes and gave a look of dismay, but it is hard to read faces in campfire light. My dismay was that Beep seemed to be accepting the man as the real Jesus Christ.

Beep then began saying some things that I thought might make Ribs madder than a disturbed hornet, but I was wrong.

"Coon hunting," Beep said, "is the way any man can lift himself above his environment. You take Ribs here, if he hadn't started coon hunting, he might have ended up just another shiftless black man on welfare, one who spent most of his time either stealing or trying to steal something from a white man.

"But Ribs saw the light, bought himself a coon dog and is now one of the most respected men in Dallas. In fact, if he could get just twenty percent of the black vote, he could become mayor of Dallas.

"Unfortunately, most blacks in Dallas see him as an Uncle Tom because he's not out every night robbing and raping white women. He is, instead, spending his nights either coon hunting or studying the techniques of coon hunting, the sport of kings."

The men cheered and Ribs looked a little sheepish. I think he might even have blushed, but it was hard for me to tell by firelight.

What was obvious, however, was that he considered Beep's praise something akin to receiving the Congressional Medal of Honor.

Beep added the clincher when he said, "Some of you probably don't know it, but Ribs' dog Blackie is a son of my million-dollar hound, Oklahoma Crude."

There was wild clapping and cheering, spitting and scratching of crotches. Some men were so excited that they swallowed their tobacco or snuff. The two guys who had been fighting over whether the new Beechnut was moister than it had been went at it again. A bucket of icy water was thrown on them to break up the fight. Two roosters came out of nowhere and started fighting. It was a beautiful example of freedom-loving Americans and roosters expressing their First Amendment rights.

After order was restored, Beep said, "At our Saturday night coon hunt prior to Christmas Day, it has been our custom to name someone as Coon Hunter of the Year. I'm pleased to announce that this year's recipient is Ribs Davis."

The men cheered, spit, scratched their crotches and the two who had been fighting about Beechnut hugged each other.

After Beep raised his hand and restored order, he said, "Ribs is the first black man ever to receive this honor and, of course, the only token black member of the Dallas Chapter of the American Coon Hunters Association."

Ribs was an emotional wreck, weeping openly when Beep said, "Ribs' picture, along with his dog Blackie, will be on the cover of the January issue of *Coon Master* magazine. And the feature article in the magazine titled 'Black Boy Makes It Big' will be the story of

Ribs' climb to the pinnacle of the coon hunting world."

Beep also said he had bought the back cover of the magazine to advertise his Oklahoma Crude Coon Jerky.

Turning to the man who called himself Jesus, Beep said, "Jesus, we currently don't have any Jew members, but I'd be willing to sponsor you for membership."

To what was obviously as honor, the man simply said, "Let me think about it."

I could not believe he was so flippant about such a grand invitation. It made me believe the guy was neither Jewish nor the real Jesus.

By this time several fights had broken out, icy water was thrown on the combatants, and Beep made each of the men share from the same pouch of Beechnut. That calmed everyone. I would learn that night that Beechnut had a calming effect on people.

Beep then continued, "Ribs, we have a few gifts for you. And, gentlemen, I would appreciate it if you would hold your applause until I'm finished.

"First, we want to present to you a year's membership to the National Rifle Association, the only decent gun-loving organization in these United States. I'm glad to be on the organization's board along with Moses, aka Charleston Heston.

"I know you're already a member, Ribs, along with everyone who truly loves America, so this membership is a renewal. The member ship is courtesy of WBAP radio in Dallas, the official coon hunter station. Anybody who doesn't like country music, or the Houston Astros and Texas Rangers baseball teams is a communist and isn't welcome in this association."

The men could not control themselves. They broke into wild applause, spitting, crotch scratching, and hitting each other on the shoulder. Again, a few fights broke out and the combatants rolled around on the ground away from the bonfire. The fact that they stayed away from the roaring fire told me that coon hunters were smart cookies.

Beep, who was on a roll, then said, "And the same goes for the Dallas Cowboys and Houston Oilers."

Luke, this was before the Houston Oilers became the Tennessee Titans and before there was an NFL team named the Houston Texans.

Beep then ignited some of the wildest applause and fighting of the night when he said, "Here's some of the best news of the night. Ribs told me earlier that he's getting rid of that kraut wagon he's been driving and buying himself a pickup."

After order was restored, Beep continued, "That makes this next gift for Ribs very special. It's a gunrack for his new pickup."

The men cheered, spit and pounded each other on the arms. A few began dancing a jig, while Beep announced, "And the final gift, Ribs, is a year's supply of my special coon jerky, the regular and Jap-flavored teriyaki. Each order of my coon jerky comes with a KILL A COMMIE bumper sticker."

Tears welled up in Ribs' eyes and he was speechless, which was understandable. There was no greater honor than being named *Coon Hunter of the Year*.

I wish I could say that Ribs simply remained silent, but he decided to respond to the great honor bestowed upon him with a musical salute.

Unknown to Joe Don or me, he had brought his accordion, which he retrieved from the trunk of the VW. With it he proceeded to play the *National Anthem*, so everyone stood with their right hand on their heart. If it had ended there, all would have been well. But he insisted on doing a complete concert of polka rap, which he had composed.

During the concert, Ribs revealed that the accordion he was using had once belonged to Lawrence Welk. He had bought it from Chico. I did not doubt the authenticity of the instrument, since I recalled a story about Welk's accordion disappearing when he was doing a show in Las Vegas.

The man who called himself Jesus may have had the best line of the night when he said, "Now you know why God issues angels' harps instead of accordions."

After Ribs played the final chord of his concert, it was time for Beep to do one of his coon hunting seminars. This was the highlight of the evening, why most of the men had showed up for the coon hunt.

Beep would be speaking on the difference between carbide lights and battery-operated lights for coon hunting. It was an advanced course at the University of Oklahoma, where Beep was a full professor and held the Chair for Advanced Coon Hunting. I learned that most of the men had already received a certificate for his seminar on Coon Hunting Ethics.

Many of the nation's top athletes chose OU for their educations because of its undergraduate and graduate programs in coon hunting, but mostly because of Beep. While many schools had programs in coon hunting, none had a faculty member like Beep, who was world renown. He set the standard.

In the short time I had known Beep, I had found him to be one of the most objective men I had ever met. He began his seminar saying, "Your Bluetick, Redtick, English, Black and Tan, Plott and Walker are all good coon hounds, but a Redbone is by far the best coon hound money can buy.

"All these different breeds of dogs, if they have choice, prefer to hunt with a man using a carbide light. And more important, if God didn't want us hunting with a carbide light, he wouldn't have given us carbide."

I looked at the man who called himself Jesus, who just shrugged his shoulders and chuckled. Now at the time I did not know where carbide came from and still do not, but I have always been willing to accept the word of experts. And Beep was for sure an expert.

He continued, "Depending on the time of night, the season, and whether persimmons are ripe, a coon will look at a carbide light a lot quicker than they will expose their eyes to a battery-operated light. A coon knows when something is artificial, and batteries are artificial, whereas carbide is natural. The carbide light is not too bright and it's not too dim, like the baby bear's bowl of porridge, it's just right."

Now most of the guys there had heard Beep before, and they, possibly, were not as awed by his insight as Joe Don and I were. However, they all seemed to be hanging on to his every word. I think everyone realized we were in the presence of greatness.

"I think modern, always have," Beep said. "That's why I have an air-conditioned and heated dog trailer. Before a real coon hunter beds down for the night, he sees to it that his dogs are fed and comfortable."

I recalled hearing similar advice in a western movie, but I think it had to do with a horse rather than a dog.

Someone in the crowd asked, "You ever use a mule for coon hunting?"

"Of course, I've hunted coons on muleback." he replied, making the questioner's question seem a little ridiculous. There was no method of coon hunting that Beep had not engaged in.

"Up around Wichita Falls just about everyone who hunts coons rides a mule," he said. "This terrain isn't conducive to mule riding, but I have a friend in Oklahoma who has a mule that trees coons."

This got the attention of everyone, so someone asked, "Why don't you bring him down here sometime?"

"Can't," Beep said. "Can't get that old mules to cross the Red River."

Another voice questioned, "Why not?"

Beep joked, "Anytime that old mule gets close to water he goes crazy, because he likes to fish more than he likes to coon hunt."

I started to laugh but noted that everyone else was taking Beep's mule story seriously. He had to say, "It's a joke, boys, you can laugh," before the hunters guffawed. It was then that I realized that everything Beep said was gospel truth to these coon hunters.

One of the hunters asked Beep what he thought about the recently formed American Association of Women Coon Hunters. His brow furrowed and he said, "It's Communist-inspired, no doubt about that. They'll ruin a lot of good dogs and a lot of the terrain we hunt on. Scripture is very clear that God didn't intend for women to coon hunt."

No one questioned Beep's reference to Scripture because, after all, we had learned that the man had doctorates from several seminaries and had been the only non-Democrat on Jimmy Carter's religious council when the Georgia peanut farmer was President. It was why the American Association of Coon Hunters had adopted the peanut as its official nut.

I had many questions about coon hunting but was reluctant to ask them because it would have shown my ignorance. Joe Don, obviously, did not fear showing his ignorance, so asked, "What kind of gun is best for coon hunting?"

Beep pondered his question momentarily, then said, "I'd have to say a twenty-two-caliber rifle and long rifle shells. However, I think the light that you use to spot a treed coon in a tree is more important than the weapon."

"I have a three fifty-seven magnum pistol," Joe Don said. "Is that too much gun?"

"I have a twenty-two and backup forty-five," Beep said, "because sometimes your dog will tree a bobcat or mountain lion. You need a little more firepower for a big cat than you do for a coon. Communists have also brought a lot of Russian boar into Texas."

"I'm ready to shoot something," Joe Don said. "When are we going to hunt?"

Beep took out his pocket watch and said, "It's ten o'clock and time to hunt. Coons are most active between ten o'clock and midnight."

One of the perks Ribs received as "Coon Hunter of the Year" was that he had the honor of hunting with Beep Jenkins and Oklahoma Crude. On this occasion it also meant that Joe

Don, the phony Jesus and I shared in that honor. Blackie and Cowboy were also included.

We were no further than a hundred yards from the bonfire when the dogs picked up a trail and started barking. Beep said it was Oklahoma Crude who first picked up the trail and started barking. Ribs agreed. I, of course, being a novice could not tell one dog's bark from another.

All coon hunters know the bark of their dog, or dogs, and even if they do not, they claim they do. Beep taught a seminar on bark recognition, which I was told was as intense and deep as his seminar on the best type light to use for coon hunting.

We, of course, were using carbide lights because Beep had some sort of vendetta against Energizer, Duracell and Rayovac batteries. All three companies had refused to sponsor his worldwide seminars, which some said, without any concrete evidence, was why he so strongly recommended carbide. The three companies justified not sponsoring him because he lived in Oklahoma.

Many people persecuted Beep because of his genius intellect. He had doctorates from all the Ivy League schools but said none of these highly acclaimed schools were as strong educationally as Broken Bow, Oklahoma High School.

He said the Oklahoma school offered classes in trapping, animal skinning and hog scraping. "I don't see how anybody can say they're educated if they don't know how to process a hog," he said.

After about three minutes of frantic barking, the dogs went quiet. It prompted Joe Don to say, "They must have lost the coon's trail."

I had learned early in my life that when you did not know anything, you did not say anything. Joe Don had not learned the same lesson.

Beep kind of chuckled at Joe Don's observation but did not say anything until the dogs started barking again. He then explained, "Oklahoma Crude is so well trained that he doesn't bark, or allow dogs that are with him to bark, when he's crossing posted land."

Finally, it became obvious that the barking was stationary. That is when Beep and Ribs high fived and declared in unison, "They've treed."

For what seemed an eternity, we battled our way through thickets and briars toward the barking dogs. By the time we arrived at the tree where the dogs said the coon was located, I was as winded as if I had run five miles. That was speculation, of course, since when in the Marine Corps I had always reported for sick call on days we were scheduled to run or march long distances.

With their flickering carbide lights, Beep and Ribs searched the tree for the coon the dogs were sure was there. Joe Don stood anxiously by with his three fifty-seven magnum at the ready position.

After several minutes Joe Don complained, "There's no coon up there."

Then Beep explained, "The dogs must have beat the coon to the tree."

"Should we wait for the coon to show up?" Joe Don asked.

"Probably not," Beep replied. "The coon might get sidetracked on the way here."

I looked at the man who called himself Jesus and he observed my gaze. He said for my benefit and hearing only, "You would expect me to be on the coon's side, wouldn't you?"

The dogs treed twice more before we got back to the campsite, but we did not see a coon. Joe Don was more than a little perturbed, but what I noticed was that he had not lit up a cigarette.

One hunter suggested that Ribs' accordion concert might have sent all coons in the area into hiding, since none of the hunters had seen a coon.

As for me, I thought it was a good hunt. The only negative was having to deal with Blackie's rear end on the way home.

ELEVEN

I was awakened on Sunday morning by someone gently shaking my shoulder. Initially, I thought I was dreaming. My world was not in focus.

"Wake up," a voice said. "Breakfast is ready."

Early in the morning my mind does not work like a computer, rather like an old Royal or Underwood typewriter with irreplaceable parts and worn keys that tend to stick. When I finally got one of those keys unstuck, I recognized the voice as being that of the man who called himself Jesus, groaned, rolled to the other side of the bed and pulled a blanket over my head.

He laughed and chided, "C'mon lazybones, you asked me to wake you up at six."

That was true, but I had made the request at a time when I was groggy from the coon hunt and not in complete control of my faculties. I also think it was shortly after Blackie had gassed me.

"C'mon," the man said. "I made grits for breakfast."

To any southern boy the word grits will cause him to get chill bumps all over and want to break out singing a rendition of *Dixie*. Had there not been a shortage of grits in the South during the Civil War, the Confederacy would not have allowed the North to think they had won. When you cut a southerner's grits ration, you get a listless individual who wants to sit on a creekbank all day fishing for catfish.

So, I robed, house-shoed and staggered to the breakfast table where coffee, grits, bacon, eggs, gravy and biscuits were waiting.

After a generous helping of grits and a couple of cups of coffee my voice came back to me and I thanked him for breakfast and for waking me up. I needed to start barbecuing ribs and brisket early to feed the crowd coming to watch the Cowboys game.

Slow cooking is the key to good barbecue. If ribs do not fall off the bone, they have not been cooked enough. If brisket cannot be cut with a fork, it has not been cooked enough.

"You are, obviously, a connoisseur of grits," my house guest said.

"I'm sure you read my *Texas Monthly* magazine article *The Greatest Grits Restaurants in Texas*. It was one of the best investigative pieces of journalism I've ever done."

"No, I can't say I read it," he said, "but I know everything you wrote."

His response made me even more certain than ever that he was not who he claimed to be. If I remembered the Bible correctly, grits, also known as manna, was what God fed his people when they were in the wilderness.

And I do not blame anyone for leaving Egypt. I spent some time there and cannot think of a single place in the U.S. that is worse, not even College Station, Texas.

The man called Jesus shook his head in resignation and said, "I can't believe what you've been thinking. You give God so little credit."

"I give God lots of credit," I argued. "I don't know what you're talking about."

The man said, "You give him credit for things that don't matter, which means you give him credit for nothing."

I did not understand what the guy was getting so uptight about, but not being one to argue on the Lord's Day, I decided to give him a pass. Besides, I had to get the ribs and brisket going. Burgers and dogs could be cooked while my guests were present.

I also had to start psyching myself up for the most important touch football game of the season.

"Hey, I hope we can count on you to play for us this afternoon," I said. "We're going to need some depth to beat this bunch."

He laughed and said, "I don't care anything about football."

"That's un-American," I said. "And even more important, it's un-Texan."

"I didn't say I wouldn't play," he said. "I'll play, but football isn't important to me."

That is what I wanted to hear. Although I did not believe he was who he said he was, if I was wrong and he was the real Jesus, I figured it would give us an edge over our opponents. I was not opposed to having a ringer like Jesus play for us, if it would help us win.

The guy gave me a look of resignation, as if he could read my mind.

I questioned, "I guess you're going to church?"

"Yes," he replied.

"I hope you'll catch an early service, get home and be rested up for the game," I said.

"I can do that," he said, then questioned, "I don't guess you're interested in going with me?"

"Normally, I would," I lied, "but I've got so much to do here that I'm going to be busier than a beaver all morning."

He said a bit sarcastically, "Well, I wouldn't want church to interfere with a touch football game."

"This isn't just another game," I said. "These guys annihilated us early in the season."

He shook his head in resignation and said, "I'm quite familiar with these guys and that all of them are going to church this morning."

I questioned, "Really? Do you think that will have any effect on the game?"

He shook his head in that "I give up" manner, which did not bother me a bit. I simply poured myself another cup of coffee and began preparing the ribs while he read the paper.

I figured if he was who he said he was, he would not need to read the paper. He would already know what was in it.

"Anything interesting in the paper?" I asked.

He replied, "I was reading here where Texas has a problem with overpopulated prisons and planned to put some inmates in a National Guard barracks in West Texas.

"Sounds like a good idea," I said.

"Evidently not," he said. "A federal judge over in Tyler denied using the barracks, claimed it would be cruel and unusual punishment."

"Must be a Jimmy Carter appointed judge," I said. "The barracks is good enough for people defending the country, but not good enough for criminals."

"You're right about who appointed him," the man said. "And I agree with you that if the barracks is good enough for American soldiers, it should be good enough for criminals."

Slurring my words, I said, "Brother, that's disgusting. Has the spread changed on the Cowboys game today?"

"It's good you have your mind on things that matter," he said.

"Hey, if you were from Dallas, you'd know that the Cowboys game is the only thing that matters," I said. "We're talking playoffs here, the most serious time of the year."

I admit that I have always been a homer, and no one can shame me about it. I had only one bumper sticker and it read LOVE NEW YORK? TAKE I-30 EAST.

I have always been a "love it or leave it" person, not only about Texas but also about America.

During that first week that the man who called himself Jesus lived at my house, I noticed there were times when he did not seem to pay much attention to what I said, as if what I said was not all that important. Of course, my friends did the same thing. And it bugged me that the man always seemed to know what I was thinking.

"Where are you going to church today?" I asked.

"We're having church at Chico's place," he replied.

I questioned, "You're kidding?"

"Why do you think I'm kidding?" he asked.

"Church among the hubcaps, "I questioned, "and especially among used hubcaps. The place doesn't exactly reek of reverence."

He said, "Your problem is that you think church is a place and not people. Church isn't a building. It's not stained glass, high ceilings and organ music. True believers can worship anywhere, and under any conditions."

I shrugged and questioned, "Okay, but what kind of people are going to worship at Chico's place?"

"The same kind of people who worship in the most elaborate buildings in the city," he replied. "People who need God."

I responded, "You know what I mean."

"I know exactly what you mean," he said. "The people who worship in the Church Among the Hubcaps, and by the way I like the name you gave the church, won't have fancy clothes or cars, and they may not have respectable professions or be able to give much, but God doesn't look at who a person is but at what's in his or her heart."

I crawfished and said, "I'm not being critical."

He laughed and said, "Yes, you are."

I responded, "As I stated previously, I'm not one to argue religion, especially on the Lord's Day. I'm more concerned about the Philadelphia Eagles than what people are wearing to church, or about where they're going to church. The Eagles are going to be primed for the Cowboys."

He sighed, straightened the newspaper, laid it on the table and left the room. He was dressed in an old robe I had given him, was barefoot and a bad case of five o'clock shadow clouded his face. I understood that he was going to shave, shower and get ready for church, although where he was going did not require much in the way of getting ready. The idea of a Church Among the Hubcaps was ridiculous to me.

It never occurred to me that he left the room because he was teed off because he had never shown himself to be that kind of guy. I certainly felt no animosity toward him for his lack of understanding of the modern church and contemporary Christians. He seemed intelligent enough, but there was a lot that he did not comprehend, which was another reason I questioned his authenticity, that and the fact that he did not have a beard.

It was my feeling that the real Jesus would never have given up his beard, no matter in what century that he decided to visit earth. I also figured Jesus for a robe and sandal man, no matter what style the rest of us chose. But phony Jesus' clothes were not unique or stylish in any way. His attire could well have fallen off the back of a Salvation Army truck.

Some of the preachers I had seen on TV were dressed to the hilt; suits, shirts, ties and shoes costing more than five thousand dollars, whereas this guy wore used outfits that could be purchased for five bucks.

Priests also put him to shame with their colorful robes. He was an opposite to everything I thought religion should be.

Well, at that moment I was too tired to worry about who he was or who had sent him my way. The coon hunt had been an enjoyable experience, except for having to ride with Blackie, but it had wiped me out. If I was going to be ready for the game, I needed some rest. So, I laid down on the couch to rest my eyes, with the grits I had consumed weighing heavily on my stomach.

The next thing I remember was the doorbell ringing. I glanced at the clock on the fireplace mantle and saw that it was eleven o'clock. Although startled by the time, I did not exactly leap to my feet. I groaned, sort of rolled off the couch and house-shoed by way to the front door.

It was Mary Lou, who greeted me with, "You look awful. I came early to help you in the kitchen."

Mary Lou was more a pain in the rear than helpful, and especially in the kitchen. I needed her help as much as I needed to find mold on a loaf of bread. She could not be trusted to wash a head of lettuce for a salad.

I grunted and asked, "Want a cup of coffee?"

"I'd rather have a wine cooler," she replied.

"You'll find one in the fridge," I said.

"Where's Jesus?" she asked.

"He went to church," I replied.

"I know that," she said. "I was there."

I questioned, "You went to the Church Among the Hubcaps."

"Whatever you want to call it, I was there," she replied. "And Jesus brought a wonderful message."

In the years I had known Mary Lou, I had never known her to attend church. So, I was a little shocked."

I questioned, "The guy preached?"

"Yes, and I've never heard anyone better," she replied.

"That's no surprise," I said, "since he's probably the only one you've ever heard."

"That's not true," she said. "When I was a kid, I attended church regularly."

"I'll take your word for it," I said, "but right now I need to shower and dress for the game. Make yourself at home and watch the tube. Everything is under control in the kitchen."

I retired to my bedroom, brushed my teeth and got the shower going. Rivulets of water were soon pounding my head, but they did nothing to wipe the cobwebs from my mind. My mental processes were in disarray, which some have always thought was the norm for me.

I knew that I would be mentally ready for our game and the Cowboys game later in the afternoon, but for the moment my mental dexterity was at a low point. It would have to be sharper if we were to stand a chance again the animals that we would be playing at one o'clock.

Proper dress is critical for a touch football game and for watching the Cowboys on TV, so I selected my mesh green and gold Baylor shirt, matching athletic pants, white socks with gold trim and white Nike running shoes.

At the time I did not know that Nike was using slave labor in China to make its shoes, or that some clown quarterback for the San Francisco Forty-Niners would one-day refuse to stand for the National Anthem. Had I known this at the time, I would have played barefooted or in my house shoes.

Mary Lou, obviously, was not impressed with my outfit. She laughed and said it clashed.

"With what?" I asked.

"With everything," she replied.

I wanted to attack what she was wearing, but it was hard to do. She was an impeccable dresser and liked to show off her legs. She had the legs to do pantyhose commercials. And even though it was colder than the proverbial well digger's rear end, she had shown up wearing shorts and a cashmere sweater. This was acceptable because she was one of our cheerleaders.

Since I was not in the mood to argue, I asked, "Anyone we know show up for services at the Church Among the Hubcaps?"

"All your alleged friends were there," she replied, "plus a lot of people I didn't know. There was a weird guy there that talked about coon hunting as a ministry."

"That would be Beep Jenkins," I said, "and he's not weird. He's one of the most brilliant men in the country."

She rolled her eyes and said, "I understand he's coming over here today."

"I invited him," I said.

"I can see why you wouldn't consider him strange," she said.

There is one thing about which Mary Lou is extremely sensitive, and I used it against her at every opportunity. Although she was at the time in her thirties, she still suffered from an occasional attack of teenage acne.

Through keen observation, I detected a small blemish on Mary Lou's chin, which I joyfully called to her attention. She scurried away to the bathroom to try to cover it with makeup, giving me great satisfaction and probable assurance that she would not, at least on this day, again make fun of the way I was dressed.

Sue Beth was the next to arrive with her new beau Chigger Dodgen in tow.

"You look awful," she said.

I began, "Just because you don't like green and gold…"

She interrupted, "It's not your school colors. It's your bloodshot eyes."

"Well, Chigger," I questioned, "don't you want to say something negative about the way I look."

"Not really," he replied. "I don't know how you looked previously. You look pretty bad, but I figure that's normal."

"I'm tired," I said. "I went coon hunting last night."

Chigger said, "I wish I had known. I would have gone with you. There's nothing better than a good coon hunt."

"Sugar, I don't think he's talking about the same kind of coon hunting you do over in Louisiana," Sue Beth said.

Chigger looked a bit baffled, but I got the impression that he always looked that way. "I didn't think you were going to be able to make it," I said. "I thought you were going to pick up aluminum cans with your kids to earn Christmas money."

He grunted and said, "That was the plan, but things just didn't work out. There are a few logistics problems when you have to coordinate things with twelve ex-wives."

I could empathize with Chigger. I had never been able to coordinate things with one ex-wife, so figured even the Pentagon would have trouble coordinating twelve scenarios.

"I wouldn't think all twelve ex-wives would necessarily be involved," I said, "just the mothers of the children."

"That would require all twelve," Chigger said. "I had one child with each ex-wife."

Chigger was maybe four-feet, eleven inches tall, not impressive size-wise even with his jockey hat atop his head. He always wore his jockey outfit, which included a cup to protect his crotch from the top of his boots. He sometimes even wore his goggles, although most of the time they were above the bill of his hat.

I suspicioned that Chigger was bald but had no proof of it. I just know that some people are sensitive about baldness, especially Congresswomen and female movie stars, and Chigger always impressed me as being a very sensitive person.

Although Chigger wore his jockey outfit and goggles almost twenty-four seven, he downplayed being a jockey. Unlike a golfer or someone taking flying lessons, he did not want to talk about riding horses all the time. His parents, in fact, never knew he was a jockey. They thought he was a brain surgeon with a practice in Shreveport.

He did have other attire, which he wore when singing on the *Louisiana Hayride* or *Grand Ole' Opry*. His country music attire included reptile cowboy boots, Wrangler jeans, a rattlesnake belt with a saucer-size Jack Daniels belt buckle, double breasted cowboy shirts like Wild Bill Elliott wore, and in winter a sheepskin coat. Chigger attached special sentiment to the coat because it was his pet as a child. He donated it to Texas A&M for cloning.

His parents were Baptists, very much against gambling, so he kept his profession a secret because the truth would have broken their hearts.

He also said that if they had known that he danced while in college and was involved in a sport that depended on wagering, it would have killed them.

Chigger's folks lived in a South Louisiana swamp and his dad was an alligator farmer, meaning he caught and sold the toothy creatures for his livelihood.

When he visited his parents, he always wore his jockey outfit, which his mother thought was what all brain surgeons wore.

"I'm glad you could come," I told Chigger, "because we need all the help that we can get against this team that we're playing today."

"You can count on me," Chigger said, "as long as no one tells my folks that I played football on Sunday."

I assured him that his participation would be kept a secret. Of course, I could not promise the same for our opponents. They were nasty and used every trick in the book. But given that Chigger's folks lived deep in the swamp where the primary means of transportation was a pirogue, I figured the only way they would hear of his sin would be if some TV sportscaster heard about the game. Anyway, I was willing to take that gamble.

"Anything to eat?" Sue Beth asked.

"Lots of chips, dips and salsa," I replied, "even some leftover grits, biscuits and gravy."

"Grits," she squealed, excitedly. "Lead me to them."

Sue Beth's squeal of excitement brought Mary Lou back into the room. I greeted her with, "I see you covered up that pimple." She gave me her killer look. She also launched some well-chosen expletives at me that I felt more than heard.

Sue Beth found what was left of the grits, gravy and biscuits, which she devoured before starting in on the chips, dips and salsa. Chigger watched admiringly but did not participate, explaining that he had to watch his weight.

When I heard a horse neigh in my backyard and heard Cowboy bark, I knew Bum Criswell had arrived. I had hoped he would arrive on one of his riding lawnmowers, instead of transportation that would fertilize my yard.

He rang the doorbell, I answered, and he said, "You look awful. Sorry, I'm late."

"You're not late," I said. "You're never late but always apologize for being late. And thanks for the comment on my appearance."

"You look okay," he said, "it's that green and gold outfit that's awful."

Bum, being almost an SMU graduate, did not like Baylor or the school's colors. I think it hearkened back to nineteen sixteen when his great grandfather's team lost to Baylor by a score of sixty-one to zero.

I obviously ruffled his feathers because he continued, "To tell the truth, you look as awful as your outfit. Where did you get those bloodshot eyes?"

This came from a man who was wearing his polo gear. He joined the discussion in the den, where he and Chigger found some common ground in talking about polo and horseracing.

When I came into the room, I asked Chigger how he and Sue Beth were doing in their quest to put a horseracing track on the SMU campus.

He deferred to Sue Beth, who between mouthfuls said, "We have options on quite a bit of property around SMU."

"I don't understand why you want the track on the SMU campus," I said.

"You wouldn't," Bum said. "People like you are the reason why Waco and Baylor will never have a horseracing track. Sue Beth wants the track among people with some class."

There was no doubt that people who lived in Highland Park back then considered it the most exclusive area in or around Dallas, and some people still do. And they have done a good job of convincing others. If it were possible to find an old roach-infested house in Highland Park for sale, which you cannot, it would sell for a million dollars or more. And it would simply be pushed down so that another house could be built in its place. It is the land that is at a premium, not the structure on it.

Many people in Highland Park have never been outside its boundaries. They think everything of value is inside Highland Park's city limits.

Back then many people had not heard about integration, and some still have not. They only know that their domestic help arrives on buses from South Dallas and returns to South Dallas in the evening. Bum lived in his grandparents' mansion in Highland Park, so he did not understand anything different.

"Does the Highland Park City Council know that you're planning to put a racetrack in their city?" I asked Sue Beth.

"No, but I think they will be agreeable when they learn how much money it will produce," she replied.

"You've got about as much chance of getting a track in Highland Park as the Mafia would have in getting members of the First Baptist Church in Dallas to vote for a casino on one of their parking lots," I said.

Bum grumbled, "You're a real spoilsport," Mark, "and not very progressive. I found the administration at SMU very agreeable to adding lawnmower polo to the school's sports programs."

"That's different," I said.

"Maybe so," he agreed, "but you have a bad habit of shooting down a person's dreams. You don't have to be the devil's advocate about everything."

"I'm not," I argued. "With the cost of real estate in Highland Park, I just think it's unrealistic to think you can build a horseracing track on the SMU campus, especially when there's already so little parking for students."

Chigger said, "Small people have small dreams."

"You're a big one to talk about small people," I responded, angrily.

What might have turned into a violent argument was stymied when the doorbell rang. It was Jimmy Joe Johnson, resplendent in a designer jogging suit, cowboy hat and cowboy boots.

"You look awful," was the first thing he said to me.

I countered, "Your outfit doesn't look all that great either."

"I'm not talking about your outfit," he said. "I'm talking about your eyes. They're bloodshot."

Draped on one of Jimmy Joe's arms was Bumps Ann Grinds, who always looked and dressed like a *Fredericks of Hollywood* model. Of course, she really was a model for *Fred's of Frisco*, a sleazy discount garment store in Frisco, Texas, which at the time was a small town north of Dallas that specialized in alleged massage parlors. Fred was later arrested for massage bartering, escaped jail and relocated to Mexico.

Anyway, Bumps was about as sultry a dish as you would ever want to see and served as one of our cheerleaders. She had natural blonde hair with black roots and used more makeup in one application than most rodeo clowns used in a season.

As always, she insisted on giving me a kiss, which cosmeticized one entire side of my face and caused it to tilt at a dangerous angle. I excused myself, went into the garage, and used a gallon of gasoline to remove the evidence of her kiss.

Bumps tolerated Jimmy Joe, but never dated him. She did allow him to give her a ride to my house on Sundays.

Bumps liked Mary Lou, but the feeling was not mutual, which made for some interesting conversations. Bumps never caught on to Mary Lou's sarcasm, which was about as subtle as a squadron of flies during apple cider season in New Hampshire.

So, I said, "Bumps, Mary Lou is having a little problem with her acne. I would appreciate it if you would tell her what you do to keep your skin so nice."

Mary Lou's killer eyes nailed me, but Bumps was already into a discourse on proper facial care, which basically consisted of just covering everything up with makeup.

Billy Bob arrived next and greeted me with, "You look awful."

I responded, "I went coon hunting last night, which is why my eyes are bloodshot."

"It's not your eyes," he said, "it's that awful outfit. But now that you mention it, green and gold doesn't go with red."

I questioned, "Don't you care about our school colors? Doesn't that *Good Old Baylor Line* give you chill bumps?"

"No," he replied, matter of fact.

There are times when I think Billy Bob is too blunt. But most of the time he engages in long, meaningless discourses to explain his position, which never make any sense. If there had been a degree at Baylor in senseless dialogue, the law school faculty would have exempted him and just given him the degree.

And, as I said previously, many judges just agreed with Billy Bob rather than listening to him in court.

"I don't understand you," I said. "Everything you are, everything you've achieved in life, is a result of being educated at Baylor University."

He sighed and replied, "I know. I'm just frustrated because it is taking so long to get a statue of me erected on campus."

"I think that's all going to change when you argue Ribs' lawsuit against the Ku Klux Klan before the Supreme Court," I said.

"You would think it would be a slam dunk," he said, "him being a member of the American Coon Hunters Association. But with the liberal judges on the court, you never know how things will go."

I checked on my other guests and found that Sue Beth had created a shortage of chips and dips. She had also gone through six bottles of beer.

I was aware of her abilities in that department, so had laid in a huge supply of Frito-Lay products and gallon containers of dip, this despite the company's refusal to buy touch football uniforms for my team.

My guests were also being treated to some of the finest wine ever stomped in Jasper, Texas. It came in milk cartons and had an expiration date. I had gotten a good buy on the wine because it had exceeded the expiration date by a little more than a week. While some would have discarded it, my experience was that the expired vintage was superior to the newer wine.

Mentally I likened myself to Joseph, who was put in charge of Egypt's food supply. Fat chance that a Jew would today be put in charge of Egypt's food supply.

Having the man who called himself Jesus in my house had caused a lot of biblical thoughts to drift through my mind. Of course, I have always been more religious than people have credited me with being. Although I have not flaunted my knowledge of Scripture, when I put my mind to it, I am the equal of any man when it comes to religious thought.

Chigger, who was filling in a crossword puzzle in the newspaper asked, "What is a three-letter word for divine being?"

"I don't have a clue," I replied.

Bum was in a serious discussion with Jimmy Joe concerning professional lawnmower polo leagues, suggesting that he might want to sell lawnmower polo franchises rather than oil leases.

"People are tired of oil," Bum said, "and almost everyone I know already has an oil well."

Jimmy Joe's response was, "I hate to deal in something that's speculative."

Billy Bob asked Bum what he knew about the Mideast Polo League, which used camels instead of horses or lawnmowers.

"I'm a consultant to that league," Bum said, "and I advised them that riding lawnmowers was not ideal for their terrain. I suggested that if they wanted to rid themselves of camels, and the problems they cause, that they should probably go to dune buggies. However, that would eliminate them from competing in the World Lawnmower Polo Championship. But I couldn't get them to understand the difference between riding lawnmowers and camels or dune buggies.

"Where is the Mideast?" Bumps asked. "Is it in New Jersey?"

Jimmy Joe, embarrassed by her ignorance, gave her a look of disdain and said, "My gosh, Bumps, you should know the Mideast is in Philadelphia."

"Where's Philadelphia?" she asked.

Jimmy Joe looked at me for help, but I was not giving any. I was building myself a frozen margarita and did not want to get into an argument, especially on a Sunday.

Chigger looked up from his crossword puzzle and said, "Philadelphia is a football team. They're playing the Cowboys today."

"I knew that," Jimmy Joe said.

"The Mideast Billy Bob is talking about is like Israel," Bum said.

"It can't be Israel," I said. "The Jewish religion forbids riding a camel."

"Where in the hell did you get that from?" Bum asked.

"It's in the Bible," I replied.

Bum questioned, "Where in the Bible?"

I replied, "Book of Solomon, chapter twenty, verse six."

I was bluffing, of course, but do remember reading something about Jews and camels, although it may have been in *National Geographic* instead of the Bible.

"Do you have a Bible around here?" Mary Lou asked.

"I loaned my Bible to a friend," I replied.

"How convenient," she said. "If you had a Bible it was one the Gideons put in a hotel room and that you stole."

Jimmy Joe questioned, "You stole a Bible?"

I denied stealing a Bible, but I had borrowed one from a hotel room and had not yet returned it.

"Have you ever eaten camel fries?" Sue Beth asked between bites of chips and dip.

"Are camel fries like calf fries?" Billy Bob asked.

"I think so," Sue Beth replied. "They're little round things. I don't think they're much bigger. The ones that I had were cooked just like calf fries and sheep fries."

"How are they cooked?" Jimmy Joe asked.

Sue Beth gave him a disbelieving look, like he was the most ignorant of men, and replied, "Chicken fried, of course."

"Where in the world did you have camel fries?" Mary Lou asked.

She replied, "I had them a couple of years ago when I took that boat trip up the Nile."

"Is that in Ohio?" Bumps asked.

"Well, I can tell you this," I said, "eating camel fries is a sin, no matter how they're cooked. The Old Testament specifically forbids people from eating the balls of any animal."

"Is it a sin if you didn't know?" Sue Beth asked.

I shrugged and replied, "I think the Bible says that God once winked at ignorance, but no more."

"Then I need to go to a priest and ask for forgiveness," she said.

"You're not Catholic," I said.

"I know," she said, "but they're the only ones who forgive sin. It's why most Mafia people are Catholics."

"I didn't know French fries were made of animal balls," Bumps said.

Jimmy Joe explained, "French fries aren't made of animal balls, Bumps. The fries we get at McDonald's are made of potatoes."

"I heard there's a company raising potatoes that taste like chicken fried steak," Billy Bob said. His statement got the attention of everyone.

"Now that's a company I'd like to represent," Jimmy Joe said.

"The company is under attack from *Vegans Opposed to Altering Potatoes*," Billy Bob said. "And, as you know, the Vegans have one of the strongest lobbies in Washington."

"This will be a political football, no doubt about that," I said. "And if Congress gets involved, there's no telling what a potato will taste like."

From the taste of potatoes, we went to a conversation about the man who called himself Jesus. I learned that all my alleged friends had attended the *Church* Among the Hubcaps earlier that morning, and all raved about the preaching of the phony Jesus.

Then out of the blue Bum said, "They use really long polo sticks."

"What are you talking about?" Mary Lou asked.

"I'm talking about playing polo on camelback," he replied.

"I sure wish we had a Bible here," Mary Lou said. "I'd like for Mark to show us where it says eating camel balls is a sin."

I said, "I wish I had my Bible here, too, because I could sure show you."

"I'll be glad when Jesus gets here," she said. "He can tell us if you're lying."

"Are you saying that you're going to take his word over mine?" I asked. "You're always trying to catch me in a lie, but you never have."

She rolled her eyes and said, "You're like a Democrat. I've never caught you telling the truth."

The doorbell rang and interrupted our conversation. It was Bobo. "I'm empty," he said.

I informed him, "There's a tub full of iced down beer in the kitchen."

As he was heading that way, he said, "I like your green and gold outfit. It goes well with your red eyes."

Bobo got three bottles of beer and sat down on the couch beside Chigger. It was quite a contrast.

"Do you know a three-letter word for divine being?" Chigger asked.

"Try Tom," Bobo suggested.

"Why Tom?" I asked.

He shrugged his shoulders and replied, "Tom Landry."

Chigger, excited, said, "It works."

Bobo asked, "How are you doing, Mary Lou?" He was always fascinated with her and could not understand why the two of us could not get along.

"I've been doing fine," she said, "and I want to thank you for the column you did on the Texas seed tick. If the state doesn't protect the seed tick, they're going to become extinct."

"They're a lot of little critters like the Texas seed tick that need our protection," Bobo said, "and as long as the paper allows me, I'm going to take up their cause."

"Well, your article was beautifully written," she said.

"When are we going to eat," Sue Beth asked.

"During the Cowboys game," I replied.

"And when does that start?" she asked.

"At three o'clock," I replied.

"I don't know if I can hold out until then," she said.

"There's a bucket of Kentucky Fried in the fridge," I said. "You can munch on that."

"Hallelujah!" she exclaimed.

I laughed and said, "I figured you would approve."

"You are a darling," she said.

"Has anyone ever had chicken fries?" Bumps asked.

Everyone ignored her question, and I busied myself building another margarita. I had just completed it when Joe Don arrived, told me I looked terrible and said, "Those things are going to kill you."

"Yeah, and smoking is going to kill you," I countered.

"I don't smoke," he said.

"Since when," I asked.

"Since last night," he replied.

"Well, bully for you," I said. "Most people count the months they smoke-free. You must be counting the hours and minutes."

"I'm serious," he said. "You need to get off the sauce."

Ribs, Chico, Beep Jenkins and the man who called himself Jesus all arrived at the same time. Beep had been invited to spend the night in Ribs' apartment but had slept in his bus. He parked his bus on my lawn and turned a dozen dogs loose in my back yard.

"I hope you don't mind," Beep said. "They need to stretch their legs."

"I don't mind," I lied, dreading all the dog poop I was going to have to shovel up. "I'm hoping the horse back there doesn't kick any of your dogs in the head."

Beep questioned, "You have a horse back there?"

"Yeah," I said.

"I just hope the dogs don't eat him," Beep said.

Somewhat alarmed, I asked, "What do you mean?"

Beep explained, "Well, I had a couple of burros and the dogs ate them. Of course, burros aren't as big as a horse. They're not much bigger than an old rogue coon."

"Well, the horse is pretty big," I said.

"Then they probably wouldn't eat all of him," Beep said. "I fed them this morning."

Beep was still wearing the same clothes he was wearing at the coon hunt, causing me to suspicion that he had slept in them. It was hard to tell because they had looked slept in when I first met him at the coon hunt. And he still had not bothered to shave.

I was planning to introduce Beep and the man who called himself Jesus to everyone present, but they had already met at the Church Among the Hubcaps. By the way, I figured *The Church Among the Hubcaps* was a Baptist church. Baptist churches often leave the word "Baptist" off their names so as not to scare people. I do not know why the word scares people, but it does.

I said to Ribs in a questioning manner, "So you were all down at The Church Among the Hubcaps and heard this guy who claims to be Jesus speak? So, what did you think?"

Beep replied, "Jesus makes a lot of sense. He has the makings of a fine coon hunter."

So, I said to the man who called himself Jesus, "Well, it looks as if you're developing quite a following."

"Believe it or not," he said, "I've had quite a following for a couple of thousand years."

"I haven't been much of a churchgoer," Beep said, "but I'd be more regular if I could go to one like we went to today."

I said sarcastically, "Being among all those used hubcaps has to give a person a sense of reverence."

He answered as if my comment was serious. "No, it was more than the hubcaps. There was some real serious spiritual movement there today. You could feel it."

"Beep led the singing," Ribs said.

Beep added, "and if I have to say so myself, I'm a pretty fair country singer. Of course, Ribs did a good job of accompanying me."

I laughed and questioned, "Ribs played the accordion?"

"His chords were like they came right out of Heaven," Beep said.

I laughed again and said, "I might have opted for acapella."

The man who called himself Jesus smiled and said, "People who preferred acapella went to the Church of Christ."

I asked, "What do you think about that, people who don't use musical instruments for worship?"

"I don't think it matters," he replied.

"That brings up another question," I said. "What denomination is The Church Among the Hubcaps going to affiliate with?"

"Why do you think it's necessary for the church to affiliate with any denomination?" he asked. "As I told you before, denominations are man's idea, not God's."

I argued, "If you're not part of a denomination you won't be able to go to a convention or have a theological doctrine to defend. That means you won't get much press every year for attacking something that nobody cares about or have a bunch of missionaries appointed to do stuff church members won't do."

The man who called himself Jesus guffawed and said, "You certainly have a grasp of what the church is all about. Is there anything else you'd like to add?"

He was teasing me, and I knew it, but someone had to set the guy straight about the contemporary church. So, I said, "Well, the least The Church Among the Hubcaps can do is to take up an offering for you to go to the Holy Land. Without a trip to the Holy Land and some slides, you're doomed to failure."

He laughed again, then said in all seriousness, "There's no such thing as a specific Holy Land. God's Spirit is everywhere, which means the Holy Land is everywhere."

I argued, "People tell me they've gone to places like the Mount of Olives and experienced a special feeling about the presence of God."

"That's good," he said. "But if you must go to a special place to feel the presence of God, there's something wrong with your relationship with God. The Holy Spirit is with a Christian twenty-four seven, no matter where he or she may be."

"Is the church going to join a softball league?" Bobo asked. "I might like to be a member if I can play softball."

"Before the church gets into a softball league, it needs to start a building fund, buy some land and build a facility," I said. "That's the only way the church can grow."

"Now I might be able to peddle some church bonds," Jimmy Joe said. 'What's the commission on those things?"

The man who called himself Jesus sighed and said, "The Church Among the Hubcaps does not require a building of brick and mortar to survive. It will require much more than cosmetic appearance."

"I know you mean well," I said, "but I don't think you know much about growing a contemporary church. To grow you're going to need the right kind of people, a different location and a new building. And you must have a lot of youth concerts with music that they like, and kid programs where parents can drop their children off and go do things. Entertainment and childcare are where it's at in the contemporary church."

He questioned, "The right kind of people, huh?"

Mary Lou chuckled and sarcastically said, "As soon as you get Jesus and his church organized, you might want to start thinking about getting yourself organized."

I responded, "Nice shot, Mary Lou."

Bum said, "I haven't really pushed a church riding lawnmower polo league, but if I can help in that regard, don't hesitate to let me know, padre."

"Thanks," the man who called himself Jesus said. Then he said to me, sarcastically, "Would polo players be the right kind of people?"

Before I could answer, Bobo said, "Church polo is a dumb idea."

"Oh, I don't know about that," Chigger said. "I don't know how anyone could object to playing polo for Jesus."

Sue Beth was supportive, saying, "Chigger's right, and church polo leagues would offset some of the bad religious press that horses and riding lawnmowers have been getting."

"I didn't know horses and riding lawnmowers were getting bad press," Beep said. "Now I did know mules were getting bad press when it came to coon hunting, but I didn't know about horses and riding lawnmowers."

"I didn't know about it, either," I said. "But I'm not surprised. It takes a while for new ideas to catch on."

"Mules have been a staple of coon hunting for centuries," Beep said. "At least since the first century A.D. when Romans used them for that purpose."

"I didn't know the Romans coon hunted," I said.

"Oh, yeah," Beep said. "And Moses used a mule back when he herded sheep."

Beep was a wealth of knowledge, teaching stuff that most people had never thought about.

It was at this point that the man who called himself Jesus left the room. I assumed it was to get ready for out touch football game, which was fast approaching.

I was a bit nervous about the game because I knew our opponent would test us to the very limit of our physical and mental abilities. We would all have to give a hundred and ten percent to have any chance of winning, but I was willing to give a hundred and fifty percent.

"Well, what do you think of my guest?" I asked, after he was out of earshot.

"He's nice, very genuine," Mary Lou replied. "If he wants to call himself Jesus, I don't see why you should object. In fact, I think he probably is the real Jesus."

"You have to be kidding!" I exclaimed.

Mary Lou countered, "I think everyone here, other than you, thinks he's the real Jesus."

"Now is the time for one of you to confess," I said. "The joke has gone far enough."

Everyone responded with a blank stare, which was not unusual. Their failure caused me to think that all of them wanted to keep the joke going. I decided that if that was the way they wanted to play the game it was okay with me.

Bobby Jack Lewis finally arrived with the explanation that he was late because he had been forced to tear himself away from several women. If nothing else, Bobby Jack was predictable.

He greeted me with, "You look awful," which had also become predictable.

"Are you ready to meet the Jesus imposter?" I asked.

"I've already met the man," Bobby Jack replied. "I met him at church this morning."

I questioned, "The Church Among the Hubcaps?"

"Yes," he replied. "I think he's real, but I brought stuff to test him." He had a brown paper bag, which he patted with assurance.

"He isn't real," I said, "and when your test proves it, maybe it will bring the clowns responsible for the charade out in the open."

I took Bobby Jack to the closed door of my guest bedroom, knocked, and a voice inside said, "Come in."

The man, with a twinkle in his eye asked, "Did you bring your lunch, Bobby Jack?"

Bobby Jack chuckled nervously, then said, "No, I just wanted to show you something."

"Okay," the man said.

From his sack Bobby Jack pulled out a small piece of cloth and a splinter of wood. He then asked the man, "Do you recognize these items?"

"Am I supposed to?" the man asked, smiling.

"I would think so," Bobby Jack replied.

"Well, I'm sorry to disappoint you," he said, "but what you have there is an ordinary piece of cloth and an ordinary splinter of wood."

He seemed amused by it all, as if he knew what was coming.

Bobby Jack shocked me when he said, "The splinter of wood is from the cross on which Jesus was crucified, and the cloth is from the grave clothes he was wearing before He was resurrected."

Flabbergasted, I asked, "Where did you get those things?

"From a radio evangelist," he replied. "I paid a good chunk of money for them, too, which I was able to deduct from my income taxes."

For those unfamiliar with religious radio, there was a high wattage station across the Rio Grande River and Del Rio, Texas, that carried religious broadcasts twenty-four hours a day and seven days a week. The evangelists on the station had shaped Bobby Jack's theology and a little of mine.

The man laughed and I asked, "What's so funny? It looks to me as if Bobby Jack has nailed you."

"Other than calling attention to your poor choice of words, I think it's important that you know the splinter of wood Bobby Jack took from his sack in from a mesquite tree just across the border, and the cloth is polyester made in this country," the man said.

"Strange, but I don't recall the cross being made from mesquite or the death shroud being made from polyester."

Bobby Jack had been duped by a radio evangelist, and it had been brought to his attention in a less than subtle manner. He was, obviously, embarrassed by the incident and I felt sorry for him.

Of course, I had known all along that what he had presented was not a splinter from the cross or a piece of cloth from the death shroud. I have never been a gullible person.

Although Bobby Jack had fired his best shot and it had been a dud, he did not fold.

"What is your sign?" he asked the man.

"Are you asking about an astrological sign?" the man questioned. "And, if so, what difference does it make?"

Bobby Jack replied, "It makes a lot of difference. It's how I match people up in my dating service."

The man laughed and questioned, "Whatever happened to marriages made in Heaven?"

"You don't have to get married to get a date," I said.

"Brilliant," the man said.

"Anyway, what's your sign," Bobby Jack asked again.

"It makes no difference," the man said, "but from an earthly standpoint I would be a Gemini."

Bobby Jack said, "The real Jesus was born December twenty-fifth, which would make him a Capricorn."

The man shook his head in resignation and asked, "Have you ever been in Bethlehem in December?"

"Can't say that I have," Billy Jack replied.

"Well, in addition to this astrological stuff being stupid, shepherds wouldn't be out in fields tending their flocks in December," the man said.

"Are you saying the Bible is lying about Jesus being born on December twenty-fifth?" I asked.

"That's not in the Bible," the man replied.

"I was just testing you," I said.

He laughed and said, "I'm sure you were. Now, would you mid giving Bobby Jack and me some privacy?"

"No problem," I replied, then said, "Just remember the game starts at one. You guys need to get ready."

When I came back into the den Mary Lou intercepted me and questioned, "Well?"

"Well what?" I asked.

She questioned, "Did Bobby Jack prove that he's not the real Jesus?"

"I've already proven that," I replied.

"How?" she asked.

I replied, "In lots of ways."

"Name one," she said.

I said, "C'mon, Mary Lou, I don't have time to jack with you. I've got to put some sauce on the ribs. But if you must know, I gave him the thumb truth test."

She laughed and said, "You're lying."

Even though I was, I did not like it brought to my attention. I was upset because Bobby Jack's test had been such a dud.

She kept bugging me with her incessant chatter, but I ignored her and took care of kitchen duties, which were much more important than anything she had to say. Blackie and Cowboy, who were not with Beep's dogs, came in the kitchen and had a snack.

I had just given Blackie some mouthwash when Beep came in the kitchen and asked, "Mind if my dogs come in and use your bathroom? They're not used to going outside."

His dogs were well-mannered and came in by twos. Then Bobby Jack showed up, his face a little flushed.

"Well?" I asked.

"He's the real Jesus," Bobby Jack replied.

I questioned, "How can we be sure the cross was not made of mesquite, or that polyester had not been discovered in the first century?"

TWELVE

There was something about dead brown grass, grass burrs and a crisp winter day moments before a game that brought out the best in me. Those moments before kickoff were a time of reflection, of regret for not having better prepared for a moment in sports history that could never be repeated, and for the determination within my soul to give one hundred and fifty percent.

Butterflies, of course, were fluttering aimlessly and without direction in my stomach. I always prayed that the kickoff would come to me, because I knew that after being touched for the first time, the butterflies would go away.

Prior to previous games, it had been my responsibility to give the pre-game pep talk, a responsibility that had always weighed heavily upon my mind. After all, it is the coach's pre-game talk that puts the team's mood in motion. And how the team responds in the first few minutes of a conflict often sets the mood for the entire game.

So, for this upcoming and most important game of the season, I had asked Beep Jenkins to give the pre-game and halftime talks to the team. Since he was from Oklahoma, I knew he had a solid grasp of both cow chip tossing and football, and what should be said to the team. And I was not disappointed.

Winning this game, I must add, was the most important thing in my life, even more important than the Cowboys beating the Eagles.

The field on which we played was a few doors down from my house and was an undeveloped area of a neighborhood park. It was uneven and had a slope to it. You were either running uphill or downhill. And the terrain accommodated numerous patches of grass burrs. If a player did not get grass burrs in his socks, you knew he was not hustling.

Our team gathered at the upper end of the field for Beep's pre-game talk. Each of us found a place to sit devoid of stickers. Bobo had dragged the big Igloo cooler from our sideline to what could be considered an end zone. He had a can of beer in each hand.

Beep put a fresh chew of Beechnut in his mouth before beginning, spit a brown stream of tobacco juice onto the ground and said, "Men, you know why we're here. Down at the other end of this field is a team that wants to beat the snot out of you. It's an anti-American team that knows nothing about the sacredness attached to a good coon hunt, a team that doesn't have this country's best interests at heart. Hell, it wouldn't surprise me if they were all Communists."

We all glared downfield at our opponents, and some of them waved at us. It was like they were mocking everything for which our team stood, which was truth, justice and the American way.

"Boys," Beep continued, "a good coon dog never gives up, no matter what the odds are against him. That good coon dog of which I speak has set an example for you, so follow it. If people were more like coon dogs the world would be a better place to live in.

"If there is ever going to be any peace in the world, if there is ever going to be any understanding, it's going to be when people start following the example of a good coon dog."

I cannot speak for any of my teammates, but Beep's words put a lump in my throat and tears in my eyes. His emotionally charged words were enough to make any grown man cry.

He continued, "Most of you boys haven't been around the horn like me, but you're all good lads with lots of heart. And you must have heart, the heart of a good coon dog. It's a good coon dog's heart that will bring you victory today.

"Look upon your opponent collectively today as a mean vicious coon that must be brought to bay. Run your hearts out, block and touch with all your strength and victory will be yours."

By this time Ribs was sobbing openly and Chigger was choking back his tears. None of us had ever been so touched.

The old coon hunter straightened his bent frame, spit another stream of tobacco juice and said, "The entire free world is watching what is happening here today and counting on each of you. It's not just a quest for victory, but it's your sacred duty to leave everything on the field."

It was then that I noticed that the man who called himself Jesus seemed amused by Beep's words. He seemed to be holding back a real guffaw. Seeing that he had not been touched by Beep's words made me angry. I decided then that the man had no shame in him, and no heart.

"I've never asked for much in life," Beep said. "Sure, I've made a few million in the oil business and have the best coon dog in the country, which God in His infinite wisdom gave me. But like Job was cursed, my curses were seven wives who stole me blind and made life a living hell for my coon dogs.

"Now I'm not one to blame God for my lack of judgment about women, just grateful that I don't have a bunch of boils festering up all over me like Job did.

"Hopefully, I won't get all emotional like a crybaby when I tell you this, but even though I've known you boys for only a short time, you're like family to me. If any of my wives had seen fit to give me sons, I would have wanted them to be just like you boys, with a couple of notable exceptions, of course.

"No offence to you Ribs, or to you Chico, but if any of my wives had given me sons colored up like you two, I would have shot them right between the eyes."

Both Ribs and Chico nodded that they understood. They knew Beep was not making a racist statement, merely emphasizing that he could not have been responsible for any off-colored kids.

Beep put the final touch on his inspiring speech saying, "It's time, boys. Go out there and put them up a tree. Win one for the Old Cooner."

The team was on an emotional high, but before I went to the center of the field for the coin toss Bobo pulled the Igloo cooler back to our sideline and popped the tab on another can of brew.

That was when Sue Beth sang her special rendition of the *Star-Spangled Banner*, accompanied by Ribs on his accordion.

Scoot Bailey and I met in the center of the field and stared at each other like two heavyweight boxers. He immediately tried to take me off guard saying, "Hi, Mister Luther. Nice day, huh?"

Scoot was one of the meanest twelve-year-old kids in the neighborhood. as evil as a caged rattlesnake. I was not about to be deceived by the likes of him, so said, "Forget the weather report, Scoot. Let's play ball."

I was pumped up by Beep's pre-game talk and ready to play some ball, not engage in meaningless conversation with Scoot.

"I could only get five other guys and my sister to play," Scoot said, attempting to elicit my sympathy.

"Tough," I said, "we're eleven strong."

Scoot questioned, "Why not loan us a couple of guys so it will be even?"

I gave him a disbelieving look and replied, "No way, Scoot. It's not my fault you can't field a team. We're coming after you with all eleven guys."

Scoot seemed surprised by the strong stance I had taken, then used the oldest touch football line in the history of the game. "I thought we were going to choose up sides and play."

Those who did not know Scoot and his twin brother Skate, could easily be fooled by their calm and seemingly good manners. But Bill Bailey's sons were very dangerous and intimidating touch football players. They asked no quarter and gave none.

There was a lot of speed, anger and muscle packed into their four-feet, eleven-inch, hundred-pound bodies. Anytime they got a chance, they put a hard touch on you.

Snuff McGrew, who lived across the street from the playing field and usually officiated our games, came ambling off the sideline to where Scoot and I were standing. He was wearing his officiating clothes, had a beer in one hand and a whistle on a cord hanging around his neck.

"How are you boys doing?" he asked. He followed up with, "Do either of you have a coin?"

Snuff, who had what might have been called a squatty body, always had a pinch between his cheek and gums. He drank beer on the side of his mouth opposite from his snuff. He was a former NFL official who gave up officiating rather than have his judgment questioned by instant replay.

Snuff was a man of great principle whose decisions were law on the touch football field. He knew the game and loved it.

There were those who ignorantly claimed that Snuff always sided with my team because we had an ice chest full of beer on our sideline. There was no truth to such a tasteless comment. Snuff was of all men most honorable.

When he had been officiating NFL games, he had never steered me wrong on the game he was officiating. He even had me make a few bets for him.

To Snuff's question about a coin, Scoot replied, "I have a quarter."

Snuff said, "Give it to me."

Scoot did as he was told. Snuff put the coin in his pocket and said, "The weather being what it is, I don't see any need for a coin toss. "What do you want to do, Mark, kickoff or receive?"

"We'll receive," I said.

"Which end of the field do you want to defend?" Snuff asked.

Scoot said, "We'll take…"

"Shut up, Scoot, I'm talking to Mark," Snuff said. "Your lack of respect for your elders is going to cost you a penalty right off the bat. You're going to have to kick off from your goal line."

I appreciated the fact that Snuff was taking no guff from Scoot.

"We'll defend the high end," I replied. This was a smart move on my part, since we would be running downhill and Scoot's team would be running uphill.

"Let's Play ball," Snuff said.

Beep called us all together and we all stacked a hand on top of a fist that he had made. We expected him to say something profound and he did not disappoint.

"Sic'em," he said.

The way he said it sent chills running up and down my spine.

We took our positions on the field, except for Ribs, who stood on the sidelines and with his accordion played a polka rendition of *That Good Old Baylor Line*.

It was a moment of rare ecstasy, and I could not understand why our cheerleaders, Mary Lou, Sue Beth and Bumps, were plopped down in lawn chairs chatting, eating and drinking. But I always suspected cheerleaders know nothing about the game.

Snuff, who had sat down on our Igloo cooler, gave the signal for the kickoff and Scoot put his foot into the pigskin. The ball took flight toward Bobo. I ran downfield looking for someone to block.

The Ludlow boys, eleven-year-old Trike and ten-year-old Bike were racing uphill toward Bobo. The Dunkin boys, no relation to the donut Dunkin family, both ten-year-old Porky and eleven-year-old Frog were, along with Scoot and Skate, bearing down on Bobo.

But it was the leader of the pack, the most dangerous toucher of them all, that I chose to block. I tried to put a rolling block into nine-year-old Sue Boo Bailey, but she deftly juked me with an illegal move, and I rolled into a patch of grass burrs.

I first looked toward Snuff to see if he had seen Sue Boo's illegal move. But he was cradling a beer in one hand and waxing eloquent with the girls.

Then I looked upfield at Bobo and watched in horror as he, holding a beer in his left hand, attempted to make a one-handed catch of the ball with his right hand. The ball bounced off Bobo's head and tumbled toward Scoot, who pounced on it.

Fortunately, Snuff saw what happened and blew his whistle. Careful not to spill his beer, he hugged his chest with his arms and declared, "Illegal fumble recovery."

"Sir, I don't understand," Scoot said.

"That will be a fifteen-yard penalty for abusive language," Snuff said. Snuff knew how to quell a riot before it got started. He began stepping off the penalty downhill, slipped and rolled the last ten yards, losing his beer.

Ribs and Chigger helped him get back on his feet and to the sideline and the cooler.

Offensively, I had the man who called himself Jesus and Ribs at the end positions, Jimmy Joe and Chico at tackles, Bobby Jack and Bum at guards, Bobo at center, Billy Bob and Joe Don at halfbacks, and Chigger at fullback. It was a very impressive lineup.

In the huddle I told Ribs to run a fly pattern and the man who called himself Jesus to run a crossing pattern. I told everyone else to block. Looking downfield beyond the end zone, I saw a neighbor holding a "John Three-Sixteen" sign.

We ran what some would call a spread or short punt formation. From my position in the backfield, I looked across the line of scrimmage to determine what kind of defense Scoot's troops were in, thinking I might have to change the play, which was often the case. The kid was a master of disguise.

Bobo's snap back to me took a nice bounce and was only a foot or two to my left. But out of the corner of an eye I saw my worst fears being realized. Sue Boo was blitzing.

Bobo missed his block on her, and I had to release my pass sooner than intended, and in the general direction of where I thought the man who called himself Jesus would be running.

Although it was a few feet behind the man's back and a few feet over his head, it was a good pass. He jumped, twisted and made what some of my teammates called an unbelievable catch. Then, with moves my teammates thought would have been the envy of Walter Peyton, he juked Porky and Frog and raced into the end zone.

Frankly, I was not that impressed. I thought my teammates should have been slapping me on the back for delivering the pass, instead of the guy who caught it and scored. But I should have known. Quarterbacks never get any credit.

For the extra point we let Chigger run a sweep to the right with everyone blocking. But Sue Boo catapulted Jimmy Joe and gave Chigger a hard touch to the head, knocking off his jockey hat. I thought it was an illegal touch, but Snuff was not watching. He was enjoying a beer and talking to the girls.

At four-feet, six inches, and upwards of sixty pounds, Sue Boo was not your average nine-year-old. Her ponytail, freckles and sweet face fooled most people, but not me. She had a mean streak, and more than once Snuff had been forced to thrown her out of a game for being too aggressive. Some excused her behavior to the fact that she had two older brothers, but I was not willing to give her meanness a pass.

When Snuff noticed that we were lining up to kick off to Scoot's team, he came onto the field and asked, "What happened?"

"We scored," I replied.

He questioned, "Seven to nothing, huh?"

"No," I replied, "we didn't make the extra point."

He grumbled, "Damn, next time you're trying for an extra point tell me and you might make it."

Although the rest of the team had high-fived the man who called himself Jesus, I had been too busy preparing for the extra point. And, of course, with the perfect pass that I had delivered, I did not think his scoring was any big deal.

But, being the team player that I was, I told him, "Good catch and run."

"Thanks," he said, "next time lead me a little so that I won't have to make like a pretzel to catch the ball."

I figured he should have been more grateful for the pass I delivered with the type pressure that Sue Boo was putting on me, but I should have known. Quarterback is the most misunderstood and underappreciated position in touch football.

Bum was our kickoff man, and he really pounded the football. It bounced down the hill and to our opponent's goal line where it was field by Trike Ludlow.

The speedy Trike's feet pedaled straight upfield until our entire team descended on him, then he streaked toward the sideline and back up the field. With a rolling block Skate had wiped out Ribs and Chico, and Sue Boo leveled Jimmy Joe, Billy Bob, Joe Don and Bobby Jack. The rest of us had been left in Trike's wake, so I feared he would score.

But Trike had not figured on Bobo's guile. Our big center had gone over to the Igloo to get himself a beer, so as Trike sped up the sideline he ran right into Bobo as he was coming back onto the field.

"Nice play," I yelled at Bobo.

"Huh?" he replied. Bobo was not one who required praise for his guile.

Frankly, I though Sue Boo's block that took out four of my guys was illegal, but I did not call it to Snuff's attention because he was entertaining our cheerleaders by balancing a can of beer on his nose. Snuff became irritable when anyone interrupted one of his tricks.

Snuff was still busy with his trick when Scoot, Skate, Bike and Trike pulled what any official would have called an illegal triple reverse that ended with a pass to Sue Boo for a touchdown.

With exception of the man who called himself Jesus, my guys were all winded by the time the play ended. That was why Frog Dunkin was able to hop into the end zone for the extra point, giving Scoot's team a one-point lead.

I suspicioned that the man who called himself Jesus could have stopped him, but I have never been one to judge, especially on Sunday.

As we lined up to receive the kickoff, I glanced over to the sideline and saw Beep pacing up and down like a caged coon. I could see the worry etched on his face.

I am sure it bothered him that our cheerleaders had not done a single "fight team" yell during the entire game. Sue Beth was working on a bag of popcorn, and Mary Lou was arguing with Bumps, who had offered to pop a pimple on her chin. Snuff was taking a nap, a can of beer balanced on his forehead.

Scoot's kickoff was one of those low bouncing jobs that is hard to handle. But Chico scooped it up and started racing downfield. He was in the process of picking up big yardage when he suddenly stopped in his tracks, dropped the football and raced toward the sideline.

Porky Duncan recovered the ball for Scoot's team.

Chico's attention had been diverted by a shiny hubcap in the grass just off the field, which I was sure had been placed there by someone on Scoot's team. I screamed at Chico, but he paid no attention to me. He picked up the hubcap, examined it, then took it over to our sideline and asked Beep to keep an eye on it for him.

Sue Boo's devious smile did not go unnoticed. I noticed it was a BMW hubcap, so made a mental note to check the hubcaps on my car when the game was over.

Although we had been touched hard and often, I was proud of the team's play. I do not think the man who called himself Jesus was putting as much into the game as the rest of us. He had, of course, caused considerable suspicion with his statements that God did not care who won football games. But I knew in my heart of hearts that God would not allow a bunch of juvenile delinquents to beat us.

Scoot's team started pounding away at us, but we defended the hill with honor. It took another illegal triple reverse by Scoot, Skate, Bike and Trike, who pitched back to Porky, who passed to Frog, who lateraled to Sue Boo, before they were able to score.

We knew they had that special play in their playbook, and we thought we knew how to defend it, but they executed it to perfection.

If Snuff had been awake, the play would have been a fifteen-yard penalty against Scoot's team, but on this day, he was letting us down bigtime.

With an all-out blitz, we were able to stop the extra point.

The first fifteen minutes of play ended with us trailing thirteen to six. Scoot thought we would be changing ends of the field, but Snuff arrived on the scene in time to inform him that we were playing thirty-minute halves, not quarters. So, we would still be running downhill, Scoot's team would be kicking off to us and running uphill.

Scoot's kickoff came skittering up the hill where it was fielded by Chigger, who started running downhill and suddenly disappeared. Scoot, Skate, Bike, Trike, Porky, Frog and Sue Boo must have lost sight of him, too, because they began wandering aimlessly as if they were hunting Easter eggs.

Then Chigger darted from behind Bobbo, where he had been hiding, and raced for the end zone. He had only Sue Boo to beat, but she was in hot pursuit.

Billy Bob Raintree, bringing all his legal training to bear, tried to clip her from behind. He, instead, ended up burrowing his head in the ground and into a patch of grass burrs.

Chigger, in fear for his life, darted and dodged, but could not shake the tenacious Sue Boo. Granted, like most short people Chigger always looked like he was running faster than he was, so Sue Boo was suddenly in front of him, slapping him upside the head and again sending his jockey hat rolling.

The girl was the Dick Butkus of touch football. After Chigger was on the turf from exhaustion and being hammered upside the head, with mock concern Sue Boo asked, "Are you okay, Mister Dodgen?"

She did not give a gnat's rear about Chigger, but the fact that she even knew his name made me realize what a strong scouting cartel Scoot had at his disposal. The CIA could have taken lessons from this touch football bunch.

Although Chigger did not score, he gave us good field position, so I figured it was time for the first gimmick play of the day. I was somewhat like coaches Tom Landry of the Dallas Cowboys and Mike Shula of the Miami Dolphins in that I always had a special play for a critical point in the game. So, I called quadruple reverse, shovel pass, triple lateral.

We were forced to run the play a man short, since Chigger was on the sideline being checked for a concussion by our cheerleading trio. Fortunately, Beep was there to help them. He had considerable experience checking coon dogs for concussions.

The play was not as complicated as it sounds. Bobo snapped the ball to me, then I ran to the right and handed off to Ribs, who ran to the left and handed off to Billy Bob, who ran to the right and handed off to Joe Don, who ran to the left and handed off to the man who called himself Jesus, who ran to the right and shovel passed to Jimmy Joe, who lateraled to Bobby Jack, who lateraled to Bum, who lateraled to Chico.

Granted, it was a slow developing play, but very deceptive. From the play we ran several variations.

Anyway, I called the play, took a two-hop snap from Bobo, and before I could even take a step to the right Sue Boo had broken through our line and slapped me upside the head. I was sure she was offsides, but Snuff was over on the sideline watching Chigger be checked for a concussion.

The man who called himself Jesus said, "You should have known that play wouldn't work."

I glared at him and angrily said, "Do you want to call the plays?"

"Sure," he replied. "Just throw to me across the middle and we can go in tied at halftime."

There are those who say that I threw the ball about twenty yards in front of the guy, but that cannot be true because he easily caught up with it and galloped into the end zone. Our guys were so excited that they all ran into the end zone, high-fived him, and made him the bottom man of a dogpile.

I did not join my teammates, primarily because I was still ticked at the way he challenged my authority. But, of course, no one has any respect for a starting quarterback. It is always a backup who gets all the accolades.

The guy who called himself Jesus came out of the pile grinning, which irritated me. It was as if he was gloating, something I cannot stand in a grown man.

But since we still had to make an extra point to tie the score, I kept my cool.

For the extra point I called a fake reverse and, thanks to Billy Bob's clip of Sue Boo, carried the ball into the end zone myself. This enabled me to stick my tongue out at Sue Boo and to spike the ball at her feet.

It was halftime. We had scored on the last play of the half, which usually is the death knell for the other team. They lose heart and cannot get it going in the second half.

Beep gathered us on the sideline where Mary Lou, Sue Beth and Bumps were still rubbing Chigger's head, trying to get the knots out of it. We toweled ourselves, drank Gatorade and listened attentively as Beep analyzed some of the problems that we experienced in the first half. We had to move our huddled mass a few yards because of Snuff's snoring.

As a head coach, I have one objective," Beep said. "It's up to me to dig, claw, wheedle ad coax a fanatical effort out of you boys. I want you to play like you're planting the flag on Iwo Jima."

Back then, Luke, we were patriotic and proud of our country. We were not goofy like the NFL players of today, who will not stand for the *National Anthem*. So, a low rumble of appreciation filtered through the team, which I attributed to our commitment to excellence. In that moment I believed Beep was the most inspirational speaker I had ever heard.

I do not think any of the rumble of appreciation came from the man who called himself Jesus. He always seemed to find Beep's talk amusing, not inspirational. I got the impression that he was the kind of guy who would go off half-cocked and could easily be led by false prophets. The fact that he did not seem to see Beep as a prophet, as I did, was another reason I did not believe he was who he said he was.

Knowing how much victory meant to us, Beep had gone over to my house and brought Oklahoma Crude to the sideline. He gave each of us opportunity to rub the dog's head for luck. We all did, except for the man who called himself Jesus.

Ribs also offered to let us rub his head, but we declined. We chose, instead, to rub Blackie's head. He and Cowboy had watched the entire first half. Both dogs were avid touch football fans.

Beep continued, "The game's tied, which means you have the advantage. I remember back in the day when I was the Oklahoma University quarterback. In the first half we fell behind sixty-three to nothing to the University of Texas. Back then I had a coon dog named Red River Sam, and although coon hunting wasn't as advanced as it is today, for the times he was on par with Oklahoma Crude.

"Anyway, we rubbed Sam's head at halftime, went out and tied the game in the last couple of minutes of the fourth quarter. With ten seconds left in the game, I kicked a field goal to give us an eighty to seventy-seven victory.

"Most people attributed the victory to my skill as a quarterback, but being the modest person that I am, I attributed it to the team rubbing Sam's head, prayer and some good officiating.

"I want you to bow your heads, and we're going to pray fervently for victory. "Lord, there are times when we haven't done what you wanted to do, haven't called the plays you wanted us to call, but these boys here are playing their hearts out for you, not themselves. They want to win this game for your glory, Lord. That's why I don't feel bad about asking for your help to subdue the evil empire represented by the other team.

"Help them defeat the Red Menace, the Communist Party that is supporting their opponent. You wouldn't want the Communists to get a foothold on this field, would you, Lord? I'll answer that for you. No, I know you wouldn't. We know you hate Communism the way a good coon dog hates an old rogue coon. So, give us victory, Lord, and we'll give you the praise and glory now and forever. In Jesus' name, amen."

All of us, except for the man who called himself Jesus, were so touched by Beep's prayer that we were weeping opening. But the Jesus phony was chuckling.

Before we unstacked our hands to go back on the field, Beep gave us his scintillating "Sic'em." I think all of us except for the phony took the field committed to win one for the *Big Coon Hunter in the Sky.*

Snuff had awakened for the second half and another beer. He met Scoot and me in the middle of the field and asked, "Either of you have a coin?"

Scoot remained quiet, but I responded, "All I have is a ten-dollar bill."

"That'll do," Snuff said. He took my bill, put it in his pocket and asked, "Mark, you have the choice of kicking or receiving, and of which end of the field you want to defend this half."

Scoot objected and Snuff said, "That'll be a fifty-yard penalty for abusive language to an official."

I reminded Snuff that the field was not a hundred yards long, so he said, "Okay, Scoot, you're penalized all the way to your goal line."

After carefully pondering my options, I chose to receive and to defend the hill. This meant we would be running downhill the entire second half, whereas Scoot's team would always be running uphill on both offense and defense. It was a calculated and smart move on my part.

From his goal line, Scoot got off a good kick, which was fielded by Bum Criswell. He began running downhill, his polo riding boots pounding the sod in the chill winter afternoon. Here he was, one horseman minus a horse, but with the determination of the *Four Horsemen of the Apocalypse.*

We all crowded around Bum, forming an impenetrable flying wedge that I thought would enable him to knife through Scoot's team. But Sue Boo went around the wedge, came in from the back of it, and slapped Bum upside the head.

The way she got inside the wedge was, obviously, illegal, but when I looked to Snuff for help, he was again asleep, a can of beer balanced on his stomach. Sue Boo's disregard for the accepted rules of touch football made me angry, but I was determined to not let her rattle me.

Mary Lou, Sue Beth and Bumps had finally gotten out of their lawn chairs, I thought to give us a cheer. But they were only stretching. They were soon back in their chairs, oblivious to the importance of what was happening on the field of play.

Beep, on the other hand, God bless him, was pacing back and forth, clapping his hands and yelling words of encouragement. Oklahoma Crude, Blackie and Cowboy, probably tired of female yapping, were napping at the feet of the girls.

I again took control in the huddle, calling for the quadruple reverse, shovel pass, triple lateral.

The Jesus phony chuckled, but I paid no attention to him. Although the play had not worked the first time that I called it because of Sue Boo Bailey's interference, it was a good play and worthy of repeating. Bobo told me that this time he was going to cream Sue Boo. I believed him because when Bobo set his mind to it, it was as fine a touch football player as ever walked onto a field.

Maybe it was his obsession with creaming Sue Boo, or maybe a perspiring beer can had made his hand wet and slippery. Bobo centered the ball over my head.

Whatever, he also missed his block on Sue Boo and creamed Bobby Jack instead. Sue Boo raced right past me and caught Bobo's center snap in midair. She then trotted into the end zone. So, the advantage we had enjoyed by scoring just before the half was gone. Momentum had swung back to Scoot's team.

Fortunately, we were able to foil the extra point attempt. Scoot tried to hit Frog with a pass in the flat, but Joe Don stuck out his foot and tripped Frog.

Scoot protested, of course, but by a vote of ten to eight we overrode his contention that it was pass interference. The phony Jesus voted with Scoot's team.

With the score nineteen to thirteen, I knew we faced a downhill battle. But I knew we were capable of roaring back to tie the score, then go ahead by converting the extra point.

On the ensuing kickoff, Scoot boomed the ball deep up the hill where it was fielded by Joe Don. He lateraled to Chigger and, with Bobo, tried to level the fast-charging Sue Boo. Their plan was to catch her in a vise block, but she slipped between them and they crashed into each other.

Whether they were knocked senseless is difficult to say, given that was their normal state. Regardless, Sue Boo slapped Chigger upside the head sending his jockey helmet rolling before he could get going.

And by the way, Luke, my suspicion was right. Chigger was bald.

In the huddle, I was about to call the play when Bobby Jack asked, "Why don't you let Jesus call the play?"

There was a chorus of "Amen" from the other players, which angered me. Even if the guy was the real Jesus, which he was not, I considered myself better qualified to call plays. I did not mind praying to God for victory, but I did not think it right for Him to call the plays.

The real hurt came from the sideline when Beep hollered, "Let Jesus call the play."

"Yeah, let Jesus call the play," came a chorus from Mary Lou, Sue Beth and Bumps. Then Oklahoma Crude, Cowboy and Blackie started barking in unison, and the girls started chanting, "We want Jesus. We want Jesus."

It was humiliating, having Beep, coach for a day, on a whim wanting to make the man who called himself Jesus the offensive coordinator. And Mary Lou, Sue Beth and Bumps, who had not bothered to provide a fight yell all day, with my teammates calling for the phony Jesus to take control of the team.

Snuff, of course, slept through this entire exchange.

First and foremost, I have always been a team player, so with my best sulking look and voice I said, "I don't care who calls the plays. I just want to win the game."

So, this Jesus character called a hook and ladder play that I was sure would not work. The snap came back to me, which I fielded on two bounces. I then threw a button-hook pass to Ribs, a tight spiral that he caught at his shoe tops, then he lateraled to Jesus, who ran untouched into the end zone.

I became so caught up in the emotions of my teammates, the fact that we had tied the score, that I forgot my anger. The way the phony Jesus could run, the way he could catch the ball, the fact that he played what most would consider mistake-free touch football, caused me to momentarily believe that he might be the real thing.

The guy called the play for the extra point, which seemed almost an afterthought. It was a guard-around pass from Bobby Jack to Bill Bob, and we suddenly had a one-point lead.

But Scoot's team was not ready to give up. After we kicked off and touched Frog Dunkin down about midfield, Scoot initiated a relentless ground attack with Sue Boo carrying the ball behind some devastating blocking.

I did not think anyone could run through our defensive line, and I was right on that score. The cunning Sue Boo, playing her usual brand of dirty touch football, kept running around our line.

In short order Scoot's troops marched up the hill, with Sue Boo scoring on an end sweep. She defiantly spiked the ball and my feet.

I got in the last taunt, though, when Bobo fell in front of Trike Ludlow, accidentally touching him before he could run the ball into the end zone for the extra point. Scoot claimed Bobo was offsides, but we overruled him by a vote of ten to eight. The phony Jesus voted with Scoot's team.

We were down twenty-five to twenty, but with time for one more drive. I was confident that with the phony Jesus on our side, we could march down the hill and score.

Scoot's kickoff was a dribbler that came right up the middle of the field. Bobo tried to field the ball, but when he could not, he fell on it. All the air went out of the football.

Scoot had brought his ball. It was new and suspicious, and it did not have the character of Bobo's ball, which we had been using. Before putting Scoot's ball into play, Beep inspected it to make sure it was American made.

"You never know what a Commie might try to pull," he said. "To hear them tell it, they invented coon hunting and football."

I did not like the feel of the new ball, but I have always handled any type adversity with grace. Having to deal with a strange ball was just another obstacle to overcome, another victory over adversity to be won. I was a firm believer in when the going gets tough, the tough get going.

I am not sure which of the prophets or apostles came up with that observation, but I know it is in the Bible.

My teammates did not object when I again started calling the plays. They were, perhaps, upset with the phony Jesus for voting with Scoot's team. He claimed he wanted to be fair, but what kind of good player wants to do that?

So, three times I called ingenious plays that should have gone for touchdowns, only to see them thwarted by the rock-ribbed defense of our opponent. Sue Boo was playing middle linebacker with a frenzy and zeal that bordered on insanity.

The game came down to one last play. It was one of those Hallmark moments, a play that possibly would determine the nation's continued freedom. So, I decided it was time for me to start believing in the man who called himself Jesus.

"Okay, Jesus," I said, "run a fly pattern and I'll hit you in the end zone."

He gave me a funny look, possibly because I had never addressed him as the real Jesus until that fateful moment.

The play worked beautifully Jimmy Joe, Billy Bob, Bobo and Joe Don blocked the blitzing Sue Boo. Bobo even delivered a perfect snap. The man who called himself Jesus was all alone when I delivered a perfect pass that landed right in his hands.

And he dropped it.

I screamed, fell to the ground and rolled around in frustration while Scoot's team celebrated. I was of all men most miserable.

I felt as if I would be rolling around in grass burrs for days. But when I looked up the phony Jesus was offering me a hand, along with the cheerless words, "Sorry, Mark, but I can't be what you want me to be. God can't be who you want Him to be."

THIRTEEN

Because of the loss, the spareribs and brisket lost their savor, although no one seemed to notice other than me. My guests all wolfed down the food with relish, whereas I had a lump in my chest and tears in my eyes that kept me from enjoying the meal. Losing was always hard for me, especially to an arch-rival like Scoot.

It did not help that Scoot's mother had him bring over a couple of pans of peach cobbler that she had made.

To my teammates and the man who called himself Jesus, it was just another game. After the game he seemed content and laid back while serving all my guests. As to my attitude toward him, I was miffed about the way he had muffed the pass and his cavalier attitude. And I was still mulling in my mind what he said, that "I can't be who you want me to be. God can't be who you want him to be."

Hell, all I expected him to be was a decent pass receiver. I did not expect him to be who he claimed to be, not the Son of God. And as for God not being who I wanted Him to be, I did not understand what he meant by that statement.

I know this. If we had won, I would have been more than willing to give God some of the credit. After all, I believe in praying to God before a game and asking for His help in winning.

It was the phony Jesus, not me, who said God was not interested in football. I have always thought of football as being a priority item with God, although I doubt that God is as interested in the point spread as I am.

I happen to know that some of the gamblers who establish the point spread pray long and hard before coming to a decision. I do not find that unusual, since many people pray for success in their professions.

The thing I could not understand following our loss was everyone congratulating the man who called himself Jesus for the game he had played. Sure, he had scored three touchdowns, but he had choked in the clutch.

My high school coach always said no matter how well you played in a game, that mistakes could negate all the good you had done. He was, of course, a man who truly understood football, the serious implications of the game.

One of the greatest character-building lessons he ever taught me was when we were preparing for a championship game. Our opponent had a great running back, and he assigned some of us to take him out. We were fortunate enough to break the guy's leg on the opening kickoff.

If the phony Jesus had made the most crucial catch of the game, I might have accepted him as the real thing. However, his failure to come through when the game was on the line reinforced my belief that he was a charlatan. The real Jesus would have caught the ball. He would not have allowed a bunch of Commie kids to beat us.

Between swigs of beer, while awaiting the Cowboys and Eagles game, Bobo said, "Lighten up Mark. We played a helluva good game. Nobody expected us to win, and we did beat the spread. That put a few bucks in my pocket."

"Yeah," I conceded, "but we could have done more than just beat the spread. We could have won the game if our phony Jesus had caught the ball."

"I can't find any fault with the man," Bobo said. "He made some unbelievable catches, and he did score all three of our touchdowns."

"Maybe so," I agreed, "but he also made the bonehead play of the game, which makes me know he's not who he claims to be. And as for what you call unbelievable catches, anyone could have caught those perfectly thrown balls."

Bobo shook his head in disagreement and said, "You're dead wrong, Mark."

I said, "Bobo, the day you give up beer will be the day I believe that he's the real Jesus."

"You really know how to hurt a guy," Bobo said.

On that score, Bobo was right. I have always known how to cut up and dice people verbally. I consider it one of my virtues. And while I had gone along with the Jesus gag someone was playing, his screwing up our chance for victory was not funny. I was more than a little teed off at whoever had sent him my way.

There are those who say I became angry, sullen and abusive after the game. It is true that I hit the sauce rather heavily, but the one thing I have always been able to do is handle my liquor. For that reason, I did not give much credence to the reports about my after-game personality.

Although I never got over losing to Scoot's team, I do not believe, as Mary Lou said, that I acted like an asshole.

Now it is true that I yelled at Beep's dogs and ordered them out of my hot tub, and complained that they left the toilet seat up, but I would probably have done the same thing if we had won.

In fact, I even made a joke of it, told Beep that since the dogs were in the hot tub, they ought to share a good bottle of vintage wine.

And I think he took me seriously. He gave them a few cartons of wine, filled his plate with barbecue, went out on the deck, stripped down to his birthday suit, and joined the dogs in the hot tub. Ribs and Chigger joined him, then Cowboy and Blackie.

Although my teammates were too calloused to notice, I think the loss to Scoot's team really took its toll on Beep. He was heartbroken, said he was giving up coaching touch football and sticking to coon hunting.

"If I ever do coach again," he said, "it will be with the understanding that I call the plays. And I hope you understand that I'm not criticizing your play calling, Mark. It's just with my knowledge of the game, I'm light years ahead of everyone else."

"I understand," I said.

"Where did we go wrong, Mark?" he asked, pensively. "What did we do that caused God to turn His back on us?"

I shrugged my shoulders and replied, "Beats me. We dedicated the game to His glory."

It was during this conversation that I began suspecting that Beep had hoped coaching our team to victory might lead to a head coaching job in the NFL. The man certainly had the charisma to make that leap.

Beep said he hoped to find another outlet for his spare time, that coon hunting only took up most of his nights. "My days are pretty empty," he said. "I'm a consultant to the CIA and Pentagon, but that's part-time gig at best. And, of course, I sometimes do a daytime coon hunting seminar, but most hunters have jobs and prefer to attend nighttime seminars."

"I can see that," I said, then questioned, "What about your tenured professorship at the University of Oklahoma?"

"Teaching the art of coon hunting to young men is satisfying," Beep said. "But there's more money in administration and you don't have to know anything, which is why I don't have a prayer of moving up in the food chain. I thought this coaching gig might lead to something, but who wants a coach with a losing record?"

"Some of the most successful coaches in the NFL have losing records," I said. "Is there any chance that you're a minority?"

"Only that I'm from Oklahoma," he replied.

"I don't know if that qualifies," I said, "but it should."

"I was offered a job coaching basketball in China," he said, "but my dogs nixed the idea."

"I don't blame them," I said. "A dog doesn't have a long-life span in China or North Korea."

Beep surprised me when he said, "I've given some serious thought to a career as a male stripper," then questioned, "Do you think I have the body for it?"

I replied, "I can't say, but isn't that a night job? Wouldn't that interfere with your coon hunting?"

"I've found a couple of daytime hangouts for women near the university that hire male strippers," he replied. "The money isn't important. I just want to do something that's fulfilling. And, of course, it has to be a place where I can take my dogs."

I told him I did not see why anyone would object to him having his dogs backstage but wondered if it was the proper kind of environment for them. I also suggested that my hot tub might not be the proper kind of environment for them.

Beep certainly had no reason to think I was sullen, angry and abusive following the game. If anything, I was very supportive of Beep, even to the point of thinking he would have made a great President of the United States. While most of our Presidents have had a dog, as President he could have set a new standard for number of Presidential dogs. Coon hunting might also have become the national pastime during his tenure.

I admit to having become a bit ill-tempered with Bum Criswell, but only after he showed no concern about his horse kicking down part of my backyard fence.

Bum told me I was overly concerned about the fence, that it could be easily repaired. When I asked if he was going to pay for the repairs, he said a horse kicking down a fence was an *Act of God*, thereby negating his responsibility.

I told Bum that it was not God who put the horse in my backyard.

He whined, "I'd pay for the fence if I had the money but as you know, all my funds are tied up in riding lawnmower polo. And now I feel a deep commitment to start a Christian polo league. I plan to talk to Jesus about it."

I suggested just where Bum could stick his mallet, or whatever that thing is that they use in polo. To tell the truth, I've never seen much difference in polo and croquet.

"You have a very un-Christian attitude," he said. "I won't be inviting you to join the Fellowship of Christian Polo Players.

I told Bum that there was already a Fellowship of Christian Athletes, and that I had not been invited to join that organization either. He countered that the athletic skill required for polo was so superior to that of other sports that the players would not be satisfied with anything less than an exclusive organization of their own.

I suggested that polo players might need their own exclusive jockey itch powder, too, and that horses and lawnmowers were more athletic than the people who rode them.

Whatever the reason, Bum got that stupid hurt feelings look on his face, which caused Mary Lou and Sue Beth to get on my case. Both referred to me as a pompous ass. Looking back, I must admit that it was not my best day.

What made it worse, Bobby Jack Lewis, who had been converted from doubter to disciple of the phony Jesus, started blaming me for the loss to Scoot's team. That was hard for me to take since, because of his religious upbringing and flirtation with the charismatic movement, I had counted on his support.

I argued, "Phony Jesus had victory in his hands and lost it."

But Bobby Jack contended, "It should never have come down to the last play. If you had put together a decent game plan, we would have won by three or four touchdowns."

I grumbled, "There was nothing wrong with the game plan. I didn't know Sue Boo was going to play for Scoot's team. If you guys had knocked her out of the game, maybe broken her arm or leg, the game plan would have worked to perfection."

Chico Neiman-Marcus agreed with Bobby Jack, that it was my game plan that was responsible for the loss, not the phony Jesus. Of course, I expected that from Chico. In only a couple of days he had become completely enamored with the phony Jesus, this despite that he did not look like any of the pictures of the real Jesus in his mother's Bible.

I have great respect for artists, whether they work on canvas or black velvet. And because artists, like writers, are inspired from above, I think their paintings are a true depiction of Jesus, especially those in the King James Version of the Bible. Obviously, I do not have any confidence in some of the Communist-inspired versions. The only version authorized by God is the King James Version.

That, of course, brought up another negative about the man who called himself Jesus. He did not speak in King James English like the original Jesus did.

I turned to Ribs and asked, "What did you think of the game plan?"

"It sucked," he replied. Blackie nodded in agreement and Cowboy left the room, not wanting to get involved.

It was one thing for Bobby Jack and Chico to be critical, but I had taught Ribs everything he knew about touch football. I had taken a raw piece of talent and molded him into one of the finest touch football receivers in North Dallas. A black receiver should never question the decisions of a white quarterback. Such questioning could well be why the world is in the shape it is in today.

I said, "The game was lost because of poor execution, not my game plan."

"Wrong," Joe Don said. "My mother could have come up with a better game plan."

The guys had never been this mutinous before, so I had to think it was the phony Jesus who was responsible for their change in attitude. I was beginning to think that he was not only a charlatan but also a troublemaker. That was another strike against him, since I was sure the real Jesus would not cause any trouble.

Even Chigger got on my case, which I attributed to the probable three concussions that Sue Boo had delivered to his head. When I first met him, I perceived him to be wise beyond his height.

He had learned at a young age that the top of his head was at the perfect height to be hammered on by a five-foot, eleven-inch man. Sine I am six-feet, one-inch tall, I thought about delivering a blow to the top of his head.

The thought dissipated when I looked at Sue Beth. She was very protective of Chigger, and she outweighed me by a good fifty or so pounds. And I recalled that she had won a mud wrestling championship sponsored by a local bar and radio station.

"Let's face it, Hoss," Jimmy Joe Johnson said, "it should never have come down to that last desperation pass. We should have been so far ahead that we should have been playing prevent defense by the third quarter."

"I agree," Billy Bob Raintree said. "I don't think you could convince any jury in the country that you had a good game plan."

It was the man who called himself Jesus that came to my rescue, if you can call it that. He said, "The most important thing to remember, Mark, is that the game and game plan were not important. There are many things more important."

Easy for him to say, I thought. The man was always speaking in riddles.

On top of it all, the Cowboys lost to the Eagles.

FOURTEEN

On Monday morning, four days before Christmas, the phony Jesus made me grits for breakfast. I thought that the reason why might be that he felt guilty for the pass that he had dropped the previous day.

But over grits, his homemade biscuits, gravy, bacon, eggs and coffee, he said he felt it might be best if he moved out of the house.

I shrugged and said, "Well, you're no problem for me, but if you don't feel comfortable here…"

He laughed and said, "I think it's more a matter of your comfort than mine."

"Where will you go?" I asked.

"Chico is providing me a room down at the hubcap store," he replied.

I said, "That's a grubby place."

"It will be fine," he said.

When I got home from work that night, he was gone. In fact, the only evidence he had been in my home was that it was hospital clean. He had thoroughly cleaned both the interior of the house and the yard, including repair of the fence kicked down by Bum's horse. He had even emptied, cleaned and refilled the hot tub.

Although he had been at the house for only a week, it seemed strange that he was no longer there. Of course, I did not miss him or anything like that. Despite his domestic ability, he had been a pain and an inconvenience. But, of course, I have always liked living alone.

After a couple of drinks and feeding Cowboy, I called Mary Lou to see if she wanted to join me for dinner.

"Sorry," she said, "but Sue Beth, Chigger and I are going down to Chico's to help Jesus get settled in."

"Why are you doing that?" I asked.

"Well, since you kicked him out it's the least that we can do," she replied.

"I didn't kick him out," I said. "If he's saying that, he's lying."

"He didn't say it," she said. "But you can make a person feel pretty unwelcome."

Arguing with Mary Lou was a fruitless undertaking. Her head was so hard it was like an anvil.

"Chico's place is in a rough area," I said. "Maybe I ought to come with you."

Cold as ice, she said, "I'm sure Chigger will be more than adequate protection."

I laughed and said, "You've got to be kidding."

"No, I'm not kidding," she said. "Besides, Jesus and Chico will be there, too."

"I wish you would quit calling that guy Jesus," I said. "He's an actor. A good one, I'll admit, but just as actor."

She questioned, "You're sure of that, huh?"

I replied, "I'm sure. I'm just not sure why whoever put him up to the joke hasn't admitted to it. The joke's over."

"The joke has always been over," she said.

What she meant by that I do not know. I had learned early on to not even try to interpret her. She was a complex woman, one whose mind defied amateur analysis.

Since Mary Lou was unavailable, I decided to call Bobo. He was always interested in chowing down and having a few brews.

"Sorry," his wife told me. "He went to someone called Chico's place. I think it's down on Harry Hines."

I could not believe what was happening, but if mothing else I am persistent. I called Ribs and got no answer. I called Billy Bob and Jimmy Joe and got the same results.

Well, I knew there was one guy I could count on. I called Joe Don. He answered but sounded out of breath. When I suggested dinner, he said he had been on his way to Chico's but had rushed back in his apartment to take my call.

I told him that Chico had more than enough people to clean up and set up a room for the phony Jesus, that he would probably just be in the way.

"After tossing him out like you did, I feel obligated to help," he said.

I denied tossing the guy out of my house, but Joe Don was not buying. "I know how you are," he said. "You can make things pretty uncomfortable for a person, even a friend."

Exasperated, I said, "I don't care what you believe, there's still no point in your going down to Chico's place. Everybody and their second nephew are on their way over there. We can go to Highland Park Cafeteria and show down on their buffet. I'm buying."

"Thanks, but no thanks," he said. "I want to talk to Jesus while I've got the chance."

"What do you mean?" I asked.

Joe Don replied, "You don't expect him to hang around here forever, do you?"

"As far as I'm concerned, he can't get out of town soon enough," I said. "And I can't believe you're buying into the phony's routine. Tell me what's going on."

He said, "If you weren't so spiritually blind and arrogant, you would know."

It was obvious that I was getting nowhere with Joe Don, so I told him to enjoy his trip to Chico's and that it would be a cold day in hell before I invited him to dinner again. He just chuckled, told me he appreciated the invitation and hoped that I would eventually wake up. I told him I was awake, sober and did not need any mothering.

I next called Bum Criswell at his home. The butler answered and said he was not there. So, I called him on his cellular saddle phone. He answered and I asked, "Bum, old buddy, what are you up to?"

He asked, "Is that you, Mark?"

"Yeah, it's me," I replied.

"You'll have to speak up," he said. "I'm at a gallop on Beltline and the traffic noise is awful."

I increased my volume and few octaves and said, "If you're not busy, I'd like to take you to dinner tonight."

"I appreciate the offer," he said, "but my horse and I went through a Burger King drive-through and picked up a bag of flame-broiled burgers. My horse won't eat burgers that aren't flame-broiled."

I did not know about Bum's horse and his affinity for flame-broiled burgers, and really did not care. But ever the diplomat, I said, "A burger or two isn't going to hold you over. Meet me somewhere where we can really chow down."

"Can't tonight," Bum said, "I'm on my way to Chico's."

This left me no one to call other than Bobby Jack Lewis, the man who had betrayed me and strayed into the camp of the phony Jesus. I called and his answering service informed me that he was at Chico's.

FIFTEEN

For a few years our gang had been celebrating Christmas Eve and Christmas Day at Sue Beth's mansion in Highland Park. We had a catered supper on Christmas Eve, followed by gift-giving and lots of drinking.

Because Sue Beth had lots of bedrooms and beds, we all spent the night at her house, then had a catered breakfast and catered lunch at two o'clock. I doubt that anyone in the world had a better spread.

Our gift giving was limited to one wrapped and meaningless ten-dollar gift. Numbers were drawn and gifts were selected on that basis. I, of course, also gave everyone as autographed picture of me.

So, on Tuesday following my rejection for dinner the previous night, I called Mary Lou and asked if she would like a ride to Sue Beth's house on Wednesday evening.

"I was about to call and tell you we're not meeting at her house this year," she said.

"Really?" I questioned, "Why the change?"

"We're meeting at the church, having a supper for poor kids and their parents, and providing them gifts," she replied.

I could not believe what I was hearing and asked, "Why?" Then added, "And it's not a church, it's a used hubcap store."

She countered, "You don't understand what a church is."

"Obviously not," I said sarcastically. "I'm sure this is the phony Jesus' idea. What about Christmas Day?"

"We're going to serve dinner to any and everyone who doesn't have a place to go," she said.

"Who in the world is paying for all this?" I asked.

"Jesus," she said. "Oh, we're all bringing a toy or two and some food, but he's multiplying everything."

I could not believe what I was hearing. The phony Jesus must be claiming he could do what the real Jesus did. The real Jesus fed five thousand men and who knows how many family members with five loaves of bread and a couple of fish. Now this clown was acting as if he could multiply a few toys into hundreds, and feed everyone who showed up with Christmas Eve and Christmas Day dinner.

I laughed and said, "I think some kids expecting a toy are going to be disappointed and hungry."

She said, "Think whatever you want. You're welcome to join us."

"I'll pass," I said.

On the first night that I met the man who called himself Jesus, he had laid some heavy religious stuff on me. Of course, I had been equal to it. In any give-and-take situation, I have always been able to hold my own. But I still questioned my willingness to listen to him on that evening. It was not because I was drunk because I do not get drunk. I am as objective about my drinking as I am about my journalism and understand exactly how much liquor my system can handle without getting tipsy.

During the week that the man who called himself Jesus spent at my house I believe he tricked me into introducing him to my friends. I questioned why my friends been so accepting of him? And I especially could not believe that they were accepting him as the real Jesus.

After talking to Mary Lou, I decided to drive down to Chico's place. I must admit that I was curious.

Although it was still early in the day, I found the phony Jesus surrounded by a lot of grubby looking people that he had deceived, also some darn nice looking and well-dressed whores. When he saw me, he excused himself and came to where I was standing.

"Nice to see you," he said.

"Same here," I said.

I could not believe how the place had been transformed. Everything was clean as a pin, and everything seemed to have a place. I had noticed before coming inside that the entire building had been freshly painted.

"What brings you to this part of town?" he asked.

I figured that if he was the real Jesus, he would know why I was there. I had noticed that there was no church sign on the building, just the same misspelled sign identifying it as a used hubcap store. There should have been a "Church Among the Hubcaps" sign, with smaller lettering underneath it "Name by Mark Luther."

But no, I was receiving no credit for my contribution to the ministry that had been started there.

However, being the gracious and giving person that I am, I said, "I was thinking about giving you a birthday party on Christmas Day, in the evening, of course. I understand you'll be busy on Christmas Eve and part of Christmas Day."

He laughed and said, "I told you my earthly birthday isn't on December twenty-fifth. I probably won't be here on my birthday."

"The King James Version of the Bible says Jesus was born on December twenty-fifth," I said, "and you claim to be Jesus."

"You might want to check out those Scriptures in the Bible again," he said.

It was another of his ridiculous statements. Once you have read the Bible, you have read it. It does not change. And there are very few people who can remember and interpret Scripture as well as I can.

I questioned, "So, you're not interested in having a birthday party?"

"Not really," he said. "You're welcome to come down here and help with Christmas Eve and Christmas Day services."

"Thanks," I said, "but I'm pretty tied up in my own church's services."

I swear he knew I was lying, but he said, "That's good, but you're still welcome to come down and have dinner with us on Christmas Day."

"I'd like to," I said, "but I'm covered up with invitations for Christmas dinner and have already made a commitment."

He sighed and said, "Well, it's an open invitation."

I overslept and did not make it to church on Christmas Day. Most of the people who knew me at the time figured I was committed for Christmas dinner, so I did not receive any invitations.

On Christmas Day I had a turkey and dressing TV dinner and watched a couple of NBA games on the tube, which, as usual, were about as interesting as watching moss form on a tree. If the NBA moved to China where it belongs, along with plantation owner Nike, very few people would notice.

SIXTEEN

Some people do not know when to end a joke, whereas others will go to extremes to prove a point. While I am convinced that one or more of my alleged friends were in on the phony Jesus joke, no one ever confessed. In fact, in the years after it happened all of them did some strange things.

Mary Lou Magruder became a missionary to New York, a state responsible for bad salsa. I suggested that we might try to make a new start, but she said she preferred taking on what some deemed a spiritually hopeless situation in a different state.

Jimmy Joe Johnson founded an organization called *Dry Hole Oil Men for Christ*, comprised of men who made unwise investments, primarily with him.

Bobo Harrison gave up sports writing, moved to California and became a religion writer for a major West Coast daily. He later told me that he sometimes went for months without having to write anything.

Billy Bob Raintree founded a prison ministry, but a federal judge ruled that listening to him constituted cruel and unusual punishment. He was banned from all prisons and never achieved his dream of having a statue of himself erected on the Baylor campus. He did give Baylor a gift of one hundred million dollars, but the check bounced.

Joe Don Barnes went on to work for the surgeon general, speaking to police departments on the evils of smoking cigarettes and cursing. He was involved in numerous fights regarding his views, traveled the country with his pet bull, and had a chewing tobacco named after him.

Bum Criswell realized his dream of riding lawnmower polo becoming one of the most prestigious sports in the country and throughout the world. He became the international czar of lawnmower polo and, like a circuit preacher, rode his trusty steed to polo match after polo match throughout the world. Both man and horse traveled the world in Bum's Boeing VC-Twenty-five, *Polo One*.

Bobby Jack Lewis sold his *Apocalypse Now Dating Service* to a senior group that changed the name to *Beyond Apocalypse Now Dating Service*. He went to darkest Africa as a missionary, preaching in English to people who did not understand a word he said. The people there thought he was charismatic and speaking in tongues.

Chico Neiman-Marcus remained at his used hubcap store on Harry Hines, serving as pastor of *The Church Among the Hubcaps*.

Ribs Davis became labeled the greatest Christian accordionist in the world by his publicist. He set many hymns to polka music and became a folk hero in Poland and South Dallas. He received the *Nobel Peace Prize* and won his lawsuit against the Ku Klux Klan, becoming the organization's first black member. And, after several years, he became a thirty-third degree Klansman, and the organization's lobbyist to Congress.

Sue Beth and Chigger got married and had thirteen children. Chigger developed a pill that allegedly helped short people grow taller. The Federal Drug Administration (FDA) charged him with fraud, but he proved that his children took the pill and were growing.

Sue Beth did not realize her dream of a horse racing track on the SMU campus, but after making a substantial gift the school did place a large portrait of her in one of the school's cafeterias.

Leading music at *The Church Among the Hubcaps* led to Beep Jenkins becoming director of the *Coon Hunters for Christ* men's choir, which performed at the Kennedy Center, before the Queen of England, at the Vatican, in Russia and at the Mormon Tabernacle, the only non-Mormon choir to ever perform there.

Beep invited the Mormon Tabernacle Choir to perform at the annual *Coon Hunters for Christ* convention, but they declined.

I do not know if Beep pursued being a male stripper. We lost touch when the choir began traveling the world. I do know that the choir had a lot of prostitutes supporting it, but never thought of Beep as a pastoral pimp.

Bumps Ann Grinds established an evangelistic cosmetic company called "Makeup with Jesus." It was called "Makeup of the Devil" by the Pentecostal Church.

As for the man who called himself Jesus, I have not heard from him since the night he told me he was going to leave town. I was sitting on the same stool that I was occupying the night I first met him.

"Where will you be going?" I asked.

"I'm thinking about California," he said.

"Why?" I asked.

He laughed and asked, "Has it ever occurred to you that I might never have been to California?"

Well, Luke, when you consider what has happened, and is happening, in California, if the guy was the real Jesus, it is doubtful that he ever made it there, or to any other state on the West Coast. If he did, there is no evidence that anyone on the West Coast paid much attention to him.

I have told you the story so you can share it with your dog friends. I cannot think of anyone who wants to hear it from me.